D0310008

SEWING CAN BE DANGEROUS
AND OTHER SMALL THREADS

S.R. MALLERY

Copyright © 2015 S.R. Mallery

All rights reserved.

No part of this book may be used or reproduced in any manner without written permission from the author, except in the case of brief quotations embodied in critical articles or reviews.

ISBN-13: 978-1511529242
ISBN-10: 1511529245

DEDICATION

To Richard, Chris, and Liz

TABLE OF CONTENTS

ACKNOWLEDGMENTS

Thanks to Dorothy Gabai, who convinced me, oh, so long ago, to take these stories out of mothballs and rework them. To Dana Ryder, whose early enthusiasm was infectious, to Judith Kilcullen for always taking time out of her busy schedule to read my work, to Jaine Duber, for her wonderful editorial expertise in "Lyla's Summer of Love," to my father, Jerome Ross, for encouraging me to keep writing, to Nicola Kaftan for being my technology guru, and to my husband, Richard, for ignoring my less-than-perfect housekeeping so I could write these stories, I am grateful to you all.

SEWING CAN BE DANGEROUS

As the subway train lurched to a spark-grinding stop, the steam, billowy white from the cold October day, temporarily blocked the neon letterforms scrawled across the station signs.

On the train, Susan turned to her companion. "This is us, Mom," she announced.

Dressed in varying shades of black, the two women rose from their metal seats, quickly exited before the doors could close on them, and gingerly made their way down the rickety platform steps. Yet down at street level, they both froze, mesmerized by the view. Hundreds of tombstones and mausoleums spread out before them on either side, and with the grey stones gradating up into a grey sky, it resembled more of an architectural painting than a backdrop to the oldest Jewish cemetery in New York City.

Mourning relatives huddled around the two newcomers, offering each one silent hugs and wet cheeks. Then, wending her way over to the family plot, Susan tried hard to avoid stepping on any hallowed ground as she passed row after row of Siegelmans, Strausses, Brodskys, Kandelbergs, and Steins.

But it was the incongruous array of headstones that impressed her the most—faded names butted up against trendy 1990 tombstones with faces photo-transferred onto their slick, dark green surfaces. Just imagine, she mused, how a heavy downpour would look, splashing against their faces, beating tears down all those shiny cheeks.

Oh, that's Great Aunt Ada, she thought, focusing on their family plot's fanciest headstone. I remember hearing about her. And there's little David, run over by a trolley car. How awful it must have been for her grandmother as a girl, to be told something so tragic about her own brother.

Closing her eyes, she could still hear her bubby's voice in her head,

1

imitating all the deep wails emanating from the family parlor the night of the boy's death. Now, even as her Uncle Jacob eulogized, her mind kept drifting, conjuring up emotions she herself had suppressed for months.

After the service, still taking in the family tombstones, she zeroed in on an unfamiliar name and stepped in closer to get a better look.

"Herein lies Sasha Rosoff
Born in Russia, 1895
Died New York City, 1911
A short life in America—
A large soul in Heaven."

Susan's interest was tweaked. Who was this mysterious Sasha Rosoff and more importantly, what had caused her to die so young? She swiveled around to ask one of her older cousins, but thought better of it. Later would be a more appropriate time for questions.

Later turned out to be at Uncle Jacob's house in Queens, where the laughter, tears, and reminiscences intermingled with tray after tray of Jewish delicacies. By evening, when a secondary wave of people arrived to extend their noisy condolences, the tiny white wood and plaster house with the black roof swelled and vibrated.

Finally, Susan couldn't contain herself any longer. Approaching a four-foot-tall, four-foot-wide silver-haired woman, she rested her arm around one of her favorite relative's shoulders. "Cousin Yetta, I am dying to know something—who is Sasha Rosoff?"

The twitch of surprise was palpable. "There are a few things we just don't talk about around here. But if you have to know, ask your Great Uncle Jacob, he might tell you," she added as she folded and unfolded her cocktail napkin.

Uncle Jacob's duty as memorial host was to keep afloat just long enough to see the last guest leave. Sitting on the sofa, the lower section of his shirt half-opened, an unbuckled belt releasing his enormous belly, he was drawing slow, deliberate breaths as Susan sat down beside him. Her fingertips were the lightest of touches on his tired arm. "Uncle Jacob, are you all right?"

He smiled at her concern. "Susan, my sweet one. How are you? I didn't even ask. How's the job? Your mom told me you're so upset."

"I am, but that's not what I want to ask you." She paused, measuring her words carefully. "When we were all at the cemetery, I noticed a tombstone marked Sasha Rosoff. Who was she? Why did she die so young?"

Uncle Jacob's unexpected tears startled them both. For all his bulk and composure, his vulnerability made Susan instantly regret having brought it up.

"That poor girl never had a chance," he murmured. "So terrible to die that way…" He ended with his head resting on his right palm.

Susan leaned forward and stroked his shoulder. "Please, Uncle Jacob, tell me what happened, please?"

He sat up, pulled a handkerchief out of his back pocket and first wiping his eyes and blowing his nose, let out a heavy sigh. "What happened? Ah, well…"

**

Sasha couldn't believe how miserable the boat trip had been coming across the Atlantic. People shoved up against each other, buffering the elements; howling babies in the arms of frantic mothers trying to pacify them, and always the inevitable nausea that forced everyone to gag or lean over the railings and vomit.

Torrential rain and wind drove the ragged ship, listing it back and forth over the fierce waves and scattering passengers into dark cubbyholes. Throughout, prayers provided the only strong haven, and for Sasha and her family, they prayed every free moment they got that New York's harbor would appear before their vessel broke into wooden fragments floating in the angry sea. From the lower levels, third-class shawled women, hatless men, and grimy-faced children kept gathering up on deck, straining to catch sight of the Statue of Liberty, the ultimate Lady of Hope.

"Anytime now, it'll be there," the crew assured them, but all they kept seeing were endless miles of a relentless ocean.

Below deck, gathered around the family's makeshift table, Sasha's father Moshe held court. "Ven ve come to New York, ve vill go to our cousins, the Brodskys, on Hester Street. Ve will all act vit respect, and ve von't give dem any trouble, vill ve? Is dis understoot, Sasha?"

Sasha clenched her teeth, her green eyes hard. Being treated like a second-class citizen in Russia because she was Jewish seemed a cruel and mystifying enough punishment, but to be viewed as a third-class citizen by her own father simply because she was female was more than she could bear.

Ignoring her set jaw, Moshe and beamed at his young son. "David, balibt, my beloved one, I know you vill behave vell, and ve vill find you goot job. Dis is land of opportunity, and you can do anythink you vant. No Cossacks to shoot you down, no pogroms here. Dis is America."

"Papa, vat about me?" Sasha struggled to steady the tremor in her voice.

"Hush, girl! You vill do vat you are told! Ve vill look for somethink dat girls are meant to do. Now hush, Sasha!"

Sasha's mother Raisa bowed her head and sighed. Twenty years of living with her husband had taught her not to argue; in the end, the price was always too high. But Sasha was young, her spirit still intact, and as the ship pressed forward, she made a silent vow to herself. She would someday live her life the way God intended her to do.

By the time the boat entered the Upper New York Bay, people had scrambled over to the main deck railing, bobbing and positioning themselves to get their first glimpse of the famous statue. There she was. None of the photos or paintings had done her justice. Up close, the sheer magnitude of her green-bronzed body with the one arm reaching up towards the cloudy sky, grasping a torch while her crowned head held a steady gaze towards America, brought tears to the Rosoffs' eyes. Without speaking, each of them was silently acknowledging her significance. To Moshe, she represented the respect he felt he had always deserved; to Raisa, if her husband received more respect, he might soften towards others; to David, she evoked new, exciting adventures, and to Sasha, just landing on American soil symbolized independence.

As the ship maneuvered into New York Harbor, the sudden horn blast and swollen plumes of smoke bursting from its huge black fennels caused everyone to first jump then shriek with delight.

Their new lives were just beginning.

But the high-paid jobs for Moshe and David never materialized, and after degrading medical examinations on Ellis Island, consisting of harsh finger probes, sneers, and humiliating positions, they both resigned themselves to sweeping garbage off the floor of a local saloon for a pittance. Interestingly enough, despite Moshe's predictions, the only family member who managed to get a better paying job was Sasha.

The Triangle Shirtwaist Factory, inside the Asch building, was located on the corner of Greene Street and Washington Place in the lower east end of Manhattan. The owners, Isaac Harris and Max Blanck, prided themselves on mass-producing new fashioned shirtwaists for American women and in the process, becoming extremely rich men by hiring young Yiddish, German, and Italian seamstresses, desperate for work.

The Rosoffs were thrilled at her steady pay, but Sasha's heart sank. She found out soon enough what working conditions were really like: sixteen hour days, six days-a-week, hunched over cumbersome black iron industrial sewing machines in dense, almost airtight conditions that had her breaking out in streams of sweat on hot summer days, and teeth chattering shivers in the dead of winter.

Harris and Blanck were true believers of the new industrial age. It never occurred to them to offer decent factory conditions to their hard-working employees when they could just as easily squeeze the same amount of work out of these naïve immigrant girls. So for Sasha, each day was filled with crippling, repetitive motions that left her neck, back, and arms sore for days at a time. The fifteen minute allotment for lunch passed so quickly that some of the slower girls only had time to pull out their lunch boxes and take a couple of bites of food washed down by two or three swigs of liquid before the whistle blew, signaling them back to work. There were no other breaks and no time to socialize.

Lint particles sifted steadily throughout, settling into every conceivable surface. Microscopic fibers clogged mechanisms and filled nostrils with a dust so fine, after two hours it became difficult to breathe. Oil soaked rags, used for greasing the mechanisms, radiated their own heat that could be slightly comforting in winter for those workers near the large bins where they were dumped, but toxic in spring and summer for everyone else.

America, Land of the Free. Such a joke, such a schpas, Sasha grumbled as she hobbled home one evening, later than usual. Entering their cramped, walk-up apartment, she appeared to be alone, and grateful for the stillness, stretched out across their daybed/sofa, relishing a soundless room without the constant clatter of industrial sewing machines. She tried relaxing her throbbing back by closing her eyes and pretending she was far away in distant lands, but within minutes, she could hear Jacob Brodsky trudging up the hallway stairs from his after school job. Eyes still closed, she smiled in spite of her exhaustion and pain.

Her little cousin Jacob had become the one and only shining light in her life. He adored her and she him. Somehow, the two found solace in each other's company and without him, Sasha knew she might not have the strength to continue. More shuffling on the vestibule steps announced her Uncle Samuel, tired but excited about all the tips he had made that day waiting on tables.

The Brodskys were fortunate. They had all gotten jobs in a local Jewish delicatessen, preparing the food, waiting on tables, and dishwashing. Delighted with their work and its decent pay, they still commiserated with Moshe and his family on their lowly positions and grueling schedules. 'Remember, this is America,' they would repeat on cue. 'Land of opportunity. Just wait and see—have a little patience, have a little geduld.'

But as time went on and still no changes, Moshe's increasing bitterness garnered a single target: his daughter. "Girl, vere ist your money for veek?" he would lash out. "I told you, you give it to me right vay. Don't tink to keep it for yourself! You vouldn't know vat to do with it, anyvay. Except for sewing, you no good! Give it! Gebin!" Most times, he would end by shoving his hand roughly out towards her, palm up, waiting for total compliance.

Tonight, still lying on their couch and watching the Brodskys prepare dinner, Sasha could feel herself drifting off into a much- needed doze. Earlier that day, her shift had been particularly exhausting. Rainy spring days brought foul, rancid smells into the factory, and with little to no air, the combined odors had proved unbearable. At lunch break, she had nearly fainted from the stench, and when she had dared ask for a lunch extension, her answer came in the form of a broom handle, poking her in the ribs.

"Gebn, meidl! Give girl!" Shaken awake, she saw her father looming over her, his heavy breathing hammering her in angry waves. Moshe's day had been bad as well, culminating in his employers deliberately stomping across the area of floor where he had been carefully mopping, tracking fresh mud in from the street. In an instant, all the months of swallowed pride surfaced. Flinging his mop down, he stormed out, pushing bills and sustenance far from his mind.

Out on the street, however, his anger quickly morphed into silent desperation and by the time he had reached their apartment, he was looking for the only satisfaction he knew he could get—attacking Sasha.

"Can't I keep a little money, Papa? At least let me do somethink else. I hurt all over. Ich schatn…" Her voice cracked.

That did it. Cursing in Yiddish, he grabbed a wooden ruler and started hitting her shoulders and outstretched hands, ignoring all her feeble attempts at self-protection. Finally, with palms the color of raw meat and raised welts rubbing against the rough fabric of her dress, she cowered on the floor in the corner of their kitchen and sobbed.

Jacob, kneeling down beside her, started stroking her hair.

Just then, her Aunt Deborah entered. Her reserve this past year as she had watched her cousin's behavior with his only daughter had been based on a laissez-faire philosophy. But enough was enough. Genug is genug. Shoving her cousin up against the wall, she snarled, "Shame on you! How dare you treat your daughter like that! Vitout her money, you vould be notink, do you hear me, Moshe Rosoff? Notink!"

Moshe slowly lowered his arm, dropping the ruler onto the floor beside him. Suddenly the apartment stilled, with only the tick...tick...tick of the wall clock, echoing Sasha's soft whimpers.

A half hour later, dinner was placed on the cracked oak table as if nothing had happened, and with Raisa home, Moshe talked fervently to everyone about how things would be soon looking up, his pink face flushed with a renewed energy. Seduced by his good mood, Deborah, Raisa, Jacob, and David listened attentively while Sasha ate in silence.

Saturday, March 25, 1911, started out like so many other days. Sasha woke up in the dark, got dressed with cold, numb fingers, splashed water on her face from the porcelain pitcher and bowl set out on the kitchen table, gently kissed a sleeping Jacob, grabbed a piece of bread she had covered with jam, and let herself out the door. Feeling her way down the pitch-black hallway by running her fingers over the embossed plaster patterns, she almost stumbled on a nail peeking out of a floorboard just before reaching the front door. The gas light in the vestibule had been out for weeks, and their landlord had refused to fix it. She felt tired and depressed, but as bad as conditions were at Triangle Shirtwaist, nothing could compare with being around Moshe, and so taking a deep breath, she gratefully made her way through lower Manhattan to the sewing factory for a day of overtime and its slightly higher pay.

On the sidewalk outside the factory, she caught up with many of the girls with whom she usually worked—three hundred Italian, German, and Yiddish girls, their thread-worn dresses hanging over muddied petticoats and eyes as dark-circled as hers. Trudging up the path, they were all met at the front entrance by Joe Zitto, one of the elevator operators.

"OK girls, OK. Let's get goin'. The rest of the building ain't opened today, so I'm gonna take ya's up to the 8th, 9th and 10th floors only. Don't try to go anywheres else for lunch. The doors to the other floors are locked mostly. I guess Old Man Harris don't want no burglars comin' in. So, c'mon girls, let's go."

Bending over her assigned sewing machine was excruciating. Her entire body ached from the previous day's abuse; still, she kept working until lunchtime. She was in no mood to socialize—making idle chit-chat was the last thing she wanted to do, but when she retreated to a corner of the factory floor by herself, two of her closest co-workers, Gladie Moskovitz and Irma Delacina, came over to sit beside her.

"What'sa matter wid you today, Sasha?" Irma peered at her friend as she bit down hard on a piece of Italian bread, some crust flipping out of her mouth and onto the floor.

"Yah, you look different. Is evertink all right at home?" Gladie was more privy to Sasha's problem with Moshe than Irma was.

"I don't vant to talk about it—sometink did happen, but I not say…" Sasha feared once she started talking, there would be no stopping. Better to keep mute.

In what seemed like a mere five minutes, the whistle blew, followed by numerous deep sighs and groans. Irma threw an arm around Sasha's shoulder on the way back to their sewing machines, and handing her a delicate-looking locket from around her own neck, told her, "Here, taka dis to wear. It's a good luck charm necklace. I got it in Italy. If you wear it, maybe you getta good luck from now on." She leaned over and gave her friend a little kiss on the cheek.

Touched by Irma's gesture, Sasha instinctively pulled off a little pinkie ring of her own—a small, silver Jewish star pattern with a pink stone in the center. Uncle Samuel had bought it for her the week before at a local flea market, telling her, "Remember, Sashelah, you're American now, but always, you are a Jewish girl. Never forget the Torah, my child."

Irma's mouth curved into a huge grin as she placed the ring on her pinkie finger. Then the two girls gave each other a quick hug before returning to their stations.

The afternoon dragged on. Sasha found that by concentrating only on the rhythm of the sewing machines, she could block out her misery, at least for a little while. Closing her eyes and listening intently, she could almost hear the tapping of a marching band: click, click, slam-slam-slam, whoosh-whoosh, rattle-rattle went the machines. Soon, the entire factory room pulsed.

By 4:45 p.m., the whistle blew as if by magic, signaling the end of the workday and going home to face another round with Moshe. Turning off her machine, Sasha stood up, took a deep breath, and steeling herself, tried to remember the good people in her life, like Irma and Gladie, and of course, little Jacob.

Three steps forward, she smelled smoke.

Girls on the opposite end of the floor next to the windows were beginning to scream in a panicked chorus and someone, suddenly streaking past her, cried out, "Fire! Fire!" Still, she remained paralyzed, her arms and legs like lead, her mouth filled with a bitter, chalky taste. Then the adrenaline hit her and she broke into a dead run.

Dark gray swirls of smoke were seeping in from under the doorway cracks while dozens of girls stampeded past the sewing room, heading towards the elevator shafts or stairwells and ending up crushed together against the in-going only doorways. Hysteria rendered each girl strong. No matter how hard she tried, Sasha couldn't push her way through the group of flailing arms and legs, so she about-faced to explore other escape routes.

Outside on the street, a man walking by pointed upward and shouted, "Look at the smoke coming out of the Triangle building!"

"Yeah, it looks like it's comin' from the top floors! What's that coming outa the windows? Looks like bolts of fabric! Old Man Blanck must really want to save his precious cloth!" a woman chimed in.

"Yeah. Wait! Wait a minute!" the man continued. "That's not bolts of fabric—they're—they're—oh, God in Heaven!"

The cynical woman let out a blood-curdling shriek.

As a large crowd gathered, all eyes were glued towards the 9th and 10th floors in time to see several blackened girls in smoldering dresses hurling themselves towards the ground to join the six bodies already strewn across the sidewalk, limp, broken.

Engine Company 72 clanged around the corner and ground to a halt, but the mounting piles of corpses made it impossible for the hose wagon to get close enough to be effective. Desperate firemen started handing out bucket after filled water bucket to the foreman, some male tailors, and anyone else available, so they could run back into the building to douse out the flames. When all twenty-seven buckets were emptied, it became all too painfully obvious; the fire was completely out of control.

A few soot-streaked firemen tried to stretch out a safety net to catch one girl's fall, but before all four corners were taut enough, three more girls had jumped seconds behind her, the weight of all four ripping the net as they landed hard against the pavement. The stunned men grabbed a nearby horse blanket to try to cushion the fall of another girl, but she, too, flew down with such force, her charred body split the blanket in two, hitting the cement with a loud thud.

Up on the tenth floor, more and more girls were desperately trying to scramble down the fire escapes. Gripping the iron ladders, terror made them ignore the steam hissing out between their fingers until suddenly, yelping in pain, they let go, gliding like flying squirrels towards the ground.

Inside the building was pandemonium. Clouds of thick, bulbous smoke blinded Sasha, stinging her eyes and rendering her throat raw until she got down on her hands and knees and managed to crawl towards the elevator shaft, praying both Joe Zitto and Joe Gaspar might still be on duty. Sure enough, the elevator was working, but it kept stopping on the eighth floor below her. She could hear Joe Zitto frantically working the metal levers, shouting up to anyone within earshot, "I can only get to the eighth floor! The ninth and tenth floors are blocked off! Get to the eighth floor and I'll take ya's down."

She managed to get to the eighth floor using one of the few stairwell exit doors not engulfed in flames, but once there, found too many crazed girls jammed together, calling out for the elevator. Joe Gaspar came up next, but could only squeeze in twelve to fifteen girls at a time. Between the two men, they made fifteen to twenty trips each, but with each trip, the girls' clutches and cries weakened as their coughing from all the smoke inhalation overwhelmed them.

"Come on, Sasha, come wid me to da westa door. We can getta through dere!" She recognized Irma Delacina by voice only. The girl covered in head-to-toe soot and sizzling clothes standing next to her, looked nothing like the kind, smiling girl she had hugged just hours before. She attempted to reach out and grab her, but Irma was already halfway across the hallway, heading toward a door that Sasha knew to be locked. She called out after her friend, but Irma either wasn't listening or couldn't hear over the din of howls.

Careening around the corner from Great Jones Street, Engine Company 33 shuddered to a full stop in front of the burning building, drawing hurrahs from a crowd that naturally assumed any back up would bring miracles. But their cheers soon turned to cries of horror when everyone realized the hoses could only reach the seventh floor, leaving the upper floors of the factory engulfed in flames.

Back on the tenth floor, Sasha viewed her options. She could see three male cutters across the room running towards an open window, and decided to go with them. She didn't get far. Oxidation from the fire had turned the tenth floor into a time bomb, and as bolts of fabric imploded into popping blazes, she was knocked off her feet and onto the floor.

Dazed, she tried to get up, then fell back, unable to move.

Two minutes later, a roar erupted from the huge crowd as they witnessed three male cutters forming a human chain from the roof of the factory to an adjacent building. Slowly, one at a time, several of the girls carefully inched across the backs of the men to safety, eliciting cheers and applause each time someone made it. But the strain on their hands and fingers were too much for the cutters; someone lost their grip, and all three men plummeted eighty feet to their death.

The sudden stillness overwhelmed the crowd already in mourning. In the thousands, they remained in shock until a man finally found his voice. "Look at the roof!"

All eyes pointed upward. There, over a hundred girls, in their cumbersome dresses and singed petticoats, were wriggling across a ladder held down by New York University law students who had hatched an escape route between the adjacent buildings.

By nightfall the fire had subsided, leaving glowing embers and assuring the firemen of an end in sight. But along with their relief came the dreaded job of scouting for more girls inside the building, and as the searchlights crisscrossed up towards the hollowed floors, an even more gruesome sight was revealed: scores of burned bodies, cradled by ropes, were being slowly lowered by firemen, then gently lined up on the cobblestones to be carted away for family identification.

Nearby, hysterical relatives had descended on the Mercer Street Police station, clamoring with questions in broken English and praying their loved ones had managed to survive. Italian families wedged up tight against German families, who melded into Russian-Yiddish families, all waiting as a unit for any news.

Soon, an official shuffled into the room, his face impassive, mouth straight-lined. With his legs in riot stance, he stared at the families for several seconds before indicating a map on the south wall. "Go to the Bellevue Morgue on 26th Street," he informed them. "You can either identify your loved ones there, or obtain more information about any missing girl." Then he about-faced and marched out, as detached as when he had come in.

Moshe, Samuel, and Raisa wasted no time. Before anyone else could leave the room, they had already begun their race over to the designated morgue. Once there, the thought of waiting in another endless line was out of the question for Raisa. She stormed across the waiting room to the main registry, leaned over the green institutional counter and demanded, "Ver ist da girls?" The inexperienced secretary flinched backwards then pointed a shaky finger towards the pier, a few yards away.

Approaching the area, the smell of burned flesh overtook them, and as Raisa started to faint, Moshe quickly stepped up to hold her.

"Be brave, be brave for our little girl," he muttered repeatedly.

All the years of repressed anger in Raisa suddenly exploded. "You—you—you did dis to her!" she screamed. "She had nottink to say—you made her verk there! I never forgive you, never! Kein mol nit!"

Jerking herself free, she charged through the warehouse to the identification room, ignoring all officials, ready for any confrontation. But in the main room, she did a double-take. On the floor were dozens of bodies, burned beyond recognition. Walking up and down the rows, she scrutinized each cadaver, but it was no use; she couldn't make out anything. Then suddenly from out of nowhere, she let out an agonized sob and collapsed. Samuel rushed over to support her, cradling her as if she were Sasha herself. After a minute of rocking back and forth, he focused on something himself and cried out sharply.

"Vat, vat is it?" Moshe implored.

Samuel pointed to a charred body, unidentifiable like all the others except for one slight detail. On the right hand was a little pinkie ring, a Jewish star ring with a tiny pink stone in its center.

"It's the ring I bought for her," Samuel moaned, his choked voice almost unintelligible.

Later that night, after Moshe and Samuel had put a catatonic Raisa to bed, Moshe turned to his relative. "Samuel, come sit vit me—ve need to talk."

As soon as they were in the front room, he began. "There was something dat bother me about Sasha's body tonight. Sasha always haf frizzy hair, but dis girl haf wavy hair. Wha' kut dat mean?"

"I don't know, Moshe. But the ring, I know that ring. I'm sure it's her. It's our little girl..." He finally broke down, releasing all the pent-up emotions from an exceptionally long day.

**

"It turned out to be one of the worst disasters in the history of modern industrialization, and because of it, a commission was set up to study more effective labor practices. Dozens of witnesses and family members testified, and when details of what happened came out, it was far more horrific than anyone could have imagined. A turbulent trial ensued, with the owners never receiving convictions. However, we do end this program on a hopeful note. Conditions today in the work environment are far better than they've ever been, partly due to the tragedy that happened at the Triangle Shirtwaist Factory on March 25, 1911. This is Peter Manning, signing off for 'Investigations On the Air.'"

Susan stared at the TV a few seconds before switching it off. Suddenly, the unlit screen brought reflections on her own job, the recent memos she had seen, and the disturbing trends she could no longer ignore. Her mother had warned her not to make waves. After all, landing a buyer's position in a celebrity's clothing firm was not to be taken for granted. Count your blessings.

But that night, Susan slept fitfully. Fire and smoke-filled dreams starring a faceless girl desperately trying to slap out flames on her long skirt startled her awake every few hours. By morning, although it took three cups of coffee to get there, she came to a major decision. She was going to read the testimonies and try and get inside her cousin's world at the factory that day.

Letting Uncle Jacob in on her plan one night after dinner, she was surprised to see him disappear into the bedroom and return with Sasha's diary. "I don't know if this will be helpful, but I have always kept this. She meant so much to me." Biting his lip, he sighed, and handed over the thin, worn, leather-bound volume.

Sasha was certainly no Anne Frank, Susan mused as she skimmed through the book, but it was touching, nonetheless. Ambivalent about her own boss, she was drawn to this girl, obviously so trapped by her father and her situation. Throughout it all, Uncle Jacob appeared to be the girl's one shining star, and that made Susan feel even closer to him. The other two names that kept cropping up were Irma Delacina and Gladie Moskovitz. Obviously she had considered them to be friends, or at the very least, comrades in misery, but other than that, there was nothing too eye-opening about the factory conditions, only that she ached all the time.

The next step was the New York Public Library. Microfiching through a mountain of testimonials, she skimmed through most of the commission's report until something caught her eye. She clicked 'pause' and started reading.

One of the testimonies given was by a Marco Delacina. He stated that he was quite distraught because they had never truly been able to identify their daughter, Irma; she was presumed to be one of the group of girls who had actually melted against a locked door, yet the family had remained skeptical. Where was her good luck locket that she always wore? It must have melted the Delacinas had been advised. It was not enough to lose one's daughter, he further testified, but to have to endure being glossed over by public officials was an outrage. Besides the personal loss, the loss of income was devastating to their family. What were they to do now?

Susan's dreams turned violent that night. Eerie, ash-coated shapes lumbered after her as she tried to escape through the blocked passageway. Clawing at the door, her fingers and nails, sticky with blood, she kept stroking a little locket around her neck.

At 4:23 a.m., she bolted upright in a sweat. Oh, my God—maybe the girls had switched jewelry!

She kept remembering Moshe's testimony during the hearings, how everyone assumed it was his Sasha, but then why was the hair different? And what about the Delacinas never truly believing they had found their girl. Maybe Sasha had never been found, not Irma!

Back to the library. She poured through dozens of articles, searching for anything that had to do with young teenage girls in New York. Nothing on Sasha, but there was an interesting article about the Delacina family doing very well financially several years after the tragedy. According to a certain interview, they kept receiving an anonymous donation each month, undoubtedly through the Sons of Italy, and it had changed their lives. Because of that, they had been able to move to Queens and were living the American middle-class dream.

Watching her night after night, the librarian couldn't contain her curiosity any longer and finally approached. After hearing the story, she suggested, "Why does it have to be New York? After all, if the girl didn't want to return to her family, why would she want to stay in New York all these years?"

Susan smiled. Of course. So she plunged in again, expanding her geographical area of interest, and focusing on a 1922 article written from the Pennsylvania News Terminal, about a homeless, Russian Jewish girl making good, setting up her own bridal sewing shop, and people raving about her work, her moxy, etc., etc. Her name: Sarah Mijss. What an odd name. A faded, vintage photo of the seamstress displayed a rather plain girl with frizzy hair.

After the name was jotted down, Susan took some notes on the article, and hugged the librarian before going home for the night. Frazzled, all she wanted to do was to pour herself a large glass of Cabernet Sauvignon and tube out. She channel-surfed for a minute or two before deciding on Rosemary's Baby, playing on one of the movie networks. She had seen it numerous times before, but for some reason that night, was in the mood for the bizarre. Snuggling up against her overstuffed Saks Fifth Avenue pillows, she settled down. Two-thirds of the way into the movie, she started glancing at her pad of paper on the coffee table, unable to stop her ruminations. Casually picking up the pad, she studied the notes, including the odd name. Mijss. Weird…

Just then, one of the most crucial scenes in the movie appeared, when the leading character, Rosemary, was told by the companion of a recently deceased friend, that the answer to the problem lay in an anagram. Getting out her scrabble letters, the heroine moved the pieces around and came up with the name of the satanic leader of a cult who happened to be living next door to her. With the music swelling ominously, it was one of the high points of the film.

Susan stared down at her pad again. Mijss. Mijss. M-I-J-S-S. Oh my God!

J stands for Jacob, I is for? S is for Sasha, M is for Moshe, and S is for Samuel! I—I—I is for Irma? Yes, it would work! It definitely could be her! Maybe she's still alive and living in Pennsylvania!

The next Saturday, she purchased a railroad ticket to the little town in Pennsylvania and after booking herself into a hotel for the weekend, spent the rest of the afternoon asking around about Sarah Mijss. It seemed everyone knew of her. "Sure, Sarah, she's the town character, ninety-five and still going strong." Susan fell asleep easily that night, looking forward to the next day.

On Sunday, Susan paused just outside Sasha's door. *Oh, dear, I hope this isn't too much for her,* she thought all of a sudden. *I mean, what if it is her and she has a heart attack and dies?* She took a deep breath before pushing down the tarnished brass knocker twice. Nothing. She tried again. Soon, she could hear shuffling on the other side of the door and a "Coming, coming," echoed by an old, yet surprisingly firm voice.

The door opened. "Hello, dear. May I help you?" the elderly woman stood waiting.

Susan was afraid to proceed. "Ah—you don't know me, Ms. Mijss, but I'm here to talk to you about something that happened a very long time ago." There was a lull while she checked for a reaction. There wasn't any.

"May I come in?" she continued. "I don't really want to say what I have to say out here."

The woman locked her knees and drew herself up. "My dear, whatever you have to say to me, you can say it in the doorway."

Here goes, Susan thought. "Have you ever heard of a little boy by the name of Jacob Brodsky?"

It was as if the woman had been slapped. Her eyes watered instantly and stumbling back, she caught herself on the doorknob before lowering her head and sinking to the ground.

Susan knelt down beside her. "I'm so sorry to do this to you. Are you all right?"

Sasha Rosoff turned to her, whispering, "Someone found me at last. I can't believe it—after all these years..."

Later, over tea and homemade cookies, it all came out. The switched jewelry identities, the escape across the unfortunate cutters' backs, the despair of losing her friend Irma, and the realization that she could start a whole new life without her dominating father.

"But the Delacinas ended up doing OK. I guess they got an anonymous donation from some Italian organization because they moved to..." Then Susan caught the corner edges of Sasha's lips curling.

Her elderly cousin nodded slowly. "After all, a life for a life, I always say. She saved mine, so the very least I could do was to save her family's."

Rounding the table to hug her newfound relative, Susan could sense beneath the old woman's frail shoulders, the toughness that had served her well all these years. Yet, as they clung to each other, Sasha started to cry. "I suppose everything has come full circle," she murmured.

Wiping away her own tears, Susan shook her head. "Not quite. There's just one more thing I've got to do to make things right, and I need you to be with me…"

**

Cameras flashed as Susan's boss, the well-known actress-turned-clothing-guru, entered the room. Marching defiantly past Susan with her team of lawyers, she put on her most dazzling smile for the press. The steady flux of voices in the hearing room buzzed like a swarm of locusts, as the gavel came down hard on the judge's podium.

Seconds before Susan got up to testify about unfair, dangerous labor practices in her boss' overseas factories, she gave her cousin's hand a nervous squeeze, and even up on the mahogany stand, the blood draining from her tight face, she needed to look over at Sasha one more time for another infusion of courage.

The skin on the ninety-five-year-old was shriveled, her shoulders hunched over like the letter 'C', but just watching Susan begin her deposition, the seamstress sat bolt upright for the first time in many years.

A DRUNKARD'S PATH

It wasn't your typical wedding present. Wedged in between high-tech blenders, irons, toasters, and boxes of crystal champagne glasses, very few people could resist walking past it without running at least a finger or two over its soft, comforting texture. Several guests even placed entire hands on top of it, palms down, their arched fingers moving in tiny circles, to get the fullest tactile sensation.

"This is the quilt that my quilt group and I sewed for you two these past six months. It's called A Drunkard's Path," Deborah's Aunt Natalie explained, ceremoniously handing the 'prize' over to her niece, who was, at the moment, attached at the hip of her new husband, David.

"My group suggested doing this because of your connection to me, of course, but also because of your famous ancestry and all your ties to American history," she continued, winking at Deborah.

David beamed, looking down at his wife and giving her an extra squeeze on the shoulder. For four years, he had enjoyed bragging about Deborah being a direct descendant of Nathaniel Hawthorne, author of The Scarlet Letter. He had judged his fellow classmates well; having a girlfriend with such a lofty heritage definitely gave him leverage at Harvard, but tonight, Deborah's reaction to the gift was altogether different. Childhood memories of visiting her Aunt Natalie suddenly washed over her, reminding her that even at ten- years-old, she had always been accepted in the sewer's inner circle while they discussed quilt patterns, gossiped, and howled with laughter.

Also called to mind was an old, tattered puppet doll, smelling like a musky mildew, and always accompanied by a group member named Margaret Stinson. The crude doll seemed out of place with all those intricate quilts, but each time Deborah ventured a question about its origin,

Margaret would promptly introduce another subject.

All of a sudden, amidst a swell of cheers, the bandleader announced, "Let the bride and groom have the first dance." All eyes swiveled to the happy couple, whirling across the polished dance floor, concentrating only on good times, champagne, and bright futures.

By two a.m., cocooned in David's arms and drifting off to sleep, Deborah fingered the fluffy quilt one more time, secure in the knowledge that she had indeed married the right man. Life just couldn't get any better.

Eight hours later, she woke up and lazily rolling over towards her new husband, was met with an indented pillow and a rumpled sheet. Running shower water from the bathroom teamed in like a tropical rain forest, making her giggle and head towards David, anticipating at least another forty-five minutes of lovemaking.

Instead, opening the frosted glass door, she was bombarded with a frosty, "What are you doing here? I just want to get on with my day! Leave me alone!"

She froze. In all the time they had spent together, he had never behaved this way towards her. Arguments, yes, of course; disagreements that needed to be resolved, sure, but never this.

Backing away from the shower, she turned around and quickly grabbed her clothes off of the newly acquired Art Deco bedroom armchair. A small vial, filled with liquid, fell to the floor.

Automatically, she called out, "What's this?"

He flung open the shower door, and seeing what she was holding in her hand, charged towards her, snatching the vial away. Still dripping, he barked, "It's nothing! Just a wedding present for me from someone from my office. It's nothing!"

Her breath eked out like a quasi-hiccup. What in the world was wrong? Charging past her worried expression, David finished getting dressed and slammed their front door on his way out. She steadied herself on the edge of a chair, waiting for her heart to stop pounding and her better judgment to creep in. OK. Maybe I should leave him alone today; let him work out whatever is bothering him. Pressures from work? Newlywed jitters? Tonight we'll certainly iron things out, just like we've always done.

The shrill phone jarred her out of her thoughts. "Hey, how are you? Is everything OK?" Aunt Natalie's voice was tinged with concern.

"Of course," Deborah lied. "Oh, just wonderful. David's gone to work, and I'm going to do some grocery shopping for tonight. Why?"

"Oh, I don't know…just wanted to make sure…" Natalie's voice trailed off, but Deborah sensed her aunt had wanted to say more.

Gourmet grocery shopping became the order of the day, and because all the local vendors knew she had just gotten married, there were plenty of free samples—chocolate croissants, Quiche Lorraine, Baba Ganoush, and pickled zucchini—along with jokes and well wishes. The hours passed quickly, and by the time she returned home at five o'clock, her honeymoon mood had completely been restored.

Just inside the door, the smell of alcohol was unmistakable. Entering the living room, she could see David slumped on the couch, surrounded by a scattered newspaper, a wagon train of shoes and socks trailed across the floor, and on the coffee table, an empty bottle of Jack Daniel's and a new crystal wedding flute filled to the brim. When he gazed up at her, his bloodshot eyes reminded her of some of the street winos she had recently passed en route to the subway.

"David…what's going on? Are you OK?"

"Of course I'm fine! Married less than a day, and already you're a nag! What business is it of yours anyway?" He reached over for his champagne glass.

"You…you usually don't drink very much, and you have never talked to me this way. I…I just don't get it. Has something happened to make you want to…"

"Well, I'm just fine!" Taking a large gulp and flipping his hand upward, he gestured her away.

Dinner backtracked into silence that evening—an unheard of occurrence—and finally, after a half hour of trying to get him to respond to her, Deborah retreated into the bedroom for the rest of the night, leaving him to sleep it off on the couch. But when the pattern continued, she became truly frightened. This is what it must be like to be an abused woman, she brooded; too ashamed to go looking for outside help and always telling herself things will undoubtedly get better; they certainly couldn't get any worse.

Once a week, like clockwork, Aunt Natalie would call, cheerful, yet always gently probing until finally, one night, after a particularly nasty quarrel, the phone rang. This time, Deborah came clean.

"I don't know what's happening. It's not as if I didn't know him. After all, we've been living together for four years and he's never showed any signs of alcoholism. I just don't get it…" the phone line filled with her choking sobs.

There was a long pause on the other end. Then, "I was afraid of this…"

Deborah gasped, mid-sob. "What do you mean?"

"It wasn't my fault…she kept it from me all these years…I swear I didn't know…" Natalie whispered.

"What are you talking about?"

"It started so long ago. I don't even know how it all came about, but there's…there's been a curse placed on you and David…that quilt that I was so excited about…Martha Stinson in my quilt group kept silent until after I had given it to you, and…and I didn't want to say anything in case it wasn't true."

"Are you kidding me?" Deborah exploded. "My life is falling apart! C'mon, curses don't really happen, do they? I mean, what can I do? You tell me now!" She segued into a screech.

"Come over to my place tomorrow and I'll try to relate it all to you, I promise."

Aunt Natalie's narrow brick house, clothed in ivy and steeped in American history, was originally part of a row of common carriage houses. Nestled in the middle of a small, wrought iron gated courtyard in Greenwich Village, it was considered by some to be one of the most charming landmarks in the city.

Each room was on a different floor, so they both had to walk up a flight of stairs just to get to the kitchen quarters. There, a pot of comforting Earl Grey tea was brewing, waiting for them to begin. On her kitchen table, two books and several sheets of papers were strategically placed in a couple of rows. Deborah couldn't read the titles clearly, but just recognizing the word Salem across one of the bookbindings, immediately sparked goose flesh that crawled up her arms.

"Some tea? I have it all ready for you," Natalie managed a smile.

Deborah nodded, her eyelids swollen from another sleepless night.

"Do you know anything about the Salem Witchcraft trials?" The older woman leaned in toward her niece, as if casting a spell herself.

"No, not much, why?"

"You remember Martha Stinson from my quilt group? Well after the wedding, she showed me a journal written by a relative of hers and frankly,

I am very concerned about you. It seems one of the accused witches from the original Salem trials might have actually had a connection with a real witch, an ancestor of Martha's…"

**

Inside the packed meetinghouse, dust particles from mud-caked boots floated through the air, rendering it dense, murky. That year, April had been an unkind month to Salem Village. Rain-drenched meadows produced a sludge that clung to the edges of women's dresses, creating odors so foul that in such tight quarters, it became difficult to breathe. But people weren't concerned with such matters on this day. They had gathered for a higher purpose: the Devil was in Salem, and they wished him thwarted at all costs. Even the constant threat of Indian attacks and surviving harsh winters paled in comparison to what was happening now, in that room, swelling with apprehension.

Crammed into high-walled pews, dark wooden benches, or simply shoved up against walls, spectators filled every conceivable space in the meetinghouse. Donning black hats, cloaks, and breeches, the men angled forward, their eyes boring holes into the five men sitting up front, yet it was the women who carried the greatest burden that day; their hooded coats and muffs covering their recently unkempt hair and unwashed fingernails, couldn't disguise the uncertainty they felt about their community's loyalty to them and how it would all end.

Sitting at the head of the counsel table, amongst other magistrates in the newly appointed Court of Oyer and Terminer, John Hathorne and Jonathan Corwin quietly conferred with each other before beginning their first round of questioning. Arrogant, self-important, the black-robed magistrates assumed their positions on the political totem pole, and having been brought to Salem for such a specific purpose, they dared not disappoint. They were on a mission to deliver souls. Hathorne, displaying the greatest exhibition of self-aggrandizement, seemed the most severe. With no real legal experience, and having only glanced at Sir Mathew Hale's Trial of Witches, and Joseph Granvill's Collection of Sundry Trials in England, Ireland the week before, he nonetheless believed he was more than competent to interrogate the accused.

At the front of the room facing the magistrates, sat all the accusers, the "afflicted" girls: Abigail Williams, her cousin Betty Parris, Ann Putnam, Sarah Bibber, Sarah Churchill, Elizabeth Booth, Mercy Lewis, Susanna Sheldon, Jemima Rea, Mary Warren, Mary Walcott and Elizabeth Hubbard.

With downcast eyes and folded hands, they appeared demure; inwardly they were experiencing emotions quite different from anything they had ever known. Childhoods stocked with adult repression and fear now served as a springboard to the frenzy of accusations they had created, because on this day, along with their catharsis and even exhilaration, came the most important emotion of all: a sense of empowerment. At last, they were getting adults to listen to them, and it was intoxicating.

John Hathorne commenced with the proceedings. "Bring in the accused, Bridget Bishop."

Bridget Bishop was an open target. Years before there had been some speculation that she had indeed been a tool of Satan. When she and her husband had hurled insults against each other, they were made to stand back-to-back for an hour in the public square, their mouths gagged, their foreheads covered with papers describing their crimes.

Now, as she walked into the room, all hell broke loose. The afflicted girls began writhing on the floor, holding their stomachs, howling with pain, and pointing accusatory fingers at Bridget.

"You are hereby brought before this court to give evidence of all witchcrafts with which you are knowledgeable," Judge Hathorne stated.

"Before these witnesses, I declare I am clear," came her firm voice.

Turning to the afflicted, Hathorne asked, "Hath this woman harmed you?"

All the girls nodded. Quiet, watchful, they waited for a response.

"You are hereby accused by these girls of hurting them. What say you?" Corwin challenged.

"I never was with these persons before," Bridget insisted.

"They say you bewitched your first husband to death."

"If it please the court, I know not of it." As Bridget shook her head in disbelief, the afflicted ones started moaning softly.

"I am no witch and am not acquainted with the devil," she insisted, but with each new word, the girls' moans grew louder.

"Your very presence brings witchcraft before us and influence upon the afflicted," pronounced Hathorne, rubbing his chin with his right hand, tapping his fingers with the left.

"I know nothing of a witch, for I am clear. Indeed, Your Worship, if I were such a person, you should know it." When the accused turned pleading eyes up towards the ceiling, Hathorne noticed all the girls also looking up in the same direction, like marionettes manipulated by Bridget's motion.

His next question was directed towards Mercy Lewes and Ann Putnam. "Look upon this woman. Is it she who has hurt you?"

The two girls nodded vehemently. He turned directly back to Bridget. "What say you now? They have negated your innocence."

"In truth, I never have seen these girls. Indeed, Your Worship, I am innocent of these actions." Bridget's voice had begun to dissolve into a quaver.

She was led away from the room then, amidst a torrent of cries and shrieks, and when she was forced to touch one of the girls who miraculously appeared 'well,' everyone agreed that this was a true sign of witchcraft. Once Bridget had gone, all the rest of the girls instantly fully recovered, readying themselves for the next series of examinations.

Thoughts of returning to prison made Bridget cringe. Early spring rains had seeped through the stone walls, flooding her cell floor and carrying rat feces and urine underfoot everywhere. Dozens of other accused women huddled around her—some neighbors, others strangers, people who before now had always believed that surely God would never abandon them.

Bridget took a long hard look around her. There were Goody Good and her four-year-old daughter, Dorcas, who both slept on either side of her, hemming her in so tightly she could barely move. Night after night the neglected girl would whimper softly until she fell asleep by herself because her mother had no strength left to try to comfort anyone, let alone a frightened child. Next, Bridget stared at Rebecca Nurse in disbelief. Here was a woman whom everyone loved and respected. Could it be possible that she, too, was accused of witchcraft? And what about Elizabeth Proctor? Supposedly she was pregnant. Surely they wouldn't be so cruel as to try her as a witch with a little one growing in her belly. And Sarah Wildes, Elizabeth Howe, and Susannah Martin. Here they all were, languishing in this God-forsaken place.

Suddenly, memories of her good friend Penelope Stinson flashed before her; how, when Bridget's husband had passed away the year before, this loyal friend had brought her food, laughter, and company to help soften the loneliness of an empty house. Now, surrounded by so much misery, she missed her former confidant more than she could have thought possible.

"'Tis a visitor for you, Goody Bishop," the jailer declared, adding magnanimously, "She seems a harmless lot. I will let her pass."

Penelope Stinson stood five-feet-seven inches tall, adorned with an imposing chest. Her ill-fitting clothes draped her body and her hair was in the usual state of disarray, but as she moved towards Bridget, the accused attempted a smile, stretching her shaky fingers out through the wrought iron cell bars.

"Keep all hands to yourselves!" the jailer bellowed from across the room.

"Penelope, it does my heart good to see you."

"Bridget," Penelope started, "there is something I must tell you before you go further in this trial." Bending in towards the iron cell bars, she lowered her voice to a whisper. "I left some things in the walls of your house last spring when you had work done there."

"What...what kind of things?"

"Well, I wanted to bring your house good lucke. It were only for good lucke, I swear it." Bridget waited, trembling.

"Remember those little puppet dolls I made two years ago? Do you remember them?"

Bridget thought a moment. "Yes, I do remember. They were so simple. I knew you could do better."

"Those were speciale dolls, they were. They could bring you good lucke, I think." Penelope was close to tears. "I never meant anything more of it. I swear it."

"Why are you telling me all of this?"

"I fear for you. The builders who labored at your house last spring say they will speak against you. They will tell of these dolls, how you made a pact with...with...Satan." A tiny sob eked out her throat.

For several seconds, Bridget stared at her friend. Dazed, she suddenly wondered why she hadn't even noticed the bars in front of her before, how filthy, how corroded they looked. And when she fainted, her dress wiped up some of the sludge she had tried so desperately to avoid.

The next day proved far worse. As she was being led into the meetinghouse by the 'official transporters,' swelling with self-importance and disdain for the accused, the afflicted girls ratcheted up their laments. Hathorne began the proceeding by addressing a small, cackling group of local women nearby. "Let the accused Bridget Bishop be examined for the 'Devil's Mark'. Conduct her into the other room, undress her, and perform your thorough search."

Scared and humiliated, Bridget couldn't get her legs to move. The clerks had to hoist her up over their shoulders like a wheat sack and carry her behind the hawk-like women, eager to explore every inch of her body. Off in a side room, she could feel their heavy breathing on her skin as their prying fingers turned her around, poking, probing. When they focused on her private parts, she flinched, determined to stop them, but her thin, protective hands were cast aside, then pinned down as two other women got on their hands and knees to look up at her most intimate spot of all.

"Looks like there aren't a mark on this one, to be sure. But she's the Devil, she is," one of them proclaimed. Then, while Bridget wept, they handed her back her clothes so she could return to jail for that night and every other night for two weeks.

That winter, angry winds had whipped around structures, blowing snow everywhere—under saggy doors, into window crevices, and finally, depositing huge drifts that sloped against buildings. By spring, the full weight of the packed winter blanket had saturated through many of the wooden planks, leaving them rotted and shrunken with rusty nails protruding at least an eighth of an inch. If people listened hard enough they swore they could hear more than the usual creaks and groans that April and May.

Then the unthinkable occurred. Witnesses would claim later that on the final examination day, just as Bridget glanced up at the meetinghouse, there was a loud crash and one of the wooden planks fell, splitting in two. There was no recognition of the previous harsh winter, nor the fact that two of the nails had worked themselves out. This was simply the sign from the Devil they had been searching for.

"Whereupon said Bridget Bishop is determined guilty of Witchcraft, and therefore sentenced to Death as the Law directs and execution shall be done accordingly. In the name of King William and Queen Mary of England, said accused shall fryday next, the tenth day of this month of June, be conducted to the place of Execution to be hanged by the neck..."

On June 10th, the last morning of Bridget's life, the sky shifted from pale to cobalt blue. Cumulus clouds floated above as the prisoner was slowly carted up towards Gallows Hill, her dirty hands and feet bound, her hair falling in unwashed strings. Along Prison Lane to Essex Street, then Essex Street through the village and out to Boston Road, Bridget endured the jeers and taunts of crazed townspeople, hungry for a spectacle. She didn't even notice Penelope standing nearby weeping openly, her hands pressed together in silent prayer, nor did she realize that one of the shrieking attendees was the main accuser, Abigail Williams herself.

As Bridget took the last few steps towards a large oak tree, Abigail felt an unfamiliar stab of conscience. Suddenly, she flashed back to when she and Betty Parris had so innocently played the New England 'egg-white-in-the-glass game'. There was the floating egg white resembling a coffin and Betty's terrified look. Then there was the following day, with Betty's non-stop 'sleeping', which, Abigail surmised, had more to do with exhaustion from the trauma of the game than truly being bewitched. Now, gathered here, there was no turning back, or was there? She opened her mouth to protest the hanging, but no sound came out. She wasn't ready for her power to end.

So she closed her lips, biting down on one side until it almost bled, and after Bridget's head was covered with a simple cloth bag, and the ladder she had climbed up on was shoved aside by a clerk, leaving her legs swinging desperately one last time before her neck broke, Abigail quickly looked down at the ground, still mute.

But Penelope's voice crackled through the silence. "You shall not die in vain, Goody Bishop, you shall not die in vain!"

People turned around to stare, murmuring in agreement, unsure of what to do next.

Abigail panicked. She could not afford to let things get out of hand. She flung her arms up in the air and cried out, "Praise the Lord, I am spared. Praise the Lord!" Soon other people were shouting, "Praise the Lord, Praise the Lord," until the entire crowd was swept up, like a Greek chorus. As they moved en masse down the hill, Penelope realized Bridget Bishop had already been forgotten; soon they would all be attending a new trial and execution.

But Bridget's friend could not forget, and as the months passed and life in Salem continued, upended, the sight of the self-righteous Hathorne parading through town day after day kept the festering strong inside her head. When the witch trials were over and the townspeople had conceded that it had all been an error of tremendous magnitude, after eighteen other hangings, overflowing jails, and destroyed families, she might have forgiven him on some level if he had shown one ounce of remorse. But even on his deathbed, some claimed he had not only been unwilling to accept any responsibility for his part in the trials, he died proud of it.

Penelope did not share that luxury. Her life had stalled, filled with the slow, steady agony of losing a dear friend and several neighbors. Writing bitterly in her daily journal, she seethed at the thought of life resuming around her as if it had all been for naught, so when the time came time for her own deathbed, she gathered just enough strength to beckon her husband to her side and whisper, "I am putting a curse on Hathorne and all his descendants…"

"No, Penelope, no! Have you not learned anything from the trials? Forget your special powers, you mustn't talk about such things!" He tenderly covered her mouth with the palm of his hand.

Penelope gently, yet firmly removed his hand and uttered with remarkable clarity, "I curse him…and his children…and his grandchildren…and his great-great-grandchildren. From here on in, I curse them all." Her drooping eyelids fluttered twice, seconds before she died.

**

Aunt Natalie's kitchen was silent, save for the second hand clicking around her 1950's wall clock. Tick…tick…tick…tick it pulsed as Deborah sat at the table, numb.

"Honey, I know this is really difficult for you, but I think you've got to talk to Margaret Stinson from my quilt group. Maybe she has a solution. Are you listening to me?" Aunt Natalie reached out to stroke her niece's hand.

Deborah sat back and shook her head. "This is unreal! I mean, this kind of thing just doesn't happen in modern times. There are no such things as witches…are there?"

"Well, according to Margaret there are. In fact, unbeknownst to me, she has been part of a coven organization called Wicca for years. They claim they are benign, but I understand they do connect witchcraft with folk medicines and perform certain ceremonies.

"Yeah, but my family's name is Hawthorne with a "w" anyway. We're not even related to this Hathorne character!" Deborah snapped.

"Not true, I'm afraid. Apparently Nathaniel Hawthorne purposely changed the spelling of his name because he was so horrified at being related to the infamous magistrate. Why do you think he wrote books like The Scarlet Letter, all about the narrow-mindedness and viciousness of the Puritans? Obviously, he decided to expose that society for all it was worth, you know?"

"And what about Bridget Bishop? Is that all true about her? How did Margaret know all about the curse?"

"Margaret showed me Penelope's actual diary—the hanging, everything. It's all there."

When the doorbell rang, Deborah nearly fell off her seat.

"Ah...I meant to tell you, dear." Her aunt emitted a slight cough. "It's Margaret. She's here because she wants to try to make things right for you."

Deborah jumped up, knocking her chair over. "I don't want to see her! Not now! What if she puts a curse on me? Please don't let her in. Please, Aunt Natalie!" She frantically tried to stop the older woman before she could head downstairs.

But Aunt Natalie had already started her descent, calling out behind her, "Take it easy, it'll be OK."

Deborah could hear the front door being opened and shut, then a friendly banter between two women growing louder as they slowly made their way back up towards the kitchen.

When Margaret saw Deborah's face, she pleaded, "Please don't be afraid. I'm here to try to help you. I had no idea anything like this would happen to you, of all people." She tried to reach out to pat the newlywed on her shoulder.

"How do I know you won't make it worse?" Deborah demanded.

"You'll just have to trust me, I'm afraid." The quilter settled down at the kitchen table and placed a small, patchwork satchel on top of it.

"I've brought two things that might help you, but you're going to have to transcend belief and do as I say. Are you willing?" Deborah looked up at her aunt as if to say do-I-have-any-choice? She nodded slowly.

From her bag, Margaret extracted two objects. The first was a book entitled, The Myths and Legends of Quilts, and the other, a simple puppet doll.

Deborah recoiled, rising in horror. Margaret stretched out her right hand. "Wait, don't panic. All this is necessary to help you. Believe me, I didn't want this to happen, I swear I didn't. But it's my family's curse as well, and if you want to be helped, you've got to trust me. Please, please sit down so we can begin."

Opening the book up to a dog-eared page, she began reading out loud. "According to legend, there are certain quilt patterns that carry significance far beyond their beauty. For example, the Drunkard's Path is a lovely pattern in general, but one must be careful. It has been noted in various folklore that if a young couple gets a Drunkard's Path quilt for their wedding, the man may very possibly turn to drink, and even abuse, thus bringing ruination and possible death to the family."

Margaret glanced at Deborah's white face, gulped, and continued. "The only cure for a Drunkard's Path curse is to take out all the quilting stitches, one by one, until every last stitch is gone. This signifies the undoing of evil and thus, the curse will disappear. However, all the removal of stitches must occur while the husband is sleeping. If he wakes up while the process is going on, the cure will end, and the curse shall live on."

The quilter carefully laid out the puppet doll facing up on the kitchen table, but as she turned it over, Deborah could see two antique pins sticking out of its back. She began to tremble.

"You see, Deborah," Margaret continued, her hand outstretched towards the girl, "my coven believes that good can also come from witchcraft, and just as Penelope was convinced she was helping Bridget so long ago by placing those dolls in her house for good luck, I, too, am trying to bring good luck to you."

"Well, those puppet dolls didn't help Bridget too much, did they?" Deborah grumbled.

"I really believe that if the people of Salem hadn't been so panicked about witches, the dolls would have probably helped Bridget. Well, anyway, we'll never really know, will we?" Margaret, although used to people's skepticism, turned impatient. She switched over to a prayer. "Help this woman remove her family's curse, and let her have her husband back. Bring goodness into her life again." As she removed the pins from the doll's back and stuck them into its heart, she mumbled some unintelligible words that Deborah didn't even want to recognize.

When Margaret finally let herself out, Deborah was left in a quandary. On the one hand, by following the quilter's instructions there might be a possible end to this madness; on the other hand, the newlywed feared Margaret was all show and couldn't be completely trusted. But she did trust Aunt Natalie, and based on that, she decided to forge ahead.

Purchasing a seam ripper, tiny scissors, and a tiny flashlight, she headed home to find David, drunk in the living room, his face red, his lips in a snarl. "Where the hell have you been? I came home for a nap, and when I woke up, there washnowifearound!"

"If you must know, I went out to a movie to try to relax. Here, let me…let me fix you something to eat."

Grunting, he sank back into the down-filled couch pillows as Deborah anxiously fingered the tiny scissors, seam ripper, and flashlight in her pocket.

Night after night she picked at the quilt as he lay sleeping. She was no seamstress, but she had used a seam ripper before and each time she painstakingly extracted a thread, she would shove it into a small zip-lock baggie, to be discarded in the trash the following morning. David, dead to the world, never seemed to notice the threads slowly disappearing from the coverlet, but as his temper tantrums increased, she soon found herself praying this 'cure' was not just a big waste of time.

And then it happened.

David's slap reminded her of a minor actress getting smacked around in a Grade B movie, all filmed in slow motion. It wasn't really happening to her, it was simply that unknown actress married to some sort of demon, not David, the gentle man who would never cross that boundary. For a split second she thought she saw a flash of horror cross his face before he sank down on the couch, giving her hope. Maybe it was a curse.

The next day, David called her from work. "I don't know what's happening to me, Deborah. I can't stop drinking and I'm consumed by horrible thoughts," he moaned.

"I know sweetheart, believe me I know. It will all work out, I promise you…" she soothed, smiling with relief.

His tone abruptly changed. "I don't know when I'm coming home. Don't wait up." Click.

Deborah was exhilarated. If he could admit it to her, he couldn't be totally lost and she even considered telling him about the curse, but then she remembered. Concealment was the key. But that night, just before drifting off to sleep, she inched closer to him than she had in months.

Still, her sixth sense warned her she was not completely out of the woods. Even with most of the threads gone, she would watch her husband sitting across from her at dinnertime, distant, brooding. Plying him with nonstop wine, she figured the sooner he went to sleep, the less chance there was of him hitting her again.

It seemed to work. He got so drunk he almost didn't make it to the bedroom. Trying to balance himself, he held onto the walls of the hallway as he stumbled into their bedroom, fell onto his side of the bed, and instantly passed out.

As his snores rattled, she worked feverishly on the quilt top, spurred on by a new hope. With barely any threads to hold it together, the quilt kept shifting, but she pressed on until the last stitch was removed. When David stirred in his sleep, she quickly turned off the flashlight, excited, waiting in the dark to see what would happen next.

He began to cough—odd, half-choking sounds that made her want to reach out and stroke his back, but she paused, unsure of his reaction. His spasm had woken him, and as he staggered into their bathroom in the dark, she could hear him vomiting behind the closed door. Please, dear God. Please, dear God. Please, dear God, she mouthed.

Like a flash, the overhead light was switched on, and David was lumbering towards her, yelling, "You bitch! You bitch!"

This can't be! It can't! The cure should have removed the curse. What's happening? her brain screamed.

"How come you gave me so much wine? Now you've made me sick, you bitch! You're no good for me. I'm going to kill you!"

She clutched the quilt tightly in her hands and bringing it up over her head, waited for him to strike. Under the quilt, above her head, she could hear his labored breathing, and she could only imagine his arm raised, ready to attack.

Then she saw it. A tiny bit of the knotted end of a thread was still embedded on the backside of the quilt. She must have missed it before. Frantically, she grabbed it by the knob and with a quick tug, yanked it out.

Silence. Her heart was pounding so hard she had trouble hearing anything else in the room. When was he going to attack? Was that the sound of some sort of weapon being taken out of a sheath? She couldn't tell. She opened her mouth, but nothing came out.

Suddenly, she pictured the noose around Bridget Bishop's neck tightening, then drawn up and pulled, leaving the accused dangling helplessly in the air.

It gave Deborah the strength to howl. "Whaaaah—" she began, just as two strong arms enveloped her, holding her gently, tenderly.

The next day she threw out the quilt.

LETTIE'S TALE

Simply stated, John Beauregard was not a contented man. According to his wife, indeed, many of his neighbors, there was no reason on earth why he shouldn't be happy, surrounded as he was by mint juleps, stylish day dresses, magnolias, hydrangeas, and white Georgian-Palladian columns on his extensive veranda. Yet for him, recently it was as if a chigger had lodged itself just below his skin, depositing its venom—itching first in one spot, then in another and another, leaving him in a constant state of discomfort. If people had bothered to ask, he might have told them how he had begun to feel caught in the middle of an antiquated world; gracious and refined to be sure, but in the end, contaminated by slavery. As he surveyed his inherited plantation, the White Birches, while others gawked at his front garden, with its planting beds edged by boxwood and its gravel pathway coated with seashells, all he could focus on were his many slaves out in the distant fields, hunched over in the hot sun, their bodies forming 'n's, as they quietly and steadily picked cotton for his profit.

Dinners that included ham, boiled mutton, beef á la mode, boiled turkey stuffed with oysters, various vegetables, syllabub, plum and cheesecake pudding, and stewed apples with cream, once delightful to him, now had become intolerable, particularly when his wife Margaret would prattle on about something inconsequential one minute, then complain bitterly about the laziness of their darkies the next. He would scrutinize the faces of their house slaves then, searching for any reaction, but usually he saw none, simply impassive stares on tired, lined faces, worn by age and servitude.

"Honestly, John, sometimes you can be so exasperating," Margaret remarked one day, seconds after hearing a startling pronouncement from her husband. "Whatever gave you such an idea as that? Our darkies don't need to learn to read and write. That would simply be too dangerous. Why would you ever want to do that, Sir?"

"Because, my dear, ultimately, they are human beings, and as such, they, too, deserve to be educated, particularly our little family of house slaves. Why, Beulah has been Charles' and Charlotte's Mammy since they were born!" It was difficult masking the contempt he felt for his wife.

"Being a mammy to our children is one thing, but educating her is quite another! I simply won't have it!" Fear of slave insurrections kept Margaret narrow and strident, although her tone abruptly changed once her daughter Charlotte was carried in by her caretaker.

"My little dahlin'! Did you have a nice nap?" Ignoring her slave, Margaret snatched the toddler away from Beulah's strong, experienced arms, and with a firm "Hurrumpff!" aimed at John, retreated to her separate bedroom with Charlotte, leaving her husband alone with Mammy.

After an awkward pause, he turned to her. "How's your daughter, Lettie, Mammy? Is everything all right now?" he asked gently.

She stared up at him, recognizing the stooped shoulders of a hollow marriage. Whereas her first instincts were to blanket her owner with comforting arms, instead she provided only a weak smile. "Yes'r. She doin' gist fine."

How could she ever divulge the fact that her own toddler had had a high fever for several days now, and all her family's frantic efforts to reduce it were unsuccessful? Certain subjects were just not discussed with white masters, even sympathetic ones, like Master John.

There was no doubt she was fortunate. Just behind the main house, the house-slave quarters seemed a paradise compared to the field hands' shacks. Built on wooden stilts several inches above ground, Beulah's family could live without mud and earthworms in the fall and spring, not to mention yearlong lizards and field rodents scurrying across their planked floor. Narrow beds coddled their backs and there was even a larder, often filled with leftover tidbits, pilfered from an unsuspecting Margaret.

Indeed, Beulah had always given thanks to the Lord for her decent life on the plantation, but tonight, upon finding her mother, Minah, sobbing and wringing her hands, the sudden wrench of her stomach told her the good fortune was about to end.

"There's somethin' wrong wid dis child. She not right," Minah moaned, clutching her granddaughter and dabbing her creviced cheeks with a shredded handkerchief.

Cradling Lettie in her arms, Beulah swayed, cooed, and, clucked, anything to stop the toddler's screams. But the little girl only wailed louder, cupping her tiny ears with frail hands as spittle ran down her chin.

Her mother's eyes rolled up towards the ceiling, as if all the Powers That Be were present in the room. "Whaz wrong? Whaz wrong?" she whispered. Suddenly, Lettie went quiet.

"She better now, she better now!" Minah kept repeating, hopping from one foot to another in joy.

"Hey, little girl, hey, little girl. You's all right now!" laughed Beulah as she threw back her head and let out such a piercing, 'Hallelujah, Lord,' she thought she'd split her dress. Then, smiling down at her little daughter, she waited for a response. Lettie stared back up at her, her dark eyes shining, her mouth still.

The tiny hairs on the back of her neck were slowly rising as she peered into her child's eyes. "Hey, little girl. Give me a smile. Hey…hey!" No response.

Laying her little one carefully down on the bed, she clapped her hands together, gently at first, then harder and harder, until the little cabin echoed with each new smack. Still, no response. Gaping at one another, Minah and Beulah suddenly recognized the truth: Lettie's world had been transformed forever.

Once secure and grateful for being privileged house slaves, they now woke each morning in a heart-thumping panic. Would Lettie be auctioned off the plantation due to her hearing deformity? Deaf slaves were certainly not valued commodities. Sleepless nights brought dark circles under their eyes and tired movements as they worked hour after hour, guarding their secret.

Finally, John inquired what was the matter. When they admitted their problem, he promptly put them at ease. "First of all, you needn't worry about me selling Lettie. She has a home as long as you all do, and that will probably be for the rest of your lives. I would set you all free if I could do so, but it is not my decision—the laws forbid it. But I have decided to teach your family how to read and write. What say you to that?" He attempted a supportive smile.

He was met with utter silence; hope had never rested well with slaves. But true to his word, several times a week John schooled Beulah, Park, and even little Lettie in reading in spite of Margaret tossing her nose in the air and spitting out, "We'll see about this!" as he hovered over their slaves, sounding out words. She would disappear then, shaking her head and wondering why he had become insane enough to even keep a deaf child on the premises in the first place!

Yet, throughout, there remained one area that secured a place for Beulah and her extended family—quilts. Quilts were an integral part of their world, quilts that won awards for Margaret in the neighboring towns, and homespun, bright-colored quilts that kept them all warm at night after the evening air had chilled or in the early fog-laden mornings when the dampness superseded everything. And in time, as Lettie grew, so did her ability to sew beautiful coverlets, just like her mother and grandmother before her.

Margaret would sneer at the crudeness of the slave quilts in comparison to the exquisite appliquéd ones that the two slaves had finished for her. As for Lettie, helping to piece her family's quilts in front of a slow-burning fire became as much of a cherished history lesson about their ancestors as it did about learning how to make tiny, uniformed stitches. Her needle flying through the clothes she had cut up for their quilts, Beulah would recount endless stories to her daughter all about their relatives and forefathers from Africa. With the little girl in front of her, she would carefully mouth her words about how clever they had all been, using secret embroidered codes on many of the fabrics they had carried with them when they were being abducted from their village.

Lettie's favorite story by far was about her great-grandfather, Ksistu, a blacksmith from the Mende tribe. It was their belief that being a well-skilled blacksmith held special powers, and although the other tribesmen could communicate through their drums, he could spread his words even farther through his hammer and anvil. Even so, he was allotted no special privileges and as a young man, he, too, was kidnapped and sent to Goree, the infamous slave pen on the West African coast.

There, in a windowless cell, jammed up against countless scores of other future slaves, he inwardly raged. Twenty-four hours of human sweat, urine, feces, and vomit accosted him from the moment he awoke until he finally fell asleep. Yet watching his cellmates slowly deteriorate from the heat and rancid air, he vowed to maintain his pride above all else.

But that task proved difficult, especially when herded down a long corridor, through 'The Door of No Return', then slung into the hold of a ship bound for the Americas. Shackled, lined up head-to-toe next to hundreds of other Africans, he could feel his body aching from the weight of the heavy iron chains and neck collar. If a person died, nothing was mentioned; the corpse would simply be hurled overboard to make room for someone else.

After landing on the shores of South Carolina, Ksistu was given no time to rest. He was whisked away to a slave auction, where, beneath a blistering sun, he stood on a makeshift platform, crushed against a multitude of terrified Africans, waiting to be bought. As the slave traders greased their faces and torsos with wax to make them 'shine', Ksistu numbed. Surprisingly, he didn't have long to wait. He was immediately sold to a gentleman farmer by the name of Montgomery Beauregard, who had specifically requested a slave with blacksmith capabilities. It seemed he had had a hankering for some intricate wrought-iron work on the gates leading up to his plantation, and was told by one of the traders about Ksistu.

Lettie pointed to the beautiful gates outside the White Birches, glottal-stopping her sounds.

"Yes, child," Beulah enunciated carefully. "Dose gates was built by yo great-grandfather, and don't ever forget it!" She laughed proudly, promising to continue telling Lettie their family history, so that Lettie would be able to some day pass everything onto her own children. "Dis is how it's done," Beulah continued. "Dis is da African way, tellin' stories so we don' ever forget."

Margaret's family background provided money and breeding but little else. Although marrying such a man as John did not produce an ideal marriage, it did bring with it a certain continuity of the noblesse oblige to which she was accustomed. However, as John's attitude changed, her increasing resentment towards their slaves needed an outlet, and Lettie became the perfect scapegoat. The next time Master John was away on business for a few days, Beulah was ordered to take her skinny, ten-year-old daughter down to the slave cabins to do some real work.

The mammy did what she was told; she nodded outwardly with just the right amount of deference. On the inside, she prayed for a good, sharp hatchet.

"Now, Lettie, don't get upset," she warned the little girl staring up at her with troubled eyes. "Dese po' folks don't live like we's do. Dey can't hep how dey look o' smell. Dey's good folk, tho', and I gist don wan you t' git scared."

Down by the row of field hands' cabins, Lettie grasped her mother's hand so tightly Beulah finally had to let go and fan out her own fingers to bring back some circulation. The smell of frying salt pork wafted out of holes where windows should have been, reminding Beulah of the harsh childhood she had spent many hours trying to forget. Chickens bobbed and clucked in the tiny front area, pecking at stray cornmeal, twisting their heads around in frenetic movements before reaching down again to peck at some more. Over a line of rope stretched between two trees, crude, shoddy material from England (Negra Cloth Beulah once heard Miz Margaret call it) was hung out to dry, in an effort to remove any leftover sizing, and/or lice.

At the tin front door, Beulah rapped softly, knowing full well that if her knocks were too loud or insistent, her cousins inside might assume it was a white person and get frightened. Seconds later, the door opened and Lettie could see about eight people sitting around on wooden stools, the earthen floor, and an old barnyard crate, about to eat their meager supper. Behind them stood their chimbly, composed of sticks and red mud. Beulah shuddered, remembering how once when she was fifteen-years-old, one of these chimblies had caught on fire, filling her parent's cabin with choking red smoke and burning twigs.

One of them instantly cried out, "Cuzin Beulah! Cuzin Beulah! 'Member me? I's yo' cuzin Mattie. Mattie from da ol' days!"

Beulah peered in at the crinkled, gray-haired woman and gasped. Her cousin had aged so much over the last twenty years she hardly recognized her. The last time they had seen each other, Mattie had been an active cotton picker in the fields, Beulah just graduated from water carrier to weed puller. Now, facing one another, grinning through their tears, any thoughts of where did all those years go were brushed aside.

"Don' worry, Cuzin," Mattie comforted her after a supper of salt pork and garden vegetables. "We ain't gonna let her work too hard. She kin be water carrier only, so she ain't gonna get no hard labor. An' if dat mean ol' Miz Margaret ever come down here to check wid things, we gist gonna put Lettie right out in da field for gist dat time. Miz Margaret don' have t' know how it really be. Don' worry, Cuzin, we gonna 'Put on the Massa' and she never know'd da dif'rence!"

They both laughed, recognizing the stupidity of slave owners and suddenly, Mammy felt considerably better. And if she could see her daughter two times a week that would be more than tolerable. Still, she let her cousin know straight off that Lettie's reading was top priority.

Cousin Mattie was as good as her word. She insisted that Lettie read to herself as well as teach the others, and as the children concentrated by the firelight each night, the young ones cocooned in gunny sacks, the older ones draped in their one outfit—a soiled cloth, drawn at the waist by a roped cord—they all learned the scriptures from an old, tattered Bible Miz Margaret had thrown away. Their backs warming, their eyes burning, they all mouthed the words slowly, deliberately, taking their cues from their educated cousin as she used her own unique form of sign language. Secrecy remained uppermost in their minds; none of them could ever be caught reading.

In time, Mattie furthered Lettie's knowledge of quilting, and from the beginning was astonished by the agility of the young girl. Small, even stitches that for many might take a lifetime to perfect, came naturally to the deaf child, who delighted everyone by presenting each family member with their own, well-crafted quilt.

At first, the idea of slavery wasn't even a conscious thought for Lettie. She had been well-treated up at the Big House and even here, in the lowlands, surrounded by her cousins with whom she romped through the tall-bladed grass each sunset just before snuggling up together, heads to wriggly toes on one large, straw mat. But as they all matured, she could see how arduous their tasks had become. How being a half-quarter hand was infinitely more grueling than being a quarter hand. With the other boys becoming full field hands, Lettie watched them return from long, backbreaking days, exhausted, bitter, transformed from the carefree boys she had gotten to know.

Her narrow world was shifting and with it, an awareness of little things that now called out to her; secrets whispered between the adults behind doorways, conversations stopped mid-sentence as she approached. It also occurred to her that more and more, slaves were disappearing. Where did they go? she wondered. Was that the secret? For the first time in her life, a tight knot was growing inside her chest, keeping her on high alert.

Increasingly, Margaret would forge down to the cabins, and each time, Mattie, having pushed Lettie out of the largest window hole to the fields, assured her mistress, the deaf slave was indeed laboring tirelessly. Barely containing her triumph, Margaret would snort in pleasure then sashay back towards the house, her petticoats taking free rein as they flounced under her hoop skirt and brocade day dress.

By sixteen, Lettie truly understood the concept of slavery and how no amount of 'special' treatment could stand up to Miz Margaret's determination. If only she could talk to Master John. He had always been so kind and gentle to her. But these days, he was nowhere to be seen and word had it he didn't have long to live. So she never returned to the Big House with the huge columns and boxwood hedges, and her images of marble halls, wide staircases, mahogany beds covered with beautiful appliquéd quilts gradually faded into a hazy, childhood memory.

Still, in spite of everything, she managed to cling to her one joy as if it were her lifeline: quilting. As she grew, so did her reputation as an accomplished seamstress. Finally permitted to sit around with the women, she stayed in her own world, rhythmically plaiting her needle in and out of the fabrics while they chatted and sewed.

One night, they jolted her out of that world.

"Mattie, it be time to tell her," one of the women suggested, resting her patchwork down on her lap.

"I gist don' know. She sure smart 'nuff, but what go on in dat head of hers, I gist...I gist don' know," Mattie cautioned.

But the next week she did begin pushing Lettie towards specific quilt patterns. First, there was a Flying Geese design, where dark mini-triangles of fabric went in one direction, lighter triangles headed in another. Next, she coaxed Lettie into making a Monkey Wrench quilt, with blocks shaped like anvils. But the moment Lettie drifted off into one of her own designs, Mattie's brows would pinch and her lips tighten.

"No! Do as you's tol' chile," she would mouth.

Before long, Lettie noticed that whenever Mattie hung up a new quilt, she would spread it out on the far side fence for only a couple of days, then take it down and carefully store it under her bed. Two months later, there would be a replacement quilt, showcased on the very same fence. On these occasions, Mattie became purposeful; none of the children were allowed to sidetrack her. Month after month passed and as she watched her older cousin, Lettie sensed something significant was happening.

"Keep quiltin,' chile," Mattie mouthed. "Yo work's so beautiful. Now I wan' you t'mek a sampler quilt wid dif'rent blocks. It's impoten' you put dem in dis order." She scribbled some patterns on paper for Lettie, but once Lettie got going, Mattie crushed the papers, tossed them into the fireplace, then together they watched the flames bend and twist each pattern until the fireplace was filled with gray, chalky ashes.

'Why are you destroying the pattern, Mattie?' Lettie wrote on her chalkboard.

Mattie eyed her shrewdly. Then, "Sit down, 'chile. It's time for you t' know. Yo quilts gonna hep us git free." She chuckled at Lettie's puzzled look. "Each quilt you done fo' me give notice t' someone 'bout what deys s'posed to do to 'scape. 'Member dat Monkey Wrench Quilt yo done?"

Entranced, Lettie plopped down on a nearby stool.

"Well, dat quilt hep save Mannah, her husband, and two o' her chil'en. 'Cause of dat quilt, dey know'd dey's s'pose to pack deys tools, and git tings they needs fo' der trip up North. I done a quilt call'd Wagon Wheel, 'member? You sed somethin' 'bout it to me. Well, I put dat one on da fence, too, and den dey know'd dey was goin' ta hide in a wagon 'n 'scape."

"Yer Flyin' Geese quilt wid the dark triangles facin' west," she continued, "tol' Mannah ta go West fust. Each square on dat quilt show'd the dif'rent fiel's she had ta go past ta git off da plantation. 'Member, I says t'make da other squares in special order: first yella, den white, den brown, 'member? Well, dat's 'cause Mannah would have ta go fust past da corn fiel', den the cotton fiel', den that fiel' up da road that's fallow dis last year. Yo' understan, chile?"

Lettie nodded slowly. Everything was beginning to make sense. All those whispered conversations, stopped short when she happened by, then the disappearance of Mannah and her family—all planned!

She was anxious to learn more, but Mattie was adamant. "We do more tomorro', chile. Tonight yo' rest. You needs all yo' thinkin' for da mornin'.'" She kissed her accomplice, worrying this venture might prove too heavy a burden for such a young girl. But in very short order, Lettie understood The Code so well, she would catch things that even Mattie had missed. In fact, word soon spread that the teenager, just like a second-in-command, should also be consulted whenever escape plans were being hatched.

She also discovered that none of this would have ever come to pass had her father, Park, not accompanied Master John to town two and a half years earlier. It was then that the slave managed to smuggle out a topographical map of their entire region, and while Master John met with some business associates, Park conducted his own meeting with another slave behind the crumbling blacksmith building. The two men didn't dare speak; their Massahs were too immediate, but they did grin, shuffle their feet, and display ignorant expressions for the plantation owners, as they drew maps and deciphered codes in the dirt with their toes.

Having become well versed in this system, Lettie promptly memorized the maps Park had drawn from his own memory before destroying them in the cabin fireplace. Then, painstakingly embroidering the identical boundary lines on the next few quilts she pieced, she chose inconspicuous areas, like surrounding a wagon wheel, or outlining an Ohio Star, indicating Ohio's various safe houses.

Slaves continued to disappear from the plantation and by 1830, at least twenty slaves had vanished. Master John didn't seem concerned. He was relieved to simply make it each day without feeling too wretched, a fact he managed to keep hidden from Margaret and the rest of his family. But all the slaves knew. They had watched his health slowly deteriorate, noticed how he gripped onto the banisters, his knuckles turning white, and how it was taking longer and longer for him to rise from his dining room seat. Margaret and his children appeared oblivious to everything; to Beulah, his physical well-being was vital for all their future. If Master John died what would become of them? And what would become of Lettie?

In 1831, all hell broke loose. Nat Turner, an educated, yet disgruntled slave had had enough, and together with a band of seventy-five other slaves, slaughtered fifty-seven white men, women, and children during a bloodthirsty night of revenge. Although he was apprehended, the ever-present fear of insurrection, already fine-tuned in the minds of Southern white slave owners, now blossomed into a blanket of paranoia.

"John, I think it is abominable that this Turner fellow carried out such an evil deed! Why, I think every one of them should be hanged!"

"My dear you make too much of these things," John protested. "We don't know the particulars. Perhaps there were circumstances that…"

"Circumstances, my foot! Honestly, John, I just don't understand you at all, and frankly, I never have!" With a toss of her hand, she quickly dismissed her husband.

John, clutching onto the spiraled banister, grunted up the staircase to his bedroom. At the top, his hand missed the hand-carved newel on the top baluster, and before he could adjust his hold, he tumbled backwards, flipping around in the air like one of his cats and finally landing at the bottom of the steps in a twisted heap, motionless.

Beulah, Park, and Margaret flew over to him. "John! John! Do you hear me? Answer me! Answer me!" Margaret bent over his body, screaming at her dead husband while the two slaves nervously looked over at each other, shaking their heads.

Margaret proved to be everything Beulah had feared. With her husband gone, her power turned boundless. "That girl should be taught a few things or two!" she snapped, ordering Mattie to triple Lettie's chores on top of supposedly toiling in the fields. Once, in a fit of rage, she even swatted at the slave's legs with a riding crop as the girl was hauling a bucket of water out of their well. At that moment, Lettie turned to face her mistress, her chocolate eyes darkened with defiance. Margaret gasped and stepped back, staring at the iron-willed girl, her crop down at her side.

Indeed, at twenty, Lettie was already a force to be reckoned with. Mattie had placed her cousin in charge and soon, people were bypassing the seasoned seamstress and reporting directly to the talented girl. She thrived on this new responsibility, never complaining if she had to stay up late, sewing by candlelight, in order to finish her 'Freedom' Quilts; too many people needed her.

"What terrible workmanship this quilt has! Nothing like my quilts, I must say!" Margaret gloated, examining the odd embroidery pattern on one of the code quilts suspended over a nearby fence one afternoon. "Well, that only goes to show how careless and ignorant these people actually are!" she proclaimed, reveling in her supremacy.

"Now where is that little cripple?" she continued, glancing toward the fields, unaware that Lettie had already ducked down out of sight in the cabin.

She was about to search for Mattie when her son Charles came panting down the path after her.

"Mother, Mother! I have wonderful news! The great Jonathan Brimford from Canada has expressed an interest in visiting our plantation! Isn't that grand?" Stopping short of his mother, Charles tried to catch his breath, his doughy chest heaving, his face like ripening cherries.

"That's all very well, my dear, but who is Jonathan Brimford I'd like to know?" Margaret sniffed.

"Why, one of the world's greatest ornithologists, that's all, mother.

Don't you read anything ?"

"Of course, well, of course," Margaret lied. "But why is he visiting us, pray tell?"

"Because he intends on studying all the various birds, or aves as he calls them, on our plantation. Then, upon his return, he shall write about them in one of his scientific journals or some such thing. He's quite well known, Mother. He might even mention you in his article!" The two smiled at one another and hurrying back up the stone path to the house, discussed preparations for their imminent guest.

Jonathan Brimford conceded to two passions in his life. On his travels to various pockets around the world, he would always marvel at not only the beauty of all bird species, his primary passion, but at all the charming ladies he had encountered as well.

But it was his third passion that he had camouflaged with the same agility of the Northern Cardinals he loved so much. Being Canadian, the American concept of slavery was to him, unfathomable. Indeed, each time he heard of some horrific act being committed towards the slaves down in his neighboring country, his blood would boil. His friends and acquaintances, scoffing at the primitive nature of all U. S. citizens, conversed on the subject as if they were talking about an errant child refusing to eat his dinner. However, Jonathan took these things far more seriously and as time passed, recognized that perhaps it was time to take a stand.

Oddly enough, a brilliant idea occurred to him one night as he lay in bed reading. In a paragraph written in The American Field Guide Book of Birds, it stated, "…one of the best places to research the North American bird is in the southern United States. There, along with the various wilderness areas, are large plantations, congested with all manner of species…"

Four weeks later, he was on a train headed for South Carolina. Listening to the rhythmic clatter of wheels, Jonathan took a deep breath before settling down to work in his private compartment. Extracting several state maps from his tan leather suitcase, he quickly leafed through them, murmuring each name as they appeared: Georgia, Alabama, Missouri, Virginia, and Arkansas. Finally, coming to South Carolina, he carefully separated that map from the others.

Next, taking out a ledger and pen, he started drawing four columns on one of the entry sheets. On top of the left column, he penned the word, "STATE"; on top of the second column, he wrote down the words, "PLACES TO VISIT"; over the third column, he copied the word, "SAFE?" and finally, on the top of the fourth and final column, he wrote the word, "NUMBER."

He shifted through another pile of papers, picking up one entitled, "PLANTATIONS AND ESTATES." On that sheet, he underlined several names including White Birches, which he also circled, along with a little check mark. Finally, he began filling in more names under his first three columns along with their corresponding numbers.

Satisfied, he leaned back for a few minutes to rest. If his system went as planned, he would at last be able to sleep well at night, knowing he had done his part to free as many human beings as possible.

At White Birches, sleep escaped Margaret entirely. Having such a distinguished guest in her house the next day was certainly exhilarating, albeit nerve-wracking. In an effort to calm herself, she coveted hourly sips of her dead husband's thirty-year-old brandy, yet her heart still fluttered, her hands twitched uncontrollably. What she really needed was a tangible release. Suddenly, gripping her riding crop in her right hand, she charged down to the slave quarters to root out Lettie.

Just seeing the young slave standing in front of the cabins washing a quilt, she blurted out, "You! Always you! What right have you to be given so much? You're nothing but a deaf and dumb cripple!" Clenching her riding crop even tighter, she raised it up high to strike Lettie, but the slave did the unthinkable. Raising her own arm instinctively she caught her mistress' crop in mid-air, blocking the blow.

Years of a pampered lifestyle was no contest for someone with a history of heavy chores. Margaret dropped the crop, gasping for breath.

"You—you! I'm going to sell you, make no mistake about that!" Reaching down, she scooped up the riding crop, and bustled up to her house before anyone could witness her tears of humiliation.

Lettie could only assume this final scene was her signal to go. That night, frenetic nightmares of wild horses bearing down on her filtered in and out of her unconsciousness and in the morning, although the air had chilled, she jolted awake, doused in sweat.

The first thing Margaret did upon waking was grin. After all these years, finally, here was her chance to not only flaunt her plantation to a person of

45

some repute, but to possibly receive some worldwide recognition as well. She wanted something to show for all the years she had spent married to a man for whom she had no respect. Giggling, she felt like a sixteen-year-old, about to attend her first debutante ball.

"Why, Mr. Brimford, I do declare! They never told me you were such a handsome gentleman!" Margaret batted her eyes and lapsed into her best Southern Belle posture.

As he was about to be shepherded up the lavish staircase to one of the guest rooms in the East Wing, the scientist rapidly assessed whether or not there were any slaves nearby, perhaps hovering in doorways or polishing the marquetry floor just inside the library. It would become crucial whom he could trust. But it was during the six-course dinner that first night that Jonathan sensed how easy a mark the family truly was, and as he consumed their fine, southern food, his disdain grew as great as his excitement about launching his plan.

He set out the following morning, notebook in hand and a wave to the Beauregards, claiming that it would be best for him to be alone for the next couple of days in order to better observe all their bird species. They nodded their heads in fervent agreement. Yes, yes, of course, they chattered in unison.

Their property stretched for miles, and at first he took his time, jotting down names of real birds and even some imaginary ones, just to fill up paper. But by afternoon, he commenced his project in earnest. The first stop was one of the fields, where the rhythmic sounds of the tireless cotton pickers resonated like quiet machines. Flick, flick, flick, shwoosh. Flick, flick, flick, shwoosh they went, as they culled, then emptied newly picked Upland cotton into large sacks tied around their waists.

"I say, who is the lead man?" Jonathan asked the first slave he encountered, Mattie's oldest son Tom.

"I guess de overseer, de boss man," Tom replied.

"No, I mean, who is the best picker here, the one the others look up to?"

Now what was this white man getting at? Tom paused a second before answering. "I guess dat'd be me. I's de best picker dey got."

"I see. May I talk privately with you?"

The slave nervously glanced up at the house. "I don' know, sah. I could git in powerful trouble!" Beads of sweat were congealing on his brow.

"I shall take full responsibility," Jonathan promised, realizing that trying to get the slaves to trust an unknown white stranger might prove more difficult than he had originally thought.

There was a moment's hesitation, then from out of nowhere, the Canadian started reciting a traditional Mendes poem, one of the few African dialects he had learned when visiting Africa several years before on a business trip.

"Who is you and why is you here?" Tom finally asked.

"Believe it or not, I've come to help you. You see, being from Canada I don't believe in slavery. So I am here to help get as many of you as possible to the North and to freedom."

Tom stood still, eyes down. "You'd better talk to Lettie. She da one who knowd all 'bout helpin' others. She deaf 'n writes her words, but she can read lips. She smart. She da one." He pointed to the barn.

That night Lettie went to bed, totally drained. The two hours she had spent with Mr. Brimford behind the barn had been crammed with safe house code numbers, detailed maps of the surrounding areas, and specific Underground Railroad routes. Yet as exhausted as she was, at first sleep evaded her, and when it finally did pull her into a grateful unconsciousness, on some level she was still all too aware that her entire future lay scribbled on two lowly scraps of paper, well-hidden in a cigar box under the mattress of her bed.

In the midst of all his planning, Jonathan recognized yet another important task ahead of him—throwing Margaret off-scent. "I have to say, Madam," he cooed, "that not only do you have one of the loveliest plantations I have ever had the good fortune to visit, I've rarely encountered such a charming mistress-in-charge." He took his time enunciating 'charming,' caressing the word with a pseudo Southern drawl, his deep voice velvetized.

"Why, Mr. Brimford how you do run on! I declare, that is the nicest thing anyone has said to me in a long, long time," Margaret gurgled, her cheeks matching her handheld rose-colored fan she had begun flapping six inches from her face.

He had her. The rest of the trip would definitely go his way if he could only keep her intoxicated each evening with this kind of Southern banter she so obviously craved.

The next day, he met with Lettie one last time, making sure she had begun memorizing those codes, and asking her which slave was going to be the first to try their getaway. She looked away, then scribbled on the slate, 'I will be the first. If I don't go now, Miz M will sell me.'

Jonathan nodded, turning toward her face so she could read his lips. "Then show the others, so after you, they can go, too. I'm going into town with Miss Margaret in two days. That will be your time to go. Just follow my code numbers for the safe houses. They will lead you into Ohio. But I must warn you, ships arriving down here are currently being questioned, so it really isn't safe to travel by boat."

A couple of days later, as Jonathan gallantly assisted Margaret onto her plush carriage seat, out of the corner of his eye he spotted an old, heavy wooden wagon, piled high with processed cotton, rambling up the road two hundred yards ahead of them. Instantly, he quickened his pace—the wagon and carriage must not cross paths.

"As you can see, sir, we are a viable exporter of cotton," Margaret boasted as he tried settling down next to her wide-topped bonnet and bulky hoop-shirted outfit.

There was no such luxury for Lettie. Her legs had been bent in a grasshopper position for hours, and even knowing there would eventually be an end to her torturous hiding under the floorboards, she feared there might also be some permanent damage. Still, she dared not make a sound; the overseer, Mr. Witherspoon was too close. Taking a deep breath, she settled down for the long journey to a distant neighbor's farm, listed as number one on the Brimford map, but with each new bump in the road, she bit her lip in pain.

Margaret, on the other hand, enjoyed grandstanding. "Mr. Brimford, I declare, I feel as if you haven't seen enough of my beautiful plantation. Why, our darkies are some of the best workers in the South. You wouldn't believe the amount of cotton they've picked this past year, I swear you wouldn't!" Unexpectedly, her face shifted. "Except of course, that Lettie! She's the one thorn in my side, I declare! She was a vexation when my poor husband was alive, and she's even more of one now. Well, nothing for you to worry about! She'll be gone soon, anyhow!"

Just beyond the road's bend, Lettie's journey was interrupted by a local farmer. "Which way you headin' with your darkie, Mr. Witherspoon? Up to Macomb County? Which way? Looks like you got a fine load o' cotton there. Should fetch quite a sum, I'd say."

Tom was becoming concerned. If he didn't open up one of the floorboards pretty soon, Lettie might suffocate. If only he could create a diversion to get the overseer and the farmer away from the wagon.

Fifty yards further up the road, the farmer's dog began whimpering as it limped back over to its owner. The two men stopped their conversation, staring at the animal for several seconds before meeting it halfway. This was the opportunity Tom needed. He scrambled down from the driver's seat, and shoving his arm deep into the cotton, opened up one of the floorboards, inches above Lettie. She instantly let out an involuntary gasp, filling her lungs.

Both men swung around to glower at Tom. "Hey, boy, what's goin' on?" Mr. Witherspoon demanded.

"Nothin', suh. I's just checkin' the cotton, makin' sure it's tied tight."

The two men laughed, shook hands, and returning to the wagon, Mr. Witherspoon hopped up onto the wood-plank seat above the loosened floorboards. As they rounded another bend a half mile up the road, Tom slowed down.

"Now what you doin' boy?"

"Oh, I's just givin' the horse a rest," Tom explained, stamping his foot on the driver's floorboard one time.

This was Lettie's signal. Obviously, they had stopped near the first coded house where she was scheduled to stay. Approaching a stone wall near the homestead, Tom turned to the overseer. "I's got t' go, boss, somethin' terrible. Kin I go over dere behin' dat fence and do my bizness?"

With a chuckle and charitable nod from the overseer, Tom stepped down from the wagon and gently knocked once on its side, alerting Lettie to get ready. He disappeared behind the rock, but after a minute or two started screaming, "Boss! Boss! Com' here's quick! Com' here's quick!"

"Oh, hell! Now what's the matter?" Witherspoon grunted, climbing down from the wagon seat and trudging over to the rock.

Lettie wasted no time. Pushing her way up through the cotton blanket, she struggled out of the wagon and took off for the woods on the opposite side of the road, while Tom continued hollering, "I's cut! I's cut! How'd dat git dere?"

Five feet short of the forest, she could hear Witherspoon reacting. "Why, that's nothin' boy! That's just a little cut from a rock. What a coward you are!" Then came more unintelligible words, a loud slap, and the wagon and horse team starting up again.

She hid in the woods for what seemed like an eternity, the cotton wisps coating her clothes and wafting up around her eyes and into her nostrils. All of a sudden, she flashed back to when she was a child, when Beulah had talked about the miracle of snowflakes. It was in their cabin, with the rain outside like opened faucets, that her mother had reminisced about North Carolina and the snow she had seen one particularly harsh winter. No two flakes were the same, she claimed, each one had its own intricate design as it floated silently down from the sky.

Just thinking of her mother steadied her, and rubbing off the white flecks as best she could, she tiptoed carefully towards the house. In the distance, hanging over a fence rail, she could see a blue Log Cabin quilt, dotted with bright yellow centers. Years ago, Lettie had learned from her cousin, Mattie, how the color yellow, unused in America, meant 'life' to many tribes in Africa. Could this mean the house was a safe life force for runaway slaves? It was time to place her trust in Mr. Brimford and find out.

Twenty yards in front of her stood an unpainted house with oiled paper for windows and badly hung doors without hardware. Two seconds later, she could feel the vibration of footsteps crunching on the first fallen leaves of the season. "Hey, I's here! Don' worry—no one else know—don' worry," an elderly black slave whispered loudly.

She didn't move. Unable to hear or read his lips, she didn't dare venture from her old oak tree with the spreading limbs hiding place. But when a wrinkled hand grabbed her from behind and spun her around, she faced someone with such kind, sympathetic eyes, she instantly relaxed, assured she was in good company.

Later, over food and an ample supply of encouraging gestures, clothing, and a map leading towards Ohio, she spent her first night away from the plantation more hopeful than she had thought possible. Perhaps her journey to freedom wouldn't be so terrifying after all.

Even so, before the Snowy Egrets, Green Herons and Merlins had a chance to warble their first morning song, Lettie was already moving along in the dark, brushing the Weeping Willows, Poplars, and Witch Alders with her fingertips.

"Mr. Brimford," Margaret gushed, sipping her Elderberry wine and flashing her most winning smile. "I declare, that was such a delightful day in town! Now, how about I show you my fields tomorrow?"

Jonathan nodded and displayed a slight bow, praying Lettie would be as far away from the plantation as possible by then.

The next morning, he procrastinated as long as he could before appearing at breakfast, stalling the inevitable. But as they wandered over to the fields, Margaret blurted out, "You know, Mr. Brimford, there is something I have to attend to. Would you mind?"

Barely acknowledging him, she continued, half out loud to herself. "She must be in the fields," she muttered as she craned her neck, obviously searching for someone.

Lettie moved tirelessly without even stopping to drink—any hesitation could easily translate into danger for her. She stumbled over moss-covered rocks and fallen tree branches, but each time, she would grab a hold of a bush or nearby trunk, say a fervent prayer, and press on.

"Where is that Lettie? Where is that blasted girl?" Margaret demanded of Tom.

"She somewhere's here, Miz Margaret, somewhere's. You look in da odder fiel'?" Tom's head didn't even turn in Jonathan's direction.

Margaret couldn't control her first unladylike snort, but managed to stop another one in front of Jonathan. "Let's go to the other field, shall we, Mr. Brimford?"

As the late afternoon shafts of light slipped in between the wooded trees, it became increasingly apparent that Lettie was nowhere to be seen. Margaret's flushed face reddened with each step until finally, she had to settle down on a rock to compose herself.

"Something is wrong! I can feel it! Where is that girl?" Then her face hardened. "My God, she's gone!"

Jonathan tried to pacify her. "Now, now, dear lady, don't trouble yourself. She probably just went to a well for water somewhere, or is in a place where you least expect her. Madam, she's only a slave. Don't even bother your pretty little head about it!"

"No, no, NO! You don't understand. This one is different! I threatened to sell her the other day, and now she's gone. Escaped! I'll have to send out the hounds! I swear I will do it!" Pushing past Jonathan, she stormed over to her barking hounds, penned in a fenced-in area beyond the barn. Within minutes, Mr. Witherspoon had hitched up the cotton wagon, bridled the horses, and gathered the hounds to track the runaway slave.

At her second safe house, Lettie breathed a tremendous sigh of relief.

Soon she would undoubtedly reach Ohio. Beyond that, freedom. She smiled and wondered why in the world she hadn't attempted this years ago, maybe with her mama and papa, or at the very least, Tom and Mattie.

By the next day, she felt relaxed enough to stop by a stream to splash her sweaty face with cool, refreshing water. Bending over, she didn't hear the first few yellow leaves crackling, nor the second or third batch. But by the fourth set of crunches, she could feel the ground vibrating, as the barking hounds pawed closer, their tongues flapping sideways out of their foamy mouths.

Frantically, she clawed her way up jagged rocks, scraping her knees and ripping the skin off her palms. At the top of a ridge, she paused for a moment to catch her breath and look back down towards the stream. She only had to see Miss Margaret's two bloodhounds, opening and closing their jaws while working themselves up into a frenzy to start up again, recharged by a jolt of adrenaline.

On the other side of the ridge, she found a stable path and trotted down it towards a house marked on her map. But as she neared a cemetery adjacent to the marked home, she panicked. She wasn't supposed to rendezvous with a freed slave until later that night, and here she was, already there, far too early, with no one in sight.

As she stood in front of the wrought iron gates, she couldn't decide what to do next until she caught sight of another stream about two hundred yards beyond the tombstones. Dogs cannot track in water, she remembered, and darted towards the brook. At first, dipping into the frigid water, she couldn't stop her instinctive shivers or violent splashes, but with a watchful eye towards the distant dogs, she slowly controlled her movements and managed to glide across the water without the dogs noticing.

She scrambled up an embankment on the other side, pulling herself along by gripping large tree roots. Then, sensing movement on the ground, she broke into a sprint, but didn't get far; a tree root caught her foot and she fell hard, sprawling over leaves, dirt, and stones. She lay still, the wind almost knocked out of her, picturing dogs tearing at her body and without warning, she started to cry.

"Aw Hell! The dogs can't track across the stream! Aw Hell! Now what are we goin' to do?" Witherspoon kicked a tree in frustration as visions of his employer slapping him across the face brought a sharp chill over him.

Damn! Maybe he'd find the little troublemaker if he went further upstream.

Her body throbbing, raw hands stinging, Lettie wouldn't stop, not even if it killed her. Yet one step more and she instantly winced, as her right knee twisted out from under her. Steadying herself against a tree, she grabbed the bandana from her head to bind the wounded area, turning it into a brace. Crumbled leaves had clothed her body, making her sneeze from their fine dust and as she wiped her nose with her hand, she saw a little blood was smeared on one of her fingers.

Have to move on, she ruminated. Have to move on—have to move on—move on—move on…

The compass that Master John had given her so long ago, when things had seemed so simple, so secure, was now clutched against her like a precious Bible as she headed in a northwesterly direction. Heart-thumping fear was causing her to run with awkward, jerky movements. Hadn't she come this way before? Didn't that tree look familiar? Everything in the forest appeared identical and with each passing tree, bush, or stone, she could feel her confidence eroding until finally, she had to face facts. She was totally lost.

Mr. Witherspoon stayed determined. He understood his somewhat precarious job was on the line with this particular runaway, so he didn't dare give up. Still, he stopped briefly to let the dogs lap up some of the stream water before forcing them to surge ahead. They dutifully followed along the stream's edge, sniffing and barking until the water forked off to the north. Witherspoon knew from there, it would soon spill out into the Ohio River and his instincts told him this was where the girl might be heading.

At night, the overseer carefully weighed his options: keeping warm for a little longer versus possibly warning Lettie of his presence. He opted for warmth and as he sat there watching the iridescent flames crackle and twist up and down, he thought of Miss Margaret and shuddered.

A half-mile upstream from the glowing fire, Lettie couldn't stop shaking. Drifting around for hours in large circles in the dark, she finally gnawed on some soggy cornbread she had left over in her dress pocket, her mind clouded with panic and despair. But once she settled on a different direction, she began to smell a dank odor, accompanied by tiny gnats flying up her nose and into her eyes. She felt her pulse jump. Could I be getting near the Ohio River? She quickened her pace, the running chant in her head pounding, 'This is it, I'm here, this is it, I'm here,' spurring her on.

"Are you lookin' for the Ramblin House?" someone asked behind her. Getting no response, he tapped her shoulder, said it again, then watched her nearly jump out of her skin. The third time he repeated his question, the light from his small lantern enabled her to read his lips. She breathed a sigh of relief and nodded vehemently, yes.

They quickly climbed into an old, mildewed boat and the man began to row, smoothly, purposely, cutting through the water in silence. But her circles in the dark had cost her, and it wasn't long before Margaret's dogs were yapping furiously as they, too, neared the river. Lettie watched the man rowing, then wondered why he had suddenly picked up speed, his oars cupping the water into two giant arcs. Then, turning her head in his point of view, she gasped. There, on the other side, she could see Witherspoon's lantern swinging back and forth as the two dogs, lit by its glow, jumped up and down, snarling, anxious to capture their prey.

Instinctively, Lettie ducked down in the boat just as the overseer bellowed, "Who goes there? Who's there? Is that you, girl? I'm gonna git you, I'm gonna git you!"

Her accomplice finally reached the other side, and grabbing Lettie, hoisted her halfway up a steep embankment. As they both scrambled to the top, something whizzed by them, grazing the man's right ear. They looked at each other and bolted towards the house.

Margaret was almost hysterical. So many days gone by with no word from Witherspoon was certainly not a good sign, and all of Jonathan's obsequious goodbyes were of little consequence to her; she was too upset to speak. Her visitor was worried as well, and over the next few weeks, tried to find out through the Underground Railroad, if Lettie had ever gotten out.

In his thank you letter to Margaret, he even inquired if her slave situation had ever been resolved, but her reply came in the form of a polite, graciously polished letter, with no mention of the incident at all. So, as he continued making his trips down to the southern part of the United States, meeting with slaves and giving his codes away to those he could trust, he never stopped wondering about Lettie, his first runaway.

When Lincoln got elected to the Presidency, Jonathan, being an ambitious man, wrote him several letters, infused with flowery words and a hope that the road to permanent abolition would be the course this new administration would adopt. Lincoln finally wrote him back, kindly inviting him to the White House to visit, and adding as a postscript, how enthralled Mrs. Lincoln was with birds, and the edification of such species.

"Mr. Brimford, I realize that your interest is in studying birds primarily, but I do confess to having a couple of intense interests of my own," Mrs. Lincoln informed him at a banquet celebration three months later, as they sat shoulder to shoulder enjoying a delicious White House dinner.

Jonathan took a sip of claret. "And what, exactly, is that, Mrs. Lincoln?"

"Why, quilts. Beautiful quilts are my passion. I do not possess the ability to make them myself, of course, but I do appreciate a well-executed one. Would you care to see my collection after dinner tonight?" Her conspiratorial tone reminded him of a schoolgirl wanting to show off something private, something treasured.

Nodding politely, he realized he could easily feign interest in a subject for which he cared very little. Anything to ingratiate himself to these people and further his career.

But after dinner, when the two of them stepped into the Lincolns' personal quarters, Jonathan was duly impressed. There, locked in three majestic mahogany curio display cabinets, were at least twenty or thirty quilts, several of which Mrs. Lincoln lovingly took out and spread before him on two velvet parlor sofas. Each one was exquisitely executed, the tiny stitches perfectly spaced, the intricate patterns well thought out.

"This one here is my favorite, I have to admit," a flushed Mrs. Lincoln proclaimed. She held up a unique coverlet for him to inspect. It was made up of many silks and satins, obviously quite different from the others in design and texture.

"Yes, yes, I know what you are thinking," Mrs. Lincoln bubbled. "This one is different. It was made from my own ball gowns, and is quite unusual, don't you think?"

Fascinated in spite of himself, he asked, "Wherever did you get the idea to do something like this?"

"A servant woman did it for me. It was her idea, and I think it is charming, no? Mr. Brimford? Mr. Brimford?"

There was no reply. He was too intent on looking at a hand-embroidered name in one of the top corners of the quilt. Drawing the lettering closer, he whispered, "Who sewed this quilt?"

"Why, her name is Lettie. I don't know much about her. She was hired by my spiritual guide, Mrs. Keckley, over a year ago who later informed me of the extraordinary workmanship of this particular ex-slave. Indeed, I know nothing of her background, but it doesn't really matter, because her work is so exceptional. Why do you want to know?" Mrs. Lincoln leaned in, her hair ringlets swinging forward, her mouth curved in an invitational smile. Jonathan grinned back. "Oh, no reason. No reason at all…" He wasn't about to offer anything further.

After all, it was Lettie's tale to tell.

THE COMFORTER

Leaning back even further into the shadows, Hans' heartbeat pulsed up into his ears. Thank God the doorway was slightly indented from the street, otherwise they would have surely spotted him. Trying to remain calm, he was suddenly overpowered by the rhythmic pounding of heavy boots on cobblestone, a mere twenty yards from his labored, irregular breathing.

"Not safe to pick up the passports today; too many SS in the city for the big rally," he speculated. Instantly, he pictured his dutiful wife Marthe, carefully folding the goose down comforter over the edge of the assigned bed while she waited patiently for him to come to her. The room would be immaculate, in fact so neat and clean you could eat knockwurst off of the floor, and the family pictures would hang straight, not crooked on the walls, as was so often the case in the other boarding houses—die besteigend hausen—around the city. Indeed, everyone often commented on how much pride Marthe always took in her work.

A sudden lull on the streets prompted Hans to slowly venture out from his hiding place, but five paces out, he could see a crowd composed of men, women, and children gathering up ahead. Booing and hissing, they all seemed riveted on something and he was about to quietly slip by them, when he glanced over and stopped, appalled.

A frail, dark-haired woman stood silently in the middle of the sidewalk with a large, wooden Jewish Star draped around her neck. Laughing and taking turns, people couldn't resist poking at the cumbersome object, and with each harsh jab, she cringed, her neck twitching back and forth. Still, she remained rooted, her glassy eyes staring straight ahead, emotionless.

An elderly man attempted to walk by as inconspicuously as possible, but it was no use. As soon as an SS guard caught sight of the yarmulke he was wearing on his head, he was hauled over and handed an ordinary toothbrush.

Hans watched in horror as the Nazis kicked the old man twice, knocking him down to his knees. Dazed, pleading softly in Yiddish, the man gazed up at his tormenters, a small stream of spittle seeping out of one side of his cracked lips. But they were on a quest.

"Clean, you good-for-nothing Jude!" they jeered. "Clean the streets! That's all you're good for. Now, do your job!"

Forcing him to scrub the streets with the toothbrush, the guards kept shoving him down with their thick, black boots every time he tried to sit up or even pause. At one point, the old man stopped long enough to peer over at their other victim and for a split second, their mutual bond of despair was palpable. But in a flash it was gone, their tasks resumed.

Hans didn't dare remain any longer. For the last several months he had witnessed so much of this treatment, he had learned protesting would be pointless, so he headed home instead, his eyebrows etched in a single, determined line.

As the late afternoon light filtered through his small apartment, he sensed that by now, Marthe would be across town, so anxious she would mostly probably be nauseous. But today, there was nothing he could do about it, he reasoned, as he began his meticulous work.

From out of his top right hand drawer, he pulled out several typed papers comprised of two hundred Jewish names, all placed in his trust. Next to the papers were at least five regular German passports, and five passports with the infamous "J" written on them. He positioned each one in front of him before he carefully started transferring the Jewish names and their photos from the Jewish passports onto regular German passports. It was a painstaking process. Each passport had to be fastidiously executed, and if he made an error, he had to start all over again.

"Irene 'Sarah' Greenfeld will now be Lisle Guttman," he muttered as he omitted the obligatory 'Sarah' attached to the woman's identification and added a Christian first and last name. He glanced over at the woman's husband's old passport, and made a mental note to change his from Leo 'Israel' Greenfeld, to Ernest Guttman.

As the pendulum on the Black Forest grandfather clock slowly clicked, Hans continued, unconscious of time. By contrast, Marthe, on the other side of the city, agonized over every minute. These days, if Hans didn't show, she automatically assumed danger was imminent and already, she could feel her stomach churning. Still, she dusted and cleaned, grateful for her housekeeping job at the Sailerstrasse Boarding House with its good pay and the opportunity it afforded for their underground activities.

Every morning she would vigorously sweep, dust, and clean each room, always making sure she finished her day with the lodging that contained the designated comforter. The comforter itself was ordinary looking: a dark brown Muhldorfer, once lush in its color and texture, now faded and worn. But stitched inside its soft folds, German and Jewish passports were strategically placed, ready for the simple exchanges that Marthe and Hans made with their co-conspirator, Herr Kaiser.

So far, the system had been impeccable. Herr Kaiser was a longtime boarder, so naturally, the comforter was housed in his room. Friends for years, he and Hans had known each other as far back as 1920, when they were both new, young professors at the University. But as Hitler's power grew, they had stood by and watched the firing of their Jewish colleagues, one by one. Finally, after two Kaier's beers each in Han's apartment one night, they knew neither of them could sit idly by while their countrymen were in so much trouble. Something had to be done.

Herr Kaiser came up with the idea first about the passports, but because Hans was an art professor, it fell on his shoulders to perform the actual forgery. Soon, he had become so proficient at these fabrications, Marthe kidded him that when Hitler was gone and their world returned to normal, perhaps he could continue this as an occupation, enabling them both to retire up in the mountains, in Mittenwald perhaps, where the snow sometimes packed twenty feet, and the quaint cottages were a reminder of better times. But Hans would listen to her fantasy for only a few seconds, chuckle, then shoo her away so he could concentrate on his passports.

Standing in the doorjamb of the final room, Marthe could hear Herr Kaiser and another man ambling up the creaky hallway stairs. As each swollen step groaned, she braced herself before telling him the bad news: no new passports today.

"Good evening, Frau Hauptman. How are you this fine day?" His jovial tone indicated Herr Kaiser assumed all was well.

"Good evening, Herr Kaiser," she answered, darting her eyes towards the comforter with just a slight shake of her head.

Startled, Herr Kaiser looked concerned, but ever the consummate actor, never missed a beat. "Ah, you have done a fine job of cleaning as usual,

Frau Hauptman, fine job, fine job. Thank you very much."

His mouth opened, poised to say something else, but just then, Herr Guttermann, the concierge, walked past them on his way to his room at the end of the hall. Herr Kaiser shut his mouth with a snap, and nodding politely to Herr Gutterman and Marthe, went into his own room, closing his door and leaving Marthe to hurry home to find out just exactly what had gone wrong.

Marthe's and Herr Kaiser's cautious instincts about Herr Gutterman were well-founded. Raised by a single mother, the concierge's life had bounced back and forth from poverty and illiteracy to shame and non-stop humiliation. Winters were the most austere, when he and his brother and sisters clung together in the kitchen, a cluster of small hands, arms, and legs, squatting on a single bench, trying to keep warm enough to sit down and eat whatever meager food their mother could piece together. As they gnawed on their bread, he would watch their mother burning worthless WWI German currency in their stove to use as fuel, her face dead, her eyes hollow.

She neither read to them at night nor told them fairytales. It seemed the only time she did have the energy to talk to her children at all was at the supper table, when she regaled them with stories about the depravity of the Jews. Then she would come alive, her face animated and her eyes shiny, convinced these people were the single cause of Germany's downfall.

"Jews kill Gentile children, then use their blood to make Matzohs," she would insist, puffing up, proud that at least her children would grow up to be good, untainted Germans.

Yet her son, Peter Gutterman was different. Unlike the classic Aryan looks of his brothers and sisters, he was small and dark, a fact that had always haunted him, and by the time he was full grown, a childhood of taunts, threats, and street pummeling had filled him with enough venom to last a lifetime.

As Hitler rose to prominence, Herr Gutterman grew hopeful. Here at last, was someone who could raise Germany up from its ashes and simultaneously, punish those responsible for its ruination. And when the Nuremberg Laws were passed, he was particularly pleased; denying Jews citizenship was only the beginning as far as he was concerned. He took particular delight in seeing a neighborhood interfaith couple forced to wear individual placards over their bodies. Mimi, who had always given him and his family sugar cookies, had to wear a sign that read: "At this place I am the greatest swine: I take Jews and make them mine!" Her husband Sidney's read: "As a Jewish boy I always take German girls up to my room!" And although his early memories of her freshly baked cookies covered in a small basket had remained imprinted somewhere in his limbic brain, he still managed to turn his head the other way when passing them on the street.

Kiosks, slathered with posters announcing the boycott of Jewish-owned stores would trigger first a tip of his hat, then a chuckle to himself. He would even, on occasion, mouth the words, "Defend yourselves! Do not buy from Jews!" He was in Heaven.

Marthe's key clicking in their front door lock made Hans jump. Then, breathing a sigh of relief, he walked over to his wife, and without a word, hugged her for a good ten seconds.

"What happened today?" she finally asked.

"Because of the upcoming rally tonight, I felt there were far too many SS around to be totally safe. Don't worry. I worked on more of the passports and next week, when the city clears a little, we can continue." He stroked his wife's slight shoulders and back gently between her shoulder blades like he used to do when they were first married.

She could feel her body start to relax muscle by muscle, then froze. "Hans! What if we are caught? Is it really worth…"

He cut her off. "Don't even talk that way! Think about all the people we've known whose lives have been destroyed: Frau Greenberg, David Honig, all the professors at the University, Moishe Federman? Why, he was best man at our wedding for Gott's sake! Think about it, Marthe!"

Marthe nodded, trying not to cry. He was right, of course. She would just have to learn to conquer her fears.

They fell asleep that night huddled together and listening to the booming loud speakers that had been set up in the main square. Hitler's voice infiltrated everywhere, thundering on about his plan to take over the world. Over and over again he bellowed, until his guttural tones became less strident, less intrusive, and just seconds before they drifted off to sleep, simply a background hum, wafting in and out.

In the ensuing weeks, although fifty more passports were exchanged easily, Marthe noticed a shift in Herr Gutterman's behavior. Before, he had always tipped his hat to Herr Kaiser as a gentlemanly gesture, but now, he would only stare at the boarder and without a smile, say hello. One day, exiting Herr Kaiser's room, she caught the concierge standing on the landing watching her closely, yet when she caught his eye, he simply nodded, deep in thought. As he padded down the hallway, she could feel the tiny hairs on her arms rising alongside their goose-fleshed brothers.

She immediately brought up her concerns to Herr Kaiser, who, in his typical way, let out a deep, resonating laugh as he warned her not to worry so much. "Please go about your business," he reassured her. "Leave Herr Gutterman to me. I'll take care of things. You know, his bark is a lot harsher than his bite."

Remaining calm was not in her nature, but as she sewed each muslin 'envelope' containing a passport into the thick down batting, she repeated a little prayer, consoling herself that by the time Herr Kaiser would extract the packages from out of the comforter, she would most probably be halfway across town.

Every few days, the city was changing. Increasingly, Jewish stores were being emptied, their inhabitants either gone, or too frightened to come to work, and from out of nowhere, one of the first Jewish ghettos was instituted, a blatant reminder of the new Germany. Now, Marthe had to get to work each morning by walking past large signs posted outside several ominous, black iron gates, "Wohngebiet der Juden. Betreten Verboten—" "Living area for Jews. Entrance is prohibited." She would peer in quickly then scurry on. Sometimes, dark-circled, glassy-eyed children stood just inside the gates, and if the SS guard's head was turned away for a few moments, extend their hands, palms up, silently begging for food. But she dared not stop. Above all, she mustn't arouse any suspicion, particularly now that they were so close to their goal.

By late October, Herr Gutterman was openly hostile. Instead of any hellos to Herr Kaiser, he just glowered, and with his consistent bragging to some of the other boarders about his close connections with the SS, Marthe feared the worst. He was an important man, he would sputter, proudly displaying the bold Swastika armband he had stolen off of a truck just two days before, along with an SS dagger, an iron cross, and a frayed copy of Mein Kampf.

"Hans, I really worry about Herr Kaiser," Marthe insisted each night.

"Herr Kaiser is amazing. He has a couple of good connections. You'll see, he'll know how to take care of himself. But I do worry about you. Perhaps this shall be the last 'run' for you, Marthe."

"Why now? I have been worried for weeks!" Marthe snapped, ignoring his outstretched hand.

"Well, from what you've just told me, I do believe Herr Gutterman is getting worse and besides, these passports will be the last fifty on the list."

"Fifty! How can I possibly sew all of them into the comforter in time?"

"My dear, you'll just have to sew faster than you've ever sewn before. It appears we have no other choice."

The next day, all the rooms were less spotless than usual in the Sailerstrasse Boarding House. Rapid dusting, makeshift floor mops, and scratches on the floors from furniture being shoved hastily out of the way had allowed Marthe an extra hour and a half by the end of her shift, giving her time to sew fifty envelopes into well-hidden areas in the quilt.

Finally, hearing Herr Kaiser trudging up the old steps, achy, tingling fingers made it difficult for her to turn the knob, but she managed to fumble through and open the door to face her friend.

Suddenly, she heard Herr Gutterman calling out from down below: "Herr Kaiser, come here, if you will. There's something I must talk to you about."

Marthe hesitated. She stared at Herr Kaiser's impassive face, watched him shrug his shoulders, do an about-face and go back down the stairs. Leaning over the railing, she strained to hear any discourses, any arguments. Silence. She locked his door as quietly as possible and tiptoed down the steps, stopping each time they creaked, but Herr Gutterman did not open the door to his downstairs office, and she couldn't hear any sounds coming out of it. As she exited the front door, she thought she heard a chair turning over, but kept running.

Herr Kaiser was not so fortunate. After he entered Herr Gutterman's office, the concierge took a couple of minutes to water his one drooping plant, fix a couple of small statues on his shelves, and dust off his desk— calm, collected, no emotions on his face. All of a sudden, it was as if a blood vessel had burst, turning his cheeks red and puffy. Like a madman, he ran around his desk, knocked a chair over while he grabbed a cane, and raising it up, struck the boarder across the face.

"You Jew-lover," he hissed, "I know now you're up to no good! You swine, you will have to pay for this! Don't you realize how close I am with the SS? How dare you have anything to do with Jews!"

Stunned, Herr Kaiser managed to sputter a few words. "Wha—What are you talking about? I don't understand…"

"Frau Burger said she saw you talking to a Jew on the street a few weeks ago, and Frau Schmidt even saw you going into a Jewish store one evening. Both of them have given me their sworn testimony on this! Now what do you say to me, you swine!" His eyes almost popped out of their sockets as he staggered towards Herr Kaiser, his left hand holding several sheets up in the air. A second later, he drew a small whistle from out of his pocket and blew it, piercing the air and catapulting a terrified Herr Kaiser spread-eagled across the floor. Instantly, an SS guard appeared from out of nowhere.

The co-conspirator was led away screaming, praying somewhere inside the other boarders or Marthe, if she was still there, would go for help. But Marthe was gone, and the boarders all knew the drill too well; no one there would ever risk everything for the sake of someone else, not these days.

Later that night, nestled in Hans' arms, Marthe started to shiver.

"What is wrong, dear one?" he asked, his voice gentle.

"I am not sure, but in my heart, I feel something is not right." She turned and presented him with her back, soft, warm, in need of comfort.

He draped his right arm over her stomach. "You are not due back at the boarding house for several days. By that time Herr Kaiser will have distributed the last passports, we will be finished with our work, and we can return to our old schedule, all right, my darling?"

Closing her eyes, Marthe nodded, knowing tears would soon follow.

In the small border town of Kietz, Gertl Grynszpan couldn't sleep even if she wanted to. Wedged in next to dozens of other Polish-born German Jews, she had trouble breathing in the stifling, overcrowded railway freight car, and coupled with a full bladder, she was truly miserable. Still, she didn't dare ask a border guard if she could go to the bathroom; it was enough just to hope for decent treatment without adding special privileges. Gagging, she could see the pools of urine spilling out in circular patterns on the floor and hear the young children whimpering, as they fidgeted next to their mothers every ten seconds.

"Mama, tell me again, why are we here? Why did the police come in the middle of the night and take us away?" Her twelve-year-old daughter Berta, old enough to demand answers, was still too young to interpret her mother's frightened eyes and the changing world around them.

"I don't know Berta, but hopefully we can go home soon. Now try to sleep. Go shushy…" she soothed, using the same, comforting phrase she had always uttered when sending her children off to sleep. But as Berta and her young sister huddled against their mother, the girl's mind stayed active. If they make us go to Poland, I will write Herschel in Paris to send us money; he has always taken care of us ever since Papa died. My brother will never let us down.

Just thinking of Herschel relaxed her and she started to doze off, when suddenly, hoarse, guttural words ripped through the night air. "Get up! You must cross the border now! Your new home will be in Lodz, Poland. Now, get going!" The guard's ferocity matched his twisted face.

By the time they had reached Lodz, they were marched behind large wrought-iron gates and herded past various buildings whose shutters creaked and rattled in the wind as they trudged by. Once inside their sleeping quarters, Berta managed to scribble a quick note to her brother, "We have been picked up by the police and are penniless. Please send some money to us at Lodz. Love to you from us all, Berta."

She gently unclipped a pendant from around her neck that she had always treasured and handed it over to a woman who claimed she could get the note out safely to Herschel as an exchange. She knew she would have to lie to her mother later and claim her heirloom jewelry had gotten lost in the shuffle somehow when they were detained at the border, but for now, all she could think of was Herschel coming to the rescue.

Herschel did receive the note a few days later, and promptly threw up his consommé avec pain lunch. That afternoon, wandering the pulsing Parisian streets, he ended up at a shop where he purchased a small, but accurate gun.

He had had enough. The next day, before anyone knew to stop him, he entered the German Embassy, marched directly up to the first official he saw and shot him squarely in the chest, then turned to face four guards with pistols aimed at his head.

Ernst vom Rath, a bit player in the Nazi government, would have surely gone through his entire life unknown and unappreciated had it not been for his encounter with Herschel, which instantly engraved his name into history books forever. As vom Rath lay dying, Herschel told the police, "Being a Jew is not a crime. I am not a dog. I have a right to live and the Jewish people have a right to exist on this earth!"

But Joseph Goebbels, Minister of Propaganda, was not convinced. When vom Rath died, he blamed all Jews for Herschel's work, and devised an immediate plan of retaliation.

In the dark, Marthe dressed haphazardly, with missed buttons and an unzipped-to-the-top skirt, anxious to get to work early to make sure all was well with Herr Kaiser. But approaching the boarding house, she stalled. There, in front of the entrance, was an assortment of furniture pieces, along with boxes and trunks overflowing with clothing, knick-knacks, books, and dishes, all juxtaposed against the building and blocking the sidewalk. Passerby's, trying to edge their way through, had given up and finally, simply milled around with the boarders, comparing notes and talking excitedly.

"What is happening?" Marthe asked one of them leaning against a sofa back.

"Why, haven't you heard? They've arrested Herr Kaiser, and Herr Gutterman is leaving us to join the Gestapo!"

"Arrested Herr Kaiser?" Marthe's stomach flip-flopped. "Why?"

"They said he had Jewish connections; I don't really know the details." The boarder sounded slightly annoyed; after all, Herr Kaiser's safety wasn't nearly as important as losing a good concierge.

Barely touching the banister, Marthe flew up the stairs to Herr Kaiser's room, where she encountered the movers already hauling off his furniture piece by piece. The comforter still lay there, neatly folded on the end of the bed, but she didn't dare check for passports in front of the big, burly men. Instead, she feigned a nonchalant attitude while dusting, humming slightly as she worked her way over towards the bed. They seemed amused by her cleaning at the last minute, but she didn't care. It provided her with an excuse to stay close as they continued carrying items downstairs to load onto a large van.

Checking the comforter proved difficult; she had performed her job so well, she had to struggle to push two fingers way up into the batting. Frantically twisting her hand to the right then to the left, she couldn't feel anything. She breathed a sigh of relief and started to withdraw her fingers, when she felt it. One of the hard, leather corners blocked her hand on the way out, bending her index finger. Shoving her other trembling fingers to the left of the passport, she touched another hard edge, and another, and another until finally, she realized all fifty of them were there, intact, ready for an exchange.

"You, please, let us finish our job. Danke," one of the movers grumbled as he entered the room on his eighth trip from downstairs.

On pins and needles, she stood back and watched the rest of the furniture being carted off—his bedside table, dressing table with the beveled-edged mirror, his prized phonograph player, his Beidermeir armoire as well as a red, gold, brown, and black Oriental rug, all slated for the small moving van parked below. Angling further out of the window, her heart still hammering, she could see the men slowly filling the truck with not only Herr Kaiser's furniture, but other people's property as well. After all, decent antiques could still fetch a hefty price at local auction houses.

Back in the room, she scooped up the comforter just in time to hear Herr Gutterman's triumphant voice blasting from the street.

"I tell you, it was one of the most exciting moments of my life, Frau Lieppman. I should have joined up with the Fuhrer a long time ago. Yes, it is a very big honor to be part of his great movement!"

Marthe quickly restored the comforter to the end of the bed, seconds before a mover came into the room, grabbed it, flung it carelessly over his shoulder, and marched downstairs to toss it out on the street where it remained, along with Herr Kaiser's less important items, abandoned and unguarded.

People were beginning to stroll past the quilt, unaware of its significance and Marthe's heartbeat gathered speed. As soon as Herr Gutterman's voice faded around the corner, she double-stepped down the stairs and hurried across the street to a local restaurant, to wait for the perfect moment to seize the comforter. But with each passing hour of slowly sipped tea, Marthe became more and more agitated. She didn't dare attempt a rescue in the midst of so much activity, yet the thought of fifty Jews unable to obtain their freedom made it difficult to breathe.

"Madam, are you planning on staying at your table all day?" the waiter's tone was unmistakable.

Quickly paying the bill, she slipped a generous tip under her napkin and went scouting for another spot to wait. An old, abandoned car proved to be perfect. Near an alleyway, it was off the beaten path and crouching down behind it, she began her possibly long vigil.

As the night sky infused navy blues with a deep rose, she noticed fewer people mingling about. This was her chance. She stood up, stretched, and was cautiously inching out from behind the automobile when she heard the first sound. Unable to identify it at first, its eerie quality instantly put her on edge. Soon, tiny staccato clinks were sounding everywhere, like delicate wine glasses splintering against stone walls. At first they appeared faint and inconsistent. But as the din increased, so did the thuds and high-pitched fractures until Marthe became truly alarmed.

She raced around the corner to a neighboring street where she knew a Jewish school was located. Stunned, she could hear screams coming from inside as she watched one of the children opening up a window and yelling, "Help us, they've locked us in—please dear Gott, help us!" The girl struggled to escape onto a windowsill, but someone inside pulled her back, kicking and screaming.

"They've set fire to the synagogue down the block. Come and look!" a man bellowed as he ran by. Marthe saw other people streaming towards a freshly painted building she must have passed by hundreds of times in the past, but never noticed. Its wooden front doors were wide open and inside, men in brown shirts and swastikas were pouring gasoline on the seats, even the holy arks, then in unison, igniting everything. As the flames danced and crackled, Marthe could hear the fire trucks coming, their sirens howling so ferociously she had to cover her ears. When they arrived, their brakes shuddered and squealed as firemen leapt off of die loschfahrzeuge and sprung into action, concentrating only on the neighboring buildings. The synagogue was left to burn.

Once each section of the temple started to kindle, the white walls grayed, then blackened with smoke. Flames reached up and licked the large Jewish star, incinerating each of the six points until finally, all that was left of the symbol was a small part of its original center, hollowed out.

In his living room, Hans paced endlessly. Not having heard from Marthe all day, now, with the evening air settling in, he was beginning to panic.

After a long bus ride, he began his trek towards the boarding house, aided by hazy streetlights gently beaming down a spotted path on city block after city block. Suddenly, he heard a loud, harrowing thud followed by a scream. Barreling forward, he felt something graze his left cheek and as he raised his fingers to touch it, felt his skin there moisten. Fresh blood, he thought, what the hell is going on?

Up ahead, a mob had gathered around the old Wasserman store. Chairs, pipes, bricks, loose cobblestone, anything they could grab, were being hurled at the storefront windows and when the plate glass splintered and fell, the crowd cheered, laughing and slapping each other on the back.

Hans hurried on, his heart rapping, his mouth dry. Passing by his favorite movie house, he could feel another crowd swelling behind him, driving him inside. At first he couldn't see anything in the pitch-black theater as people pressed against him so vehemently he had to hold onto the wall for support. But as his eyes grew accustomed to the half-light, he could discern a few people down in the front row being dragged up on stage, crying and pleading.

Once the house lights were flipped on, he recognized several of the victims. It was members of the Federman family—Moshe Federman, Sadie, and Sarah cowering together Stage Right, sobbing, as two guards came forward and started beating them. Half-hearted protests burst from the front row, while Judith Federman and her sons Leo and Hirsch were forced to watch their family attacked.

Nausea instantly made Hans gag, and pushing his way out of the theater, he broke into a dead run towards the boardinghouse, gulping air and thinking of the Av Harachamin—a prayer for Jewish martyrs he had learned at the university from his Semitic friends. Around the corner, broken glass glistened on the streets as the largest mob of the night swelled and rumbled towards the Lieberstrasse House.

In front of the building, a lone man straddled several huge crates stacked together, waving his arms and shouting, "Germany is for true Germans only. Juden es Vorboten! Jews are forbidden!"

The crowd took up the cry. "Germany is for true Germans only! Juden es Verboten! Jews are forbidden!"

Reflections from the different fires bounced and flickered against buildings, cars, and faces, reminding him of a horror picture he and Marthe had seen not so long before, where a vampire's face was illuminated by the glow from people's torches. The orator's face remained hidden from view, the swell of the crowd keeping his voice unrecognizable. But then the crowd cheered again, and the man slowly turned his face in Hans' direction. It was Herr Gutterman, distorted with power and rage.

Hans gasped, and when people turned to stare at him, immediately ducked back into the shadows of a nearby alley, frantic at the thought of trying to find Marthe to extricate her from this frenzy. Seconds later, he had slowly inched his way out when suddenly two small arms encircled him from behind. Jerking backward, he nearly knocked Marthe over as they both fell hard onto an overflowing garbage can, all four legs splaying upward.

"I thought I would never find you!" Hans murmured, stroking her hair and trying to blink back tears.

"Hans, the comforter—Herr Kaiser—it's horrible..." Marthe could only string a few words together at one time as she stood up, flipping off bits of garbage from her skirt.

"What is it? What are you trying to say?" he coaxed.

Finally, she managed to spit out a complete sentence. "Herr Kaiser was arrested before he could transfer the passports! All fifty of them are still in the comforter!"

They both pivoted towards the forgotten coverlet, thrown recklessly over a dresser sitting on the sidewalk to the left of Herr Gutterman. Then slowly, they turned to face each other, their eyes the size of a Nickel 1 Reichsmark.

Krystallnacht, the Night of Broken Glass, was in full swing. Books were being yanked out of stores and libraries and thrown onto huge bonfires that hissed and crackled up towards the blackened sky as possessed people danced up and down, laughing, howling, out of control.

Marthe and Hans watched Herr Gutterman suddenly leap down from his makeshift podium to yell, "Help me people! Let's fill this comforter with more books so we can forge the largest fire in the world! We'll wipe out every Communist intellectual and Jewish book in existence!"

With the help of three other men, they dragged the comforter over to a nearby store and started loading it with dozens of books. Hoisting it up like a tent, they marched over to the fire and on the count of One-two-three—go! flipped the books up into the air and onto the fire.

The enraptured crowd chorused a one-two-three–go! with each new toss of books onto the snapping, popping fire. On the last trip, when the coverlet came dangerously close to the flames, Hans had to pin Marthe back from charging over to try and stop the proceedings.

After a while, Herr Gutterman and his cohorts had depleted all the books and were on to the next inspired offense. "Let's gather up the glass from the street and throw it all into their ghetto. Let glass rain down on all the Juden! Down with the Juden!"

People applauded and cheered before gathering shards of glass to fling beyond the ghetto walls. Bleeding hands left the glass red, but they were oblivious; this night had become far too exciting to worry about such trivialities.

Frustrated, Herr Gutterman started hunting for some sort of tool to expedite the process. His eyes lit on the comforter and running towards it, called out for everyone to bring their glass pieces over to him. As soon as he laid the quilt flat on the street, jagged fragments were dumped onto its soft folds, mounding a pile of glass at least a foot high. Then each corner was grabbed and soon, the comforter was swinging back and forth as it was shifted over to the iron gates just outside the ghetto. Crussssshhhh—crussshhh—crussshhh—crussshhh—it chimed, until at last, the men halted in front of the gates.

"One-two-three–go!" Everyone screamed, watching the glass fly up into the air, disappear into the dark, then fall like slivered rain from a noiseless sky onto the courtyard of the ghetto.

Craving an encore, Herr Gutterman started in again. "Let's do it again, only this time, let the comforter GO! Ready?"

The crowd followed suit, chanting, "One-two-three—Let GO!" Suddenly, the entire comforter was released, flying over the gates like an Arabian carpet floating in space.

Hans and Marthe held their breaths, waiting. From out of the ghetto came only stillness; no one stepped out or even showed their head. After a few minutes, the crowd drifted off, bored, eager for better entertainment elsewhere, and as their footsteps faded, Marthe and Hans inched forward cautiously, gripping each other's hand, hoping for any sign of life rustling behind those ghetto walls. But everything stayed as silent as a snow's first fall.

That night, safe in their apartment, Hans and Marthe collapsed together on their sofa, sobbing and promising each other they would exit Germany at the very next opportunity. But first, they had to make sure. By morning, after a hurried cup of coffee and day-old apple strudel, they gingerly walked down Lebenstrausse Street, stopping by the ghetto gates. Still, there was no sign of life.

And no sign of the comforter.

Shaking their heads, they moved on, Hans grim, Marthe tear-stained, just as fifty men, women, and children gratefully boarded a train out of Germany.

A PLAGUE ON BOTH YOUR HOUSES

As a little girl growing up in Brooklyn, it remained a mystery to Lizzy why her mother, Ruth, would always swear upon entering her daughter's bedroom. Never mind the fact that stepping into Lizzy's bedroom was similar to guerilla warfare; the land mine of socks, shoes, stuffed animals, and Barbies scattered on the floor often made Ruth trip, and one time catapulted her so far into the room, if there hadn't been a bed or chair to break her fall, her neck could easily have been broken.

"Let's face it. You're a slob. I was a slob. Hell, we come from several generations of slobs," Ruth kept muttering, shaking her head in acknowledgment of their bad family trait.

On the other hand, in Manhattan, Mark was the model child. His mother never swore at him; there was no need. By evening, after a quiet meal with the nanny, Mark was already in his bedroom tidying up, a good half hour before his mother even got a chance to visit. Anything to avoid her disapproval.

Sometimes his mother would attempt a smile at the fastidiousness of her boy, her thin, tight lips flat-lining. In her heart, she knew no girl would ever be good enough for him.

Each night after Lizzy had crawled into bed and received at least twenty hugs and kisses from her mom, her favorite thing to do was to sleep with only her undies on, wrapped up like a blintz in her treasured rose-colored satin comforter, sewn by her great grandmother. She would rub the quilt with her fingers as she wriggled around inside her soft cave until finally, she would settle down to let the 'Sandman' do his thing.

Mark would have loved to cuddle as well, but somehow his mother was never able to take enough time out of her busy schedule to stay with him for very long. He did get a goodnight kiss of course, but often it didn't quite make his cheek. Still, he knew how to keep up appearances, and being the perfect child, never complained. He had learned early about locking in his sadness.

Lizzy's mom marched for Civil Rights, toting hand-made placards and occasionally getting herself into trouble with the police. Mark's mom believed in Ivy League schools, country clubs, and Wall Street producing stable citizens. Lizzy attended progressive schools in Greenwich Village, while Mark attended one of the best prep boarding schools in New England, lonely, miserable, but ultimately, paving the way for a fine future in investment counseling at his father's firm in lower Manhattan.

When Yale happily accepted Mark as a business student minoring in math, Lizzy was thrilled to be majoring in textiles at the New York School of Design.

"Son, you do make me proud," commented Mark's mom when he graduated cum laude. She couldn't resist adjusting his cap and tassel, tweaking it just so on his head.

"Yes, and when you get your MBA behind you, you will be able to join our investment firm, just like my father before me and then, the sky's the limit," his father chimed in, searching the crowd for prospective clients.

Secretly, Lizzy's mom wondered about the validity of a Masters in Textile Design, but was grateful that at least it wasn't some inane business degree. Flashing back on her own college experience, she shuddered at the thought of her haughty roommate, Lucille Hartford, a business major who always made sure Jewish girls understood the rules: they were tolerated, but never completely welcome.

During the past four years, Mark had taken some mental notes on the co-eds at Yale—smart, chic, and slim, similar to the girls he had grown up with, and that was the problem. The boredom factor kept seeping in. Even before these co-eds spoke, he instinctively knew what they were about to say. Going to bed with any of them didn't generate any spectacular sparks, either, simply reflexive passion, then release.

Most of Lizzy's art student boyfriends were laced with tattoos and earrings, and housed in the same ongoing outfit: tattered jeans, encrusted with strategically placed paint spots, and a torn, thrift store T-shirt. Completing the ensemble was either a heavy flannel lumberman's coat or a replica of a 1940's bomber jacket.

One of them stayed on, devouring Ruth's food and irritating her to no end, but after Lizzy announced she had become pregnant and her boyfriend had split, her mom could only sigh, take a deep breath, and wonder where she had gone wrong.

Yet her daughter's art quilts proved to be worth their weight in gold. Bold, innovative geometric designs, sewn with warm, vivid colors, soon landed her one of the most successful artist reps in the city. As her reputation grew, so did her promotional abilities and monetary acumen, to the delight of her rep and awe of her mother. Still, for all her 'success'—the competitions, the galleries, and the prestigious commissions—with her daughter Natalie in tow, Lizzy could never shake the feeling of 'what about me? Who's gonna take care of me?'

Charging up the corporate ladder, Mark stayed focused as the 1980's arrived and with it, mergers and acquisitions. Instinctively, he understood which lower-end clients to avoid by simply delegating them to other stockbrokers, and which high-rollers who wanted to buy companies in financial trouble to knock himself out over. His plan worked. To the envy of many of his colleagues, he quickly became "The Golden Boy," so named half-admiringly, half-flirtatiously by the women; mentioned in snide, envious tones by the men.

Nights and weekends for him were consumed by take-home work and take-out gourmet deli food from his favorite restaurant Mangia, around the corner from his office. A Spaghetti ajo-ojo one night, a Quiche Lorraine the next, and whenever his parents called up to ogle over the latest acquisition of a new client he had brought in, he remained somewhat removed.

"Honey, I have some sad, but possibly good news for you," Ruth informed Lizzy one day, watching her daughter pour over a monthly earnings spreadsheet.

"That sounds ominous," Lizzy muttered without looking up.

"Your Uncle Maury just passed away, leaving you assets in a stock portfolio. You are supposed to hear from the estate lawyers any day now and they're gonna send you to an assigned investment counselor."

Lizzy put her financial records down on the coffee table. "Wow. I didn't really know Uncle Maury all that well. That's really amazing."

"Well, sweetie, don't get too excited. Your Uncle Maury was not such a great businessman. Besides, whatever he did earn, was whittled away by that despicable, crooked investment counselor, Van de Hooten. So, when you do go in to discuss all this, be careful of the sharks."

"OK, Mom, OK." Here we go again, Lizzy sighed. The-Evils-of-the-Corporate-World. Next, her mom would launch into how her father had been robbed by greedy, corporate lawyers, and her grandfather had nearly jumped out the window during the Stock Market Crash of '29 because his investment counselor neighbor Richard Van de Hooten had sold him a bill of goods. Oh, and what about her nasty college roommate, Lucille Hartford? She was involved in business, too. Once her mother got started, there would be no end to the tirade.

When the call did come from her Uncle's investment counselors, she carefully jotted down the name of the investment firm, nestled in the heart of Wall Street and the New York Stock Exchange. She recognized the address. Gee, they're right next to that great deli, 'Mangia', she thought. It was always such a treat to go to that place on her way to Brooklyn. For some reason, whenever she went in there to order take-out, she would play a make-believe game to help pass the time. According to her, each stockbroker/ secretary/investment counselor/businessman had a rich fantasy life, so by the time she had fully analyzed people sitting in their booths, her order was packaged, ready to go.

Forty-five minutes before her afternoon meeting with the investment counselor, she was in top form, playing her game at Mangia's as she nibbled on some lunch. This one's definitely two-faced. He's got a wife, two-point-five kids out in Scarsdale, and a wild, sexy mistress in Greenwich Village. That one dresses in Armani three-piece suits during the day, and at night, cross-dresses in Versace. This one pretends she's a straight-laced secretary at work, but secretly gorges on oysters and dark chocolates while writing romance novels at night. And this one...

This one was a puzzler. Handsome, yes, stockbroker-type, to be sure, but there was also a sensitivity about his face that touched her. He ate unobtrusively, reading some sort of large, paperback book. She couldn't quite read the title, but it had something to do with the word 'Creative,' so she perked up. Any movement he initiated was graceful, yet at the same time, quite masculine.

She noticed that she and the man had finished eating about the same time, but as they both stood up to go, she hung back slightly, fidgeting with her napkin, so they wouldn't enter the revolving door at the same time. Caught off guard by her own sudden modesty, she let out a deep, resonating laugh. Several people turned to look at her, including him. She blushed at his long stare, quickly glancing down at the floor and steadying herself before looking back up at him. But he had already left. *You just need a little TLC, Lizzy, you've been without any for too long,* she mused. *Calm down. Get a grip.*

The New York Stock Exchange convulsed with flying papers, computer screens flashing every two feet, and jacketless stockbrokers yelling at the top of their lungs, fast on their way to guaranteed heart attacks. Lizzy was quietly led upstairs to the Executive Investment Counselor offices, and like Lot's wife in Sodom and Gomorrah, took one last look at the entire scene, riveted. So this was the infamous 'Shark Pen.'

Upstairs lay an entirely different world—plush, beige carpets spilled out into lavish executive suites, some with large picture windows, others with smaller, less conspicuous views. *The bigger the window, the more elevated the company stature,* she had read somewhere.

Mark Salisbury's corner office contained two enormous picture windows, a comfortable Shabby-Chic slipcovered couch surrounded by two Windsor chairs, and a Shaker-style coffee table. The two remaining walls were coated with books, stuffed into distressed wooden bookcases.

With no Mr. Salisbury in sight, Lizzy entertained herself by perusing the books, curious to find out what this new advisor was all about. There were plenty of the usual Stocks and Dividend volumes of course, but what threw Lizzy off were all the art and art history books.

It had been her experience that when people collected coffee-table art books, they weren't that knowledgeable about art, they just liked the way the covers looked in their living rooms; a touch of culture in an otherwise tasteless setting. But these books were a true art lover's find, with titles she hadn't seen since her early art school days. There was even one on the history of textile design. She was impressed. *Maybe this meeting was salvageable, after all.*

She heard a rustle behind her and spun around, expecting some corpulent, middle-aged balding man sporting a Signa Phi pinkie ring, white shirt, black striped tie, and a five thousand dollar suit. But it was him. Large, virile hands shifted papers on top of a mammoth, leathered-surfaced mahogany desk as he gazed up at her. He politely motioned for her to sit down next to his desk, stammering, "Ah—ah— haven't I met you— before?"

"Yes, in Mangia's, I believe, just now." Self-consciously, she jerked her right hand up against her warming cheek.

But it was Mark's face that flushed pink. He had definitely noticed her before; in fact, had been surprised by his own reaction to this zaftig, curly haired woman, who reminded him of some of the women in Ruben's paintings he had seen at the Metropolitan Museum as a teenager. His first instinct had been to reach out and touch their softness then, and now, so close to Lizzy's brown eyes, blanketed by such thick eyelashes, he could feel the same magnetic field drawing him in.

For a few seconds, his usual financial spiel vanished while he pulled himself together. Then, starting in on his pitch, he informed her she wasn't going to be rich, but she could definitely change her lifestyle somewhat, perhaps even move out of her mother's apartment in Brooklyn and live across the Hudson River. Maybe try country living.

Lizzy watched his lips and hands move, but had trouble concentrating. "I see you have a great collection of art books. That's very dear to my heart, you know," she inserted finally, from out of nowhere.

Immediately, the topic switched to art quilts and in particular, textile design. As they talked, it was as if he, too, were wrapped up inside her rose-colored satin comforter with her, burrowing around together, forgetting everyone else. Every few minutes she would lean forward and tap him gently on his arm for emphasis. The lightest of touches, he felt stroked in a way he had never experienced before. He was hooked.

Asking her out for a cup of coffee seemed a natural progression, and after calling her mom, she accompanied him to a little bar 'n grill near his apartment on the Upper West Side. He couldn't stop staring at her, and as he ushered her through the door, he could sense her soft skin underneath her 1940's vintage style dress. He wanted to feel more.

Coffee was followed by drinks, at which point Lizzy watched him order a very expensive Pinot Noir quickly and decisively. Unused to such capable hands, she sat back, sipping her wine, the weight of responsibility floating up and away from her. It was like a drug.

"You know, I've been wondering if Back-End Mutual funds would be a good way to go?" Lizzy's second glass of wine was even better than her first.

Mark blinked twice. "How do you even know about that?"

"Why? Just because I'm an artist, I can't read "The Wall Street Journal?""

"I think it's great, that's all. Back-Ends are OK, but bonds in general, are safer," he replied, grinning.

"Really! I heard high yield bonds are something to watch out for!"

"Junk Bonds? Yes, of course! I meant Guaranteed Bonds, Investment Grade Bonds, or just Closed-End Bond Funds."

Angling back even further in her chair, her dark, shoulder length curls bordered her face as the candlelight highlighted her eyes and cheekbones.

They ended up in bed, of course, clinging to each other like two soaked cats finally finding a warm, dry spot together in the middle of a downpour, and when the typical NYPD sirens sounded at five a.m., there was only the flutter of Mark's eyes trying to open.

"I want you to meet my Natalie," a naked Lizzy cooed later on Mark's lap, his queen size down comforter keeping their body heat warm and consistent.

"I'd have suggested that if you hadn't beaten me to it!" Mark laughed, nuzzling her throat and nibbling on her ear.

But two days later, a pinprick surfaced on their romantic bubble when Mark called Lizzy's house. "Oh yes…you're the investment counselor, aren't you?"

Cringing at her mother's tone, Lizzy rushed over to the phone and grabbed it with a snake-like hiss. She cupped the phone and started gurgling. "Hi, I was hoping to hear from you tonight. Yes—I know—I feel the same. When? Uh-oh, I have a gallery opening that night. Can we make it another? You want to come to it? Really? OK, it's at the Stevenson Gallery on 85th and Madison. Seven p.m., tomorrow night. See you there." By the time she had hung up, she couldn't stop giggling.

She took one look at her mother's arched eyebrows and grimaced. "OK, Mom, I get it! Leave me alone! Who knows where it will end. But for now, he's making me very happy. Isn't that the most important thing?"

"I just don't trust that whole business investment thing, that's all. These people are different from us. Most of them are crooks, by the way."

"For God's sakes! I know our family got burned once, but that doesn't mean it will happen again. My gut tells me this guy wouldn't try to hurt me."

Ruth shifted from one foot to the other. "Don't forget, I spent a lot of my college years dealing with business people like Lucille Hartford, and trust me, they're all alike!" Stalking off, she made sure her one short, jarring snort was more than audible.

At the exhibit, Mark appeared with a couple of his cronies. Their khaki pants, Yves Saint Laurent belts, pale blue Pierre Cardin shirts, and navy blue Armani jackets couldn't compete with the spiky hair, black leather tights, high-heeled boots topped by black leg warmers, and colorful tunics that Lizzy's girlfriends all wore. But Mark seemed oblivious. He wandered throughout the gallery, searching for Lizzy and eavesdropping on pretentious conversations.

His friends did admit her work was excellent, but questioned his sudden interest in such a woman. Where was the usual blonde executive they were used to seeing him with and envying him for? What did he see in this earthy artist and what about his parents? The Van de Hootens having this voluptuous dark-haired vixen over to their apartment for a dinner party? Yeah, right. When Mark wasn't in close proximity, his friends spent the evening making the usual insinuations and sexual wisecracks.

Lizzy's fellow artists weren't much better. 'Come on, Lizzy,' they sneered. 'You must be dating him just for the money. Are you planning on trading in your artist lifestyle for Versace accessories, Givenchy tailored suits, or Donna Karan wear for the unstoppable Power Woman Executive?'

Aware of the chilly reception, Mark kept defiantly slipping a possessive arm around Lizzy's waist whenever possible, and when her mom and Natalie arrived, just seeing the businessman with her daughter made Ruth hyperventilate. But Mark ignored everyone and knelt down to talk with Natalie eye-to-eye. Reeling him in with the same trusting, dark brown eyes as her mother, he was smitten, and with her small hand constantly clasped in his, by the end of the evening they looked as if they could have been father and daughter.

Finally, Lizzy helped Ruth on with her coat, murmuring, "See, Mom? Look how great he is with Natalie. He's not going to hurt us." Ruth made an effort to smile, but it came out more like a grimace.

There was no stopping the two lovers after that. They spent hours walking around the Wall Street area on lunch breaks, up Wall Street to William Street, left on Pine Street, left again on Nassau Street; back down to Wall Street. Weekends ended up at the Brooklyn Zoo, communing with the elephants, hippopotamuses, giraffes, and flamingos, with Natalie running back and forth between the two grownups, clutching an ice cream popsicle and shrieking with laughter.

But The War had already begun.

Her mom started in first. "I hope you know what you're doing. You have a responsibility to your little girl. It's not just about you now. You can no longer bring anyone home and assume it'll work out."

Lizzy stared in disbelief. What was wrong with her? After seeing Mark interact with their family on numerous occasions, there wasn't one act that he had done that would justify such an outburst. It was that damned obsession against the corporate world. She tried to reason with Ruth repeatedly, but it was no use; the years of resentment of Lucille Hartford and her crowd had taken its toll.

Over in Manhattan, a similar process was underway. "Hello, dear. I hear through the grapevine you have a new girlfriend." His mother tried to sound cheerful, but the tightness sifted through.

Mark stiffened. Here we go. "Yes, I have been dating someone, Mother. She's a quilt/textile designer, very artistic, a Democrat, and oh, by the way—she's Jewish."

Silence. "Oh, I see..."

"Is there anything else you need to know, Mother?"

"Now, dear, there's no need to get so snippety. I'm sure you're having fun. I wouldn't dream of interfering!" Her voice instantly reverted back to her old patterns.

He began to freeze—the little boy again, waiting up in his room for a good night kiss. But just picturing Lizzy on his bed, soft, naked, her arms beckoning, he found his voice. "What exactly is it that you object to, Mother? The fact that she's an artist, or that she's Jewish?"

"Dear, I don't even know the girl." The word 'know' arced up and down, like a member of the British royal household, invited in for a spot of tea.

"All I can say," she continued, "is that a long time ago, your grandfather had some issues with a Jewish family who claimed that he was responsible for their father almost jumping out of a ten story building during the crash of '29. It was so unfair, really. All your grandfather had done was to make a couple of stock suggestions. You know, dear, these Jews get so excited about everything. After all, they're just not our kind of people."

Explosive thoughts frightened Mark with their intensity. Still, he remained silent. What was the point? There would never be any stopping of the relentless diet of put downs, dirty glances, and comments, in his mother's effort to wear him down.

Two weeks later, when Lizzy's artist rep called early one morning, she was foaming at the mouth. "I have an extremely well-to-do couple who like your work so much they want to commission you to create a one-of-a-kind wall hanging for their living room. You won't believe how much they are willing to pay for it, too!"

"That's great! What are their names and where do they live?"

"Their name is Van der Hooten. Lucille Hartford Van der Hooten. Come to 254 Fifth Avenue, the Penthouse apartment on Thursday, two o'clock. She'll meet you there."

Nine million alarm bells blared. Don't do it, Lizzy. Tell your rep. Explain the situation. Yet the temptation to meet the enemy trumped everything. "Fine, great. I can always use the money. What time again?" She giggled impulsively. Maybe it would be up to her to finally set the record straight and convince her mom that people do change, that they shouldn't always be held accountable forever.

On Central Park East, between 77th and 78th, the doorman in the Van de Hooten apartment building sniffed at Lizzy disdainfully as she entered the lobby. His dark, maroon uniform, topped with brass buttons and gold lame tassels, exemplified crisp—the dry cleaning bill must be horrendous, Lizzy thought, flashing on a phrase she had heard from her mother her entire life, 'The better the building, the snootier the doorman.'

The elevator was decorated in the same plush decor as the lobby, with only one difference. Midway up the walls, three golden brass handrails were fastened to the mahogany paneled wood. On its floor, high-lofted beige carpeting flowed everywhere, a fact that amazed Lizzy, considering a good part of the inclement weather in New York was tracked in on muddy boots every winter. Oh, well, that's obviously the janitor's cleaning problem. How pathetically feudal. Nevertheless, she was intrigued.

"My, don't you look—well—just like a true artist. Please come in." The words and tone definitely lowered the room temperature.

Mrs. Van de Hooten proceeded to strut around their apartment in her Belgium Beige Gucci shoes, showing off their various artworks, architectural chairs, a glass and chrome dining room set, and Etruscan pottery. Then Mr. Van der Hooten entered. A handsome, gracefully aging man with salt-and-pepper hair and horn-rimmed aviator glasses, he reminded her of someone she had seen, but couldn't quite remember where or when. He was fairly cordial, 'for Goyim,' as her mother would say.

Besides, at that point, she was grateful for even a sliver of kindness.

The spacious, high-ceilinged apartment must have included at least twelve rooms, decorated primarily in a contemporary style. White walls served as a backdrop to muted grays, beiges, rusts, and olives, tastefully blended into a well-coordinated living room. Obviously, a high-priced interior decorator had had a field day, sparing no expense.

Mrs. Van de Hooten led the three of them over to a narrow, gray Bauhaus-styled sofa to discuss the new art quilt that would hang over the Solano Camino Adobe fireplace she had had shipped in from the El Dorado Stone factory in Carnation, Washington. As the upscale couple sat facing the Brooklyn artist explaining their color likes and dislikes, Lizzy realized, to her amazement, they were basically giving her free reign over design and execution. By the time she had left their apartment building, all her mother's warnings were completely forgotten. She was far too busy allowing the creative juices to take over.

For two weeks, she barricaded herself in the back of her mom's house, talking only to Mark at night, bubbling over about her new commission, with its design and all the colors she intended on using. No names were ever mentioned.

"Oh, my. Actually, this is wonderful." Mrs. Van de Hooten's reaction stunned Lizzy after delivering the piece. Standing in the living room, she could feel her face redden in the awkward silence that followed.

When her new employer did speak again, it was accompanied by the light clink of a martini glass hitting the edge of a nearby tray. "Now dear, my husband and I would like to invite you to our fiftieth wedding anniversary party tomorrow night at the Alpine Club on Park Avenue and 58th. Would you care to come?"

Again, Lizzy was taken aback. Who was this woman, really? Could she actually be a good person after all these years? Suddenly she pictured her mother in the same room with them, kvelling at her daughter's success, and laughed.

"Please feel free to bring a date. You do have someone you could bring?" Mrs. V peered over at Lizzy.

She smiled. Mark would be a perfect fit with these people. "Yes, I do have someone in mind."

As soon as she got home, she immediately phoned him, but his message machine was obviously on the fritz, so, on an impulse, she called Riley, one of her old artist friends. A true wild-man, he chortled at the thought of having to wear a tie to get into the club.

"OK-Doke. I'll meet you there," he snickered.

When Lizzy saw the free form, hand-painted tie that Natalie had painted for Riley as a Christmas gift last year, coupled with his teal blue sports jacket, she knew she had made a mistake. And just watching her fellow artist gleefully helping himself to free gourmet hors d'oeuvres and wine, Lizzy broke out in a sweat. Mrs. Van der Hooten was definitely annoyed and embarrassed by Riley's appearance; even her good breeding couldn't camouflage her disapproval. After a few minutes, Lizzy took the cue and was about to tactfully distance herself from her date when she caught sight of Mark from across the room.

"What are you doing here?" Mark asked, his grin the size of Texas.

"What am I doing here? What are you doing here?"

"I belong to this family."

"What? But—but—your name's different!" Her heart was fluttering so fast it almost outweighed the nausea.

"When I went into the stock market, I decided to change it, so I wouldn't capitalize on their, shall we say, obvious wealth?" Mark looked a little sheepish. "But what about you? Why are you here?"

"They're the people I have been working for these last two weeks, the reason I was too busy to see you." Mark shook his head in disbelief as Mrs. Van der Hooten approached.

"Mark, you know this young woman?" she coached, her Estée Lauder face expressionless.

"Yes, mother. This is the woman I told you about, Elizabeth Madsen Steinberg. Lizzy, for short."

"My, my, isn't this a coincidence!" She was thoroughly enjoying herself. Then she turned and walked away, leaving both Mark and Lizzy with drooping shoulders; they could already see the handwriting on the wall.

Things deteriorated from there. When Lizzy returned home that night, she found her mother, sitting bolt upright in the living room, angrily flipping through a magazine with Mach 1 speed. She picked up a copy of The New York Times and shook it at her daughter.

"Do I have something to show you!" she convulsed, her biting tone the worst Lizzy had ever heard.

"What is it?" Lizzy jerked her trembling hand up to her mouth.

"Come here and see for yourself. I want you to read this name and you tell me..." She signaled for Lizzy to come closer to get a good look.

Lizzy's heart sank. The name Van de Hooten was circled boldly with an extra thick red marker. "...the Van de Hootens have recently made generous contributions to the Markley Gallery, making it one of the largest collections of unknown modernists. The former Lucille Hartford was raised with a sizable knowledge of art, and after having met and married her husband Harold Van de Hooten, she simply continued on in her family's tradition. From all indications, their son, Mark Salisbury, a successful investment counselor in his own right, will also take part in this worthy cause..."

"I know, Mom, I know. I found out tonight," Lizzy said dully.

"Well, what do you have to say about this? You're not going to continue seeing this Mark, are you? This woman made my life a living hell for four years! And then she goes and marries a man who comes from a family that almost destroyed ours! You are not to see this man again, do you hear me?" Her voice morphed into a scream.

"Mom, Mom, calm down, calm down." Lizzy wrapped her arms around her hysterical mother, pulling her into a silent, davening rhythm—back and forth on the couch for almost a quarter of an hour until finally, Ruth relaxed enough to let go and bid her daughter an exhausted good-night.

It was much more peaceful the next morning, but Round Two had already been mapped out. "You understand how I feel about this, right, honey? I suppose Mark is perfectly all right but the thought of us being linked to the Van de Hootens is just impossible for me."

"Mom, listen. I can appreciate how hurt you have been by those people in the past, and I do emphasize in the past. And I do recognize that Mrs. Van de Hooten is certainly not in favor of our union. She's made that quite..."

"What's that supposed to mean? Was she nasty to you? Tell me, if she was, I swear I will speak to her, I will..."

"Now CALM down, Mom. No, she wasn't nasty, just a little cold. Obviously, my relationship with Mark isn't her first choice, either. But it's nothing that we can't handle. We love each other very much, you know. In most circles that counts for something!"

Her mother made sure Natalie wasn't within earshot. "You mean like when that son-of-a-bitch bum who knocked you up was around all the time, ummm?"

Lizzy sucked in her breath. "That was several years ago, Mother! I was very foolish and very needy. Things have changed." She tried to stand her ground, but the bombardments continued in short, stinging rounds, both in Brooklyn, and on Fifth Avenue.

Finally, one day Lizzy turned to Mark. "I love you so much, I really do, but maybe we should cool it for a little while, if only to let them think we're not seeing each other too much."

Mark sat back, flabbergasted. "Is—is this really what you want?"

Shaking her head slowly, she reached out for his hand. But her eyes said it all; she was tired of the fight. Furthermore, she explained, preoccupied as she was with an upcoming show, just the thought of more pressure made her want to escape to a desert island, away from everyone.

So they took time off from one another and Mark learned several things. He learned how pleasant his mother could be when she got her own way, and he also discovered how intertwined his life had become with Lizzy's.

Her absence hit him on all five fronts. Gone was the smell of her lavender soap whenever he had kissed her neck, face, and ears first thing in the morning, and the feel of her soft, colorful kimonos she always wore as he pulled them off to land on his tossed shirts resting on a nearby chair. No longer could he taste her lips, nor touch her luscious body draped over him at night as they languidly made love, and in the mornings, he could no longer see Natalie and her cuddling together, chanting their mother-daughter song that filled him with such unimaginable peace.

Ruth was rejuvenated. With Mark no longer in the picture, she bent over backwards to placate her daughter; hours of extra babysitting with Natalie, cooking Lizzy's favorite foods, and plenty of motherly love. But neither of them had factored in Natalie. Each time the little girl asked where Mark was, Ruth would look nervous and Lizzy ached.

"You're going to the conference with that Blackstone Group keynote speaker on Friday, right, Mark?" All heads turned towards the investment counselor, who had been coming into work later and later, his eyes saucered by dark circles, his chin, an uneven stubble.

Mark nodded and staggered into his office. If only he could sleep at night, he could get a handle on things. His date the night before hadn't helped, either. A promise to his friends, it would be a way of proving he could get his act together. But they had set him up with a young, blonde stockbroker, a woman as sharp and thin as all the others, and as he had ushered her through a doorway, his hand caught her bony shoulder. Suddenly, Lizzy's flesh seemed years away. That night in bed, after hours of flipping around and adjusting pillows, he made up his mind; he was going to win her back.

The next day he was reminded of Ruth's power. When he called, she informed him coldly that Lizzy was out of town for a few days, teaching a quilt workshop in Virginia, and there was no way she could get in touch with her daughter. He'd just have to wait until she got back. When he asked to speak with Natalie, her tone chilled to ice. "Sorry, that's not possible." Click.

The once-a-year Blackstone Group sponsored conference at the Hilton was a mega deal. In the past, it had strengthened Mark's connections and introduced new ideas and people, because everyone agreed—networking was vital. Stockbrokers and investment counselors, fueled by Sandwich Chef, Inc.'s high-power caffeinated coffee, paced up and down the aisles of the showroom, jockeying for positions next to successful men as they sweated through their Van Heusen's shirts, red suspenders, or Donna Karan shoulder pads.

For his part, Mark had never had to worry. This was an area in which he shined, where everything came naturally to him. He never sought; he was simply approached. His palms never moistened, they remained dry, but now, in a room where a keynote speaker was pontificating about mergers and acquisitions and the rise of Reaganomics, he could feel his mind drifting.

"Our President has made his new policies crystal clear. Now is the time for the Trickle Down method of government in America, and with the lowering of taxes for corporations, Ladies and Gentlemen, this might very well be our golden hour…"

Two minutes later, Marked stared down at his Blackstone Group brochure. He had coated it with doodles, trees, bushes, Van Gogh-like spiraling flowers, all gradating into geometric designs—bold, angular patterns that reminded him of Lizzy's quilts.

He stood up, and ignoring all the surprised, upturned faces, made his way out of the hall. Stopping at a lobby pay phone, this time he wouldn't take 'no' for an answer and insisted on talking to Lizzy, but just hearing her voice, his tears caught him off-guard.

They planned a rendezvous picnic in Central Park, near the New York Zoo, with Natalie along as a buffer. Once there, the little girl ran towards him, flinging her arms around his waist, like she would a long lost friend, yet Lizzy stayed restrained, buttoning and unbuttoning her coat.

The park was particularly crowded—jungle gyms crawling with children, lines for the swings, and mothers and nannies chatting non-stop. When Natalie trotted off to play, Lizzy and Mark were left on a bench trying to talk while keeping track of Natalie amidst a swarm of children. It was hard to reconnect—a mother, squeezed in next to them, competed with any confessions of love, but at one point they managed to hold hands and begin a kiss.

"Watch me, Mommy! Mark, look how high I am!" Natalie yelled from the top of the jungle gym.

Time stalled, transforming into a snail's pace. Natalie was falling and Lizzy and Mark were running to her, but it was slow, like a movie shown at half speed. As they both ran, they could see her hit the sand with a thud, her head bouncing off to one side over and over again; an instant replay of a football player's bad fall. Then, in an instant, everything sped up, leaving Natalie motionless in the soft sand.

Scooping her up in his arms, Mark raced with Lizzy out of the park to a nearby hospital and into the emergency room waiting area. He kept asking the quilter questions about their doctor, but she could only manage a few, short gasps. Still holding Natalie, he stepped up to the admissions desk and took charge.

"She's had a bad fall. She needs immediate attention!" His commanding manner made people break out running and as Natalie's small frame was hoisted onto a gurney and taken into Triage he stayed next to her the entire time, grilling the medical staff.

Later, in the waiting room, Lizzy hung limply onto Mark as the long evening dissolved into an even longer night. At dawn, after the doctors had informed them Natalie had a slight concussion, but would definitely recover, Lizzy went into a room to kiss her sleeping daughter, then folded her arms around Mark, whispering, "I love you."

Of course Ruth had to thank him, but she did it grudgingly, with little expression. Meanwhile, uptown, Mrs. Van der Hooten was horrified and saw this whole incident as yet another hurdle he would have to face in his life with this woman, this single mother.

The pressure continued, with Mark away on business and Lizzy transporting her art quilts over to the Madison Avenue Art Gallery for her new textile show. At the show, her artist friends' conversations, once exciting, creative, now seemed pretentious and unimportant. Who cared how many silk screening techniques Andy Warhol used, or which painter used Sienna brown as opposed to Copper.

In Germany, Mark attended an American symposium on Mergers and Acquisitions, a concept, which, although popular in the U.S., seemed to be falling on deaf ears in Europe. He had been sent to win hearts and minds, but ended up going out to dinner with his hosts and discussing art. Over an expensive brew, knockwurst, and sauerkraut, he bubbled on happily about Brueghel and Bosch.

"Hello, is this Ruth? Ruth Steinberg Rosenblatt?" The voice on the other end was painfully familiar.

"Yes…"

"I don't know if you remember me. I certainly remember you. We roomed together our first year at college. I'm Lucille Hartford Van de Hooten."

"I know who you are. What do you want?" The tone stayed monotonal.

"Even though we have had our differences, I believe we both do not want our children to continue this relationship. Am I correct?"

"Yes…" This was interesting, Ruth thought.

"Why don't you come around to our apartment this week, say two p.m. on Wednesday, and we can discuss this. All right?" In spite of herself, Ruth found Lucille's conspiratorial inflections enticing.

"I'll be there. Yes, I can find it, don't worry about me."

At the Van der Hooten's front doorjamb, the two women stared at each other. They had both aged gracefully—one short, dark and round, the other tall, thin and gray, and as they sat on opposite sofas, soaking up each other and transporting themselves back to a time when they could never have had any common goals, they discovered within the first half hour, that the one thing they both did have in common, was that they wanted the best for their children. By the end of two hours, not only were the matriarchs satisfied they could possibly help shape the course of events, they were rather surprised at the mutual respect they ended up feeling towards one another. As they said their good-byes, there were no hugs, but their grins spoke volumes as they separated.

When Mark returned from Europe, there were six messages on his phone, four of which were from old dates or girlfriends, and when Lizzy finished her show on the last night, an old flame suddenly appeared at the gallery from out of nowhere.

The Mother Campaign had been activated. Whenever Mark called up, if Lizzy was in another room, out of earshot, according to her mom, she 'wasn't in.' If she really wasn't in, she never got his messages.

"Mommy, when are we going to see Mark again?" Natalie asked one morning, as she snuggled up close.

Lizzy hesitated. "I don't know, honey, I just don't know..." How could she explain the makings of a relationship and how she had never heard from Mark again?

Out with friends at a local club one night, after his third Manhattan, Mark waxed philosophical. "Maybe the problem with new relationships is that both sides are so damned insecure. Do you think by the time couples celebrate their twentieth wedding anniversary they get it right and are finally at peace?" His words were beginning to slur.

"Maybe she wasn't for you. She was different from us, you know," his friends told him.

Mark smiled sadly, and nodded. He had loved her differences.

Summer came to a lazy end and with it, a free Shakespearean Festival in Central Park, featuring Romeo and Juliet. As hundreds of New Yorkers toted their blankets, coolers, and low-backed lawn chairs over roughly-mowed grass, the smell of MacDonald's happy meals along with gourmet deli meats and cheese layered on top of crackling Italian bread wafted leisurely through the balmy air.

Spreading an old, patchwork quilt out beneath her, Lizzy settled in for an evening of fine, distracting entertainment. Anything to take her mind off Mark. Another night of being at home with her mother's smirking was more than she could handle.

Twenty yards away, hidden behind a tree, an unshaven Mark sat alone on his Abercrombie & Fitch blanket, a high-priced bottle of chilled French chardonnay by his side, two thirds empty.

The play began with well-trained, top-notch actors, their interpretation of the language impeccable. Yet during its first few lines, you could still hear the crinkle of hamburger papers being crushed into throw-away balls, the psshhtt of the pop-top soda cans expelling fizz up into the air, and people shifting on their blankets as they hunkered down for the duration.

As the play wound its way towards the moment when Mercutio, who had just been mortally wounded by Juliet's brother, spoke his classic lines, "I am hurt/A plague on both your houses, I am sped..." the audience stilled, so silent a single cough sounded like a shotgun blast.

Then suddenly, a little boy, standing up in front of Lizzy, made an announcement. "Hey, why are you and that man crying?"

She looked up at him, dazed, her cheeks slippery from tears.

"Why are you and that man the only ones crying?" he repeated, hopping from one foot to the other and pointing to a nearby tree.

Lizzy looked down, annoyed and embarrassed. Who was this kid and why was he singling her out? Then she remembered his words and glanced over at the tree. A man had emerged from behind its wide trunk, dabbing at his eyes with his sleeves and staring at her.

As the play headed towards its final scene, and four hundred and ninety-eight pairs of eyes were centered on the makeshift stage built down on the south side of the 79th Street meadow, two pairs of eyes were focused elsewhere. Wrapped up together in the old comforter, Lizzy and Mark mouthed the words, "a plague on both our houses—a plague on both our houses," as they burrowed deeper under its folds and kissed.

Twelve years later, when their parents decided to renew their marriage vows in front of all their friends in their backyard in Sneden's Landing along the Hudson River, Natalie and her two half-sisters were surprised to see a couple of actors there, performing only a single scene out of Romeo and Juliet.

"Just what are our parents thinking?" Natalie looked at her siblings and shrugged as an actor playing Mercutio was mock-stabbed.

Ruth leaned in and put her arms around Natalie's teenage shoulders. "Ah, well, what can you expect from a crazy art dealer for a father and a business tycoon for a mom?" she quipped, hurrying back into the kitchen for another round of hors d'oeuvres.

BORDER WINDFALLS

Surrounding the main quad at Sunford College stood brick buildings coated with ivy so thick the windows looked more like square holes chiseled into a Chia Pet than double-hung windows. From there, bored students could gaze outside, daydreaming, while frittering away precious classroom time. Below them, narrow pathways gently twisted and turned through a staid campus, reminding one of an English university rather than a small United States college, and indeed, in 1968, Sunford might as well have been nestled in another country. No anti-Vietnam demonstrations or Civil Rights movements here; only conservative children of even more conservative business families, pretending to get a "well-rounded" education and simultaneously, spending their parents' money as fast as they could.

Peter Rosen's view on education, however, contrasted sharply from his colleagues and in particular, his roommate Jack Reinhold. No two people could have been more different. Jack descended from a Texas oil-rich family, while Peter's parents were hard-working, lower middle-class, and being Jewish, slightly insecure about their son's enrollment in so Waspy an institution. But Peter had won a full scholarship, and that was that.

"Jesus Christ, Peter, why do you have to pound the books all day, huh?" Jack's boisterous voice always broke Peter's concentration.

"Listen, I've got a chemistry test tomorrow, if you don't mind! Some people have to work hard to get good grades..." Peter, teetering on the verge of another rant about not having a rich daddy to bail him out, thought better of it, and stopped.

"Peter, someday you're gonna regret not playing with me and my pals. Life's too short, you know?" Changing into his tennis outfit, Jack warbled a low whistle, then bounded out of the room, slamming the door shut and sending several of Peter's papers flying.

"He really thinks he's God's gift…" Peter grumbled, snatching up the strewn papers littering the floor of their small dorm room.

As much as he tried, he couldn't contain himself—he was bitter. Why not? Everything always came so easily for people like Jack. Was it because he was from a wealthy family? No, not just that. After all, there was Leonard Quigley down the hall; his father was fabulously rich, yet he was a complete nerd. Nothing ever went right for him. Peter chuckled at the thought of Leonard trying to be social in the college cafeteria. It was not a pretty sight. Then, looking down at Jack on the quad talking to a co-ed, he drew a slow sigh before settling down to a long study session.

Four years later in medical school, he was still studying hard, still far too serious, and still a far cry from Jack. "Come off it, Rosen, you'll never save the world, you know," everyone laughed. But Peter was not just going to be a good surgeon; he was really going to contribute something to society.

However, picking out a specialty proved difficult. Too many things competed for his attention and indeed, if his aunt Sophie hadn't been sent to the hospital for extreme dehydration on the heels of a bout of influenza, he might never have decided at all.

"Dahlink, I expect you to come visit me here at the hospital. Now, come tomorrow, that'd be nice," she commanded over the phone, obviously puffing on a pilfered cigarette. Click.

The next day, as the elderly woman nodded off on her bed, Peter was itching to go, but just knowing that leaving without a goodbye would cause Hell-To-Pay, he picked up a copy of National Geographic and started thumbing through it, flipping the pages in time to Aunt Sophie's rhythmic snores.

God, these articles could be so much more interesting, he sighed, alternating between glancing at the pictures and checking on his aunt's progress toward waking up. The photos were really spectacular, he thought, if only the articles gave you more detail. If only…

On the spreadsheet in front of him was a little boy, displaying a horrendously disfiguring harelip and cleft palate. Staring forlornly into the camera, his tears had been caught mid-slide on his cheeks, frozen forever in the photograph. Behind him, several townspeople had been captured as well, but instead of sadness, their faces were suspended in sneers and taunts.

Children born with this condition, the article stated, not only had to contend with a real physical deformity, they had to deal with people who were convinced their malady was the sign of the Devil himself. According to local custom, they weren't allowed to live a normal life. Indeed, they were to be punished, or at the very least, not permitted to go to school for fear of contaminating the other students.

Peter could feel the energy being drawn out of his body and siphoned onto the page. This was his Eureka moment. He would specialize in plastic surgery and try to set up a small clinic to repair some of nature's damage to these poor unfortunates.

But nobody took him seriously. Sure, sure, they all snickered. You're doing this not for the tremendous-amounts-of-money-you-could-get-doing liposuction, but rather for the good of small children. Yeah, sure. Tell us another one, Rosen. His parents were no help, either. They were more than ecstatic—their son, the Beverly Hills millionaire plastic surgeon. What a godsend, our Petela!

But in his first year as a doctor, Peter chose a research position at a plastic surgery clinic in El Paso, Texas, where the job description included some hands-on experience as a craniofacial surgeon, dealing mostly with harelips and cleft palates. His salary was much lower than expected, and he didn't seem to even care about liposuction or face-lifts where the real money was. His parents were stunned.

The head surgeon at Peter's clinic was succinct. "Listen, Rosen, I know you are hoping for extra funding for your harelip projects in Latin America, but just forget it. This is 1981 with a Republican president. The new administration is not going to be receptive to your convictions."

He studied Peter for a second then continued. "If you have to pick an unpopular cause, why don't you spend your time researching this new virus that seems to be killing homosexuals? Nobody cares about your kids from other countries. Take my advice on this, I know what I'm talking about."

Devastated, Peter slunk home. It must be my karma, my touch, the non-Jack-Reinhold-touch, he ruminated. Suddenly he wondered what the rogue was up to. How was his life turning out? He switched on his television for the evening news and walked over to his refrigerator to pull out a frozen turkey T.V. dinner. He was examining the back of the package when he heard a voice that propelled him 180 degrees back towards his set.

"...Tell me, Mr. Reinhold, how can you account for this remarkable turn-around in your newly acquired cable station in El Paso? Ever since you took over three years ago, the rating charts have skyrocketed, with everyone buzzing about record sales. Isn't it true your "Give-A-Kid-A-Wallet" campaign has been the main reason for this?"

There was a deft smile on Jack's face as he leaned into the microphone. "Well, yes, the program has been a success. Give a child a wallet and they'll try to put something into it, I always say. Makes them get out there and work hard. Thanks much, and have a great day." Slipping into his brand new Porsche 911, he was off and running.

All the years of hard work and frustration finally caught up with Peter. "Goddamit!" he blared as he hurled a slipper at the TV. "It's time I had some of my goals realized! I'm a good person; I work hard. Why the hell can't I get successful? Give a Kid a Wallet! Give a Kid A Wallet! What about my kids? How about their lives?" Flinging his dinner against the kitchen counter, he watched turkey, gravied mashed potatoes, and peas catapult across the room.

That night in bed, images of Jack standing over him, laughing, made sleep impossible, but eventually, as the night shifted from pitch black to a soft, milky gray, he drifted off, his mind made up.

"WBBQ Cable network, Jack Reinhold, Managing Director," a receptionist's reedy voice warbled over the phone.

"Yes, I'd like to talk to Jack Reinhold, please." Suddenly, Peter was very nervous.

"I'm afraid he's in a meeting. Whom shall I say is calling?" Her pinched tone was beginning to lodge itself an eighth of an inch beneath his skin.

"Just tell him a very old friend from college is on the phone."

"What is your name, sir?" The tone chilled slightly. The hell with her.

"Look, just tell Jack, Peter Rosen called, and have him call me back." He hung up, sorry he had called.

He only half-expected an answer back. People like him never commanded one. Instead, he spent his nights at a nearby library, studying South American cultures, with their remarkable herbal medicines, and their abhorrence for harelips and cleft palates. The more articles he read, the stronger the gravitational pull towards these abused and abandoned children.

Two weeks later, an invitation arrived in the mail. "WBBQ Station cordially invites you to a cocktail party honoring Jack Reinhold, Managing Director. Please RSVP by February 20, 1981." Annoyed that there was no personal note to him, he was about to flip it into the waste paper basket when he caught sight of a few scribbled words on the back, "Hey, buddy, great to hear from you. Please come, OK? Best, Jack."

He felt curiously reaffirmed, as if his own father had placed a loving arm around his shoulders, telling him what a good boy he had been and how much he was admired.

The Maitre D' Restaurant was old-world, elegant, and undoubtedly expensive. Silver trays of champagne-filled fluted crystal glasses floated throughout the "Chateau Room" on the finger tips of well-dressed waiters, while caviar canapés made their way into executives' mouths, and plush carpeting muted the sounds of business deals being solidified.

Trying to juggle a canapé-filled plate and napkin along with his second glass of champagne, Peter scoured the room for his old roommate. When he spotted him from across the buffet tables, he chuckled ruefully—same old Jack, handsome, albeit with a slight receding hairline, but still vital as he extended his hearty handshake out to everyone in passing.

This man really had it all, the surgeon smiled in spite of himself. Then Jack caught sight of him. Waving his right arm wildly, he shouted, "Hey Peter! Wait there, I'm comin' over!" By the time he had reached the doctor, his simple bear hug made Peter feel truly welcomed.

"What a surprise to hear from you! Frankly, Rosen, I thought you hated my guts. I'm so glad! When this is all over, I want you to come to my apartment to catch up on old times, OK?"

Peter nodded, excited at finally being accepted. But after the party, as he entered Jack's apartment, his insecurities instantly surfaced. A glass and chrome coffee table lay on top of the plushest cream-colored textured carpeting he had ever seen. Light tan leather sofas, accessorized by woven Guatemalan throw pillows and a collection of antique sailboat models on various Stickley side tables, completed the perfect picture of confirmed bachelorhood and good taste. Peter was totally intimidated.

"Hey, buddy. Have a drink and let's catch up." Jack handed his ex-collegiate roomie a thick-walled tumbler of Jack Daniels-over-ice and motioned for them both to sit down.

"So what in the world have you been up to these last few years, huh? Still in medicine? Still so serious? Talk."

Not inclined to spill his guts, Peter hesitated. But a second later he couldn't resist. "You're the one who's gone on to fame and fortune, Jack, not me." The envy and bitterness were unmistakable.

Jack sat back for a couple of seconds before answering, his head cocked at a forty-five degree angle. "Man, I'm so tired of you always thinking everything's been handed to me on a silver platter. I mean, I created this whole cable situation on my own, without any help from my dad or the rest of my family. It's all me, kiddo, so why don't you get off your high horse for a second, OK?"

Peter could feel the blood rushing up into his brain and quickly gulped down the rest of his drink. Suddenly the room started to sway, and with it, an outpouring of his goals and dreams in a torrent of words that had been repressed for years. When he started talking about the children, he became quite emotional. Suddenly embarrassed, he asked where the bathroom was so he could compose himself.

Returning to the living room, he sat down to face a surprisingly somber Jack. "Listen, buddy, if you are serious about this business with the harelips and the kids, maybe I can work something out for you." Jack leaned in, squinting his eyes as he continued to think out loud.

"I don't know if I can swing anything, mind you, but why don't you make a list of what you would need in order to start operating. Then send it to me, let me think about it, and I'll get back to you on this in a couple of weeks. All right?"

Numbed by alcohol, Peter nodded, accompanied by a surrealistic feeling that all this couldn't possibly be happening.

But by the following day his list was preliminarily sketched out: a clinic that could hold up to five beds at a time, an operating room, x-ray equipment, surgery utensils, scopes, at least one nurse—he recognized sometimes nurses were required to help in the suturing of the nose and mouth if one side was to be symmetrical with the other. Sometimes there might be poor healing from cleft palate surgery, and that, too, might require a second operation. In addition, he knew ear infections often resulted from cleft palate surgery due to the cleft interfering with middle ear functioning. To allow proper drainage and air circulation, often a plastic ventilation tube was inserted during smaller procedures.

He thought of bleeding inoperative hemorrhaging because there was such an abundance of blood supply in the palate, so of course, a massive stockpile of bandages would be needed. Due to budget concerns, he would have to forego a geneticist and psychologist, but an orthodontist, audiologist, and an ear, nose and throat specialist would be much appreciated. A bi-lingual speech therapist would be ideal, but having scribbled late into the night, he was beginning to get anxious—his list had become so extensive. How far could he actually push Jack? he wondered.

Then it hit him. Narcotics. Drugs for anesthesiology and for pain. Oh, my God. How in the world was he going to carry narcotics across the border? He knew from experience post early tissue operations could use Tylenol or other weaker aids, but bone-grafting and post palate procedures were a different matter altogether. The very idea of all these children having to endure these operations without proper painkillers made his stomach churn.

He was thinking of scrapping the entire operation when his office phone rang. "Hey, Peter, I think we might have a go-ahead on this." Jack sounded excited.

"You're kidding! Well, I've thought of a problem." Peter said.

"What's that?" Excitement had leaned towards impatience.

"Narcotics. Those kids cannot have certain operations without them. The pain is just too great. You can't bring narcotics over the borders, you know Jack?" Peter couldn't hide his disappointment.

There were several seconds of silence. Then, "Call me tonight. I have an idea."

After a long day of anxiety, Peter finally phoned. "Hi, Jack, it's me." He waited nervously. "Well...?"

"OK," Jack started in. "I don't think it will be a problem, because my cable station has worked with a doctor down in Mexico who says he can supply morphine, etc. in exchange for helping some villagers he knows with this problem."

Peter breathed a huge sigh of relief; maybe it was all going to work out after all. He went ahead and signed his Professional Leave papers from his clinic, and contacted Jack daily about all the things he needed until at last, he felt he was ready to go.

"Oh, Rosen, there's one more thing I forgot to tell you," Jack said casually. Peter cringed. Oh, boy, here it comes.

"It seems my driver, who has been transporting all the wallets for my "Give Children A Wallet" out of this little village, suddenly quit, leaving me high and dry. Since you mentioned you're thinking of putting a clinic near there, I thought maybe you could pick up the wallets yourself. I'll be looking for a new driver, but for now, maybe you could pinch-hit for me?"

"Sure, sure, no problem," he laughed. "Just when do I start?"

From birth, sucking on his mother's breast had been an altogether different experience for Eduardo than it was for his brothers and sisters. When they nursed, their tummies were soon filled with warm, nutritious milk. When Eduardo tried to feed off of his mother, all he got for his efforts was pain and total frustration.

"Ah, Dios mio, what are we going to do?" his mama would say, tenderly looking down at her odd little one, the one many villagers claimed was the work of Satan. Her eyes would fill with tears as she watched her baby desperately try to suckle, his cheeks working furiously, his hands squeezing her flesh. But as the liquid spilled out between the two gaps on the top of his mouth, he would end each feeding session with an explosive wail.

Her husband Ernesto pronounced the boy was no good, but Rosalie wrapped him even tighter in his swaddling clothes, keeping him warm and safe, away from the world. Still, she couldn't always protect him. As Eduardo grew, she could see how everyone else treated him. Children threw things at him as he walked to school, and many of the adults in the village, when they saw him coming, would scurry over to the other side of the street, making the sign of the cross. So she shielded him the only way she knew how. He was to stay close at home, never appear in public, and with her limited education, she would teach him how to read.

In time, Ernesto admitted there was no good reason to complain about Eduardo; he was a good child, after all, with an acceptance of life far beyond his years. In fact, he was so quiet and well-behaved, his father often didn't even notice his son sitting by the big front window, his face pressed against the glass, gazing at all the other children scampering back and forth from school each day without him. It just bothered him that his son could only manage strange guttural tones that no one but Rosalie could understand.

Yet there was one joy in Eduardo's life—watching his mother weave bright, beautiful cloths. Her wooden loom took up most of their back bedroom, and it was there he would spend hours observing her shift the different threads with her hands and feet, combining colors that lingered inside his head for days at a time.

Often she would instruct Eduardo not to interrupt her, particularly when weaving her 'material especiale' for that Nice Mr. Reinhold's made-to-order wallets. Her concentration was of the utmost importance for them all; on this she would insist, reminding him how much better their lives had become since connecting up with Mr. Jack and how vital his business was to them.

Her methods were simple. She would take out several different colored strands from her parents' hand-carved trunk—navy blue, magenta, yellow, pink, red, white, and green. Threading them carefully into her loom, she would start humming. This was the part Eduardo loved the most; it meant his mother was happy and he could relax.

In and out the different shuttles flew. Up and down the foot pedals danced until soon, a beautiful striped heavy fabric would begin to emerge. And as the afternoon light angled in through the window lower and lower, Rosalie would keep weaving until finally her neck and back felt the familiar muscle tension she knew so well. Time to stop and prepare dinner. Then she would get up, and stretching into a yoga-like position, laugh at Eduardo, sleeping next to their dog, curled up like a baby, not the eight-year-old boy he really was.

"I think I've gotten everything you wanted on your list, Buddy. It's all ready to be moved into your facility in the town of Quolonga, as requested." Jack couldn't control his smug grin. "Give me a call the second you get down there, OK, Rosen?" he went on. "I wanna make sure you and all the equipment made it all right. I also want to make double sure after a week, you get over to the Gonsales house to pick up those wallets."

"Of course, of course. I promised you, didn't I? You know me. The conscientious one. Don't worry—I'll definitely pick up those wallets." Peter tossed a wave to Jack as he hopped into the front cab with the driver and the truck pulled away.

In Quolonga, a small staff of three greeted them in front of a rundown, paint-peeled clinic on one of the few paved streets in town. Inwardly, Peter groaned, but in a few days they had managed to make sure it was scrubbed, cleaned, and sterilized—at least it was sanitary and usable.

It turned out Jack remained true to his word. Not only did Peter receive most of the items on his list, his former roommate had also done extensive PR. Within the first week, Peter had patients standing in line, more than ready for their first operation. Babies, swaddled in their mothers' arms, were the easiest. It was the older children that Peter was the most concerned about and without morphine, he felt completely stymied.

When Jack phoned, he assured the doctor about a delivery soon, and speaking of deliveries, had he picked up the wallets from the Gonsaleses yet? Peter felt like snapping at him; wallets were certainly not as high a priority as these children, but he bit his tongue and agreed to go the very next day to pick up the trinkets.

Watching Peter trip over one of their chickens clucking happily in the front yard, Rosalie giggled. These gringos. They might all have money, but en realidad, they had no grace. Walking through the rusted front screen door, she greeted him politely, then motioned for him to follow her into the house where all the wallets were kept.

Stepping inside, Peter gasped. The tiny living room exploded with beautiful fabrics hung up in every conceivable inch of space—from an armoire, several cupboard doors, to even a standing lamp. He had always admired these kinds of woven cloths at the Texas open-air markets, but it was quite another thing to see that many intense colors up so close.

With a proud grin, Rosalie coaxed several members of her family to come out of the back bedroom to meet Peter. Ernesto shuffled his feet nervously, his eyes cast downward as Peter extended his hand. Little five-year-old Maria stared up at the strange man with the biggest brown eyes the doctor had ever seen, but it was Eduardo who immediately captured his attention. Just seeing that bilateral lip, he understood instantly how miserable the boy's life was and most probably, had always been.

After retreating towards the back of the house, Rosalie returned, carrying a large cardboard box. Peter took it from her, set it on the floor, and opened it up. Inside, were dozens of beautiful, hand-woven wallets. As he exclaimed, "Oh, how wonderful!" Rosalie came and went, carrying box after box, until the small room overflowed with cardboard and vibrant colors.

She pointed to an address on a small slip of paper, then to the boxes. "Muy importante, muy importante!" she insisted.

Frustrated with Jack, Peter frowned. What was he, a delivery service or a doctor?" Then he felt ashamed. After all, Jack was making his dream come true; it was the least he could do for him and the wallet campaign for kids.

Turning to Eduardo and placing his left hand on the boy's shoulder, he tapped his own chest with his right index finger first, then gently laid it over the two gaps above the boy's lip, declaring, "I can fix. Me...el doctor. Comprende?"

There was a split second before it hit her. Rushing over to Peter with eyes the size of two hundred peso coins, Rosalie kept asking, "Es posible? Es posible?"

Peter nodded. Without warning, she flung her arms around the young doctor's neck, crying and laughing all at the same time.

The next several weeks were a blur. Twenty-four-seven, Peter focused on the children, and although all the morphine had arrived, he realized he would have to divvy it out sparingly. As far as his weekly trips to the Gonsales household to pick up the wallets were concerned, they didn't bother him that much—his official driver, José, turned out to be pleasant enough. Each week, they got into a light banter about baseball and American culture while José loaded his truck with the 'wallets especiale,' as Rosalie had coined them.

Eduardo was doing remarkably well, considering, although his series of cleft repair operations had been as difficult as they had been painful. Because the child had never had the initial tissue procedure that Peter normally would do at three months, they had to make up for lost time, and then, when they saw some intraoperative hemorrhaging, they decided to perform major suturing in order to stop any excessive bleeding. But throughout the operations and his stay at the clinic, Eduardo never complained; he just kept nodding his head and gazing up at Peter with nothing less than adoration.

Even outside the clinic, life had picked up for Peter. Jack bought him a black Range Rover for his weekly trips with José and in addition, two good business suits for when he was slated to go to 'important meetings with corporate heads' back in the States. Although those meetings never seemed to amount to anything, the doctor didn't notice. He was too busy flying north with Jack on the station's Lear jet and admiring the view from cream leather-double-club seats.

Jack and his companion George began their slow descent over the sparse, arid terrain, as huge dust clouds rustled up dirt particles, paper debris, and dried plant life. After landing, they climbed out of the small Cessna and ran for cover into an old, mud-splashed building, just long enough for Jack to radio someone over his walkie-talkie.

"Get 'em all ready. We're comin' over now," he ordered into the mouthpiece. Turning around, he winked at his associate.

Soon, a bug-splattered jeep shuddered to an abrupt halt outside the building, and when the driver vaulted off the truck to reposition himself next to the window on the other side, some fine dust from the ground seeped in under the crack in the door, causing Jack to give two quick coughs before heading out.

With George in the middle, the three men rode in silence for quite some time as they traveled far up into the hills, where the habitat was bursting with vegetation, birds, animals, and humidity. Nearing the top, odd, unintelligible sounds echoed repeatedly, but as the jeep got closer, the sounds became almost familiar, until finally, the car pulled up in front of a large, Spanish-style hacienda. There, the sounds were perfectly clear.

Barking dogs clogged the otherwise peaceful air, making it almost impossible to hear oneself think. As soon as the men exited the jeep and walked behind the house to a large wired kennel, the frenetic hounds jumped up in unison, their noses twitching like rabbits as they desperately clawed the fence.

Most of them appeared to be Bloodhounds, but several were German Shepherds, and one was a Doberman. Judging from the timbre of their barks and the slight curl of their lips, he surmised they were not necessarily friendly, simply territorial.

"See, George, I told you these dogs are special," Jack announced proudly.

"OK, OK, but why? You never said why, Jack."

"These dogs are 'specially trained for border patrol guards, U.S. Marshals, and drug enforcement organizations in the states. We have also used them in Mexico and further south. They're beautiful, don't you think?"

"Yeah, so?"

"So anyone would think they do top-notch drug sniffing work, because they're smart, they look great, and they certainly have the energy. But I have a little secret. I've hired an expert dog trainer to brainwash these little fellas here, so they don't locate the drugs. They even start looking elsewhere. Great plan, don't you think?"

George stared at Jack for a couple of seconds then shook his head. "Son-of-a-bitch! That's brilliant! It must really work, you bastard, you've sure gotten rich. But what about this partner of yours, this goody-two-shoes doctor friend?"

"Don't worry about him," Jack snorted. "He's totally oblivious, and so into his kids and their operations he wouldn't be able to tell cocaine from white table salt. Forget about him."

Three months later, when Peter spotted a shiny black Mercedes parked halfway up the street from Rosalie and Ernesto's house, he didn't think anything of it. After all, his current mission was infinitely more important. He had brought with him his new young friend and together, they quietly walked up the front path and slowly opened the screen door.

Eduardo took one look at his mother and said clearly, like any other boy, "Te amo, Mama." The hushed silence lasted a good two seconds before she burst into tears.

"O Díos mio," she sobbed, clinging to Eduardo and rocking him back and forth in her arms. "Es muy claro, sí?" she finally whispered to Peter.

Smiling, he nodded. Yes, it was very clear, for the first time in Eduardo's life.

Suddenly, a rifle blast cracked through the air, shattering the front window and scattering broken glass everywhere.

"Get down! Get down!" he hollered. There was no time for a Spanish translation and apparently, no need for one. Before Peter could say another word, he watched the members of the Gonsales family crawling on their hands and knees military-style to the back of the house, with Rosalie signaling him to follow as they all bolted out the back door. In less than one minute, they had ended up at a hidden outhouse, where an old, rust-covered pickup truck was already fired up, with Ernesto behind the front wheel.

One of the children shoved Peter towards the load bed, and jumping in, he landed on a semi-soft dark green army tarp. When he lifted up a corner, he saw more bolts of the beautiful woven fabric. Stunned, all he could mutter was, "Que pasa? Que pasa?" What the hell is going on? he wondered.

"No problema. Es no problema. Paciente, por favor. Please," Rosalie begged, as one of the older daughters covered them all up with the tarp. The truck sped off, bouncing so high, Peter had to grab Eduardo to keep him from flying out.

After the first field, the truck slowed down, stalling long enough to pick someone up. Peter could hear Ernesto and another adult male in the cab, talking rapid-fire Spanish, and although the man's voice had a recognizable ring to it, he couldn't quite make it out over the rattle of the old engine and the crunch of road pebbles. His right hip bone was throbbing and edging up on his elbow, he called out to Ernesto, just as the truck unexpectedly slammed to a dead stop.

Cupping his right hand against his forehead, he tried shielding his eyes from the fierce sun as someone slowly lifted up the tarp. After several seconds, his eyes adjusted and he blurted out, "Oh, my God, José! What the hell are you doing here? What's going on?"

José grinned. "Hey, amigo, this is the way it is down here, you know? We all gotta live, we all gotta eat." With a quick shrug of his shoulders, he walked back to the cab.

Peter lay still for a moment, trying to think. Obviously the Gonsaleses were in on this whole thing, so was José, and Jack—Oh, my God! Jack had to be the ringleader, he...A wave of nausea washed over him. If Jack was up to his eyeballs in drug trafficking, where did that put him? Where did he fit into all of this?

He sat up in a panic and yelled at the muddied half-opened cab, "Hey, José, stop and answer me RIGHT NOW! Stop the truck!" The two men up front continued in stony silence for a couple of minutes, until they had rounded a bend and got into a more deserted territory before stopping.

The driver switched off the engine and Ernesto twisted his torso to look back at the doctor. "Señor, what is it you want to know, eh?"

"I want to know where am I in all of this? I don't want to have anything to do with drugs!" Peter's fist slammed down hard on the load bed's edge.

José jumped out of the cab and stamped back over to Peter. "Amigo, you always in the middle. Those wallets you and me pick up every week, eh? You always in the middle."

Peter's mouth dropped. "But...but...I'm innocent, I had no idea..."

"Señor, we gonna take good care of you. You stay with us for a few days. Then the Federales not find you, OK?" José was already heading back towards the cab.

That night, as they all huddled together in the back room of a small, dilapidated house, overwhelmed by cat urine and tobacco, an angry Peter stayed warm under a bolt of fabric he had wrapped around him by nursing his murderous thoughts.

But just one look at Eduardo, and he melted. As the moonlight beamed in through an open window, he spied a tear drying on the young boy's cheek, and he wondered what the child was thinking if he was awake, or dreaming about if he had just fallen asleep. It was the last thing on his mind before drifting off into his own turbulent dreams.

A loud knock startled Peter out of a police-filled nightmare the next morning. Seconds later, José was bending over him. "Señor Rosen, is not safe for you to return to the United States yet. Too much trouble at the borders. We can keep you for a week or two, here in town, OK?"

"Listen, where the hell is Jack Reinhold? Where is he? I want to talk to him!" Peter demanded.

"I so sorry, Señor Reinhold," he muttered, lowering his eyes. "No is here right now. I am so sorry. We do not know where he is."

"That's just great! Just what I need! He gets me involved in this mess and then disappears! Just wait until I get my hands on him," Peter growled. "What about the rest of my children? I need to get back to the clinic, and do my real work, you know?!"

"Sí, sí, Señor Rosen, I understand. Is your job. And now, is my job to protect you, so please, stay here 'til I say is OK." He heel-turned and walked out of the room.

After that, Peter's sleep was fitful, and during the day, his appetite had shrunk down to nothing. Forget José, he finally decided, I'm going to return to the clinic and complete my operations. Suddenly, he felt better than he had in two weeks.

Café Orlando was an intimate place where pretty waitresses served cafe espressos and cervezas that tasted better than the usual warm beers offered in other local hangouts. Settling down at a table in front of a large glass-plated window, Peter zeroed in on the front door of his clinic across the street and waited. Soon, a mother entered the clinic with her little girl whose head and lower face were carefully covered with a colorful Mexican shawl. When the two quickly came out again, the mother was trying to calm a sobbing, inconsolable child.

I should be there for them, Peter agonized, gulping down his last sip, and as he raced across the street to try to catch up with the mother and daughter, he smiled, knowing in his heart that he was at the right place, doing the right thing.

He never made it.

Two Mexican drug officials nabbed him as soon as he got over to his clinic, whisking him away to the border, where they handed him over to two U.S. drug enforcement officers.

"But wait, I must see my patients at the clinic. They are counting on me." Peter pleaded. The officers just laughed, shaking their heads and shuffling through papers.

His trial didn't last very long and the judge was fairly lenient with him in comparison to Jack. His doctor's license was suspended for now, but because of his charity work, there would be a possible future reinstatement based on good behavior. When they read Jack's sentence, Peter glanced over at his former partner and noticed that the suit was still gorgeous and expensive, but the face looked gray under the tan, and the knuckles were definitely white.

Most days Peter feels quite sorry for himself, sorry he ever got involved, and how he would like to kill Jack. For an innocent man, eighteen months in jail is a long time to be locked away. But then, when he really feels depressed, all he has to do is get out Eduardo's letter again for the twentieth time:

Señor Peter,

I write letter to you. Thank you for my life ever one love me now. I go to school other persons play with me now. I never forget you. I love you.

con mucho cariño, Eduardo

Sometimes in the exercise yard, Peter runs into Old Bill, the "Lifer" who manages to pull himself up onto an iron bench and pontificate about how crime doesn't pay. Once in a great while, the other inmates even stand around and listen to the old guy for entertainment. But on those occasions, just thinking of Eduardo, Peter smiles and walks away, shaking his head. Maybe, just maybe crime does pay, after all.

EMMA AT NIGHT

The women in my family, I am told, have collectively handed down our ancestral folklore as long as anyone can remember, beginning with my great-great-great-great-great-great grandmother Eugenie. She was one of the most eloquent of our clan, recounting these tales to her daughter, who then sat down with her own daughter and so forth and so on, until one day, centuries later, my mother enriched me with the life of Emma, perhaps the most gifted cognate of us all.

According to Eugenie, Emma had always felt at one with the night. She claimed it was only then that there were no class distinctions; the world mostly emerged balanced, a balance totally ignored during the day. Indeed, for her, the daylight had often brought scorn and envy from many of the villagers around her.

"Pray, pardon me, m'lady, if thou wouldst not mind. I should like to pass," sneered the teenage boy angling past her in the narrow, mildewed corridor of the local abbey. Smacking her dress aside with his right hand, he made the parchment papers she had been holding fly out of her arms. She stood still for several seconds, refusing to appear weak, but kneeling down to gather up the frayed pieces of paper, her tears came in quickly.

A gentle pat on her shoulder caused her to look up into the creviced face of an elderly monk with compassionate eyes. He spoke softly, tenderly. "I have watched thee, child for several years hence, coming here, reading, nay, devouring the words on our pages, and it doth touch my heart. Pray tell me, wherefore didst that young man be so cruel to thee? In faith, 'tis beyond my comprehension."

"Father Mathew, thy abbey hath taught me to read now for three years hence. Verily, in the village they doth loathe me for it."

"I hear tell thy embroiderie is some of the best in the village. Is that not enough pride for thee?" His words scolded, yet his demeanor remained kind.

"Yes, I am proud of that which I sew; still, I ask thee, shall we all be punished for not being noble born?"

The monk hesitated. "Pray, do not despair, child. Come here in a fortnight with thy family. If all goeth well, I shall have a surprise for thee. In addition, prithee, bring some of thy embroiderie samples."

A summons to the abbey was a true gift from God, an event so powerful if it weren't for the charitable monk coming towards them two weeks later with outstretched arms, her family would have been far too apprehensive to stay.

The monk addressed Emma's father. "I hath spoken with Lord Buckingham, and he hath agreed to help thy family. If thou, good sir, wouldst be willing to go fight in the Crusades for our King Richard, his Lordship will treat thee well in return. Taxes shalt not be collected and thy daughter shall live in his manor. 'Tis her skills in embroiderie that giveth him interest, and he hath assured me she shall be given an excellent position in the Wardrobe. She shall be expected to embroider tablecloths, pillows or the like, whatever Lady Buckingham doth desire."

To her surprise, her father acquiesced, ignoring any danger he might encounter, simply expressing gratitude for the great honor bestowed upon his daughter.

The next day, Emma set out on the long journey to Buckingham Manor with Father Jerrold. Walking down familiar roads bursting with trees, stone fences, and thick brushes dotted with wild flowers, she smiled, thinking how the countryside had never looked so beautiful. By the last bend in the road, they had passed at least two flocks of sheep grazing lazily in neighboring fields and in the middle of the Buckingham moat itself, three territorial swans flapped their wings menacingly at the travelers scurrying over the drawbridge, eager to arrive at the massive, front door.

After a few knocks the door opened, its unoiled, metal hinges groaning against the swollen wood. A tall, dark-haired servant with a close-cropped goatee appeared, took one look at Emma, and sniffing haughtily, led them both into the high-ceilinged hallway. But the seamstress took no offense; she was too occupied gawking at all the coats of arms draped over the jutting spears.

Set deep into a thick, stone wall was a staircase and as they entered into its cavern and ascended up the cold, unlit steps, they both lost sight of the stairs momentarily, moving mostly by instinct. At the top, they could see light streaming in from narrow stain-glass windows in what was obviously the Wardrobe room. There, at least twenty young women sat, sewing intently, noiselessly, their needles flicking in and out of the various cloths. They all raised their heads in unison as Emma was brought in, eyeing her suspiciously.

The manservant barked a quick order to one of the women. "Get thee to thy Ladyship and tell her the new wench is here. Be gone!"

Waiting for Lady Buckingham, Emma seized the opportunity to look around her. Intricate floral embroidery was everywhere—in pillows, long tablecloths, or chair covers, filling Emma with a wave of insecurity. She was about to turn to Father Jerrold to tell him they had made a mistake, when she heard the gentle rustle of petticoats entering the room. Looking up, she contemplated one of the loveliest women she had ever seen.

Lady Buckingham, dressed in emerald green velvet, graciously smiled. "Pray tell me, Father," she resonated, "is this the young wench of whom thou hath spoken?" She inched in closer to inspect the young seamstress. As if on cue, Emma obediently withdrew her embroidery sample from a thin cloth satchel and held it up for her ladyship to judge. Lady Buckingham caught her breath, then examined the needlework more meticulously.

Several seconds passed before she spoke again. "Thou truly doth worthy work, child. Therefore, thou shalt be my personal sewer, and will henceforth work with me both day and night."

Two weeks later, it still felt as if the seamstress were caught in the middle of a dream. Waking up each morning to clean sheets, the smell of sausage, eggs, trout, kippers, and hot bread from the nearby kitchen all made Emma realize just how changed her life was. No more hauling heavy milk pails or emptying chamber pots before dawn. No more hateful townspeople making her life wretched. Here, it seemed, all she was required to do was to behave herself and sew until her fingers ached.

And sew she did, most of which was done during the afternoon and at night, perched on a round wooden stool in front of the huge hearth by the north wall of the Wardrobe. Sometimes her back developed spasms when she stood up, making it difficult to lie down at night to sleep. But in the mornings, everything was restored once she saw Lady Buckingham's radiant smile and received such high praise for her handiwork from her mistress.

Yet within six months, she noticed the smiles had lessened, replaced by dark purplish circles under the once flawless eyes.

"Thee hast done well here, child and for that, I am truly grateful, more grateful than thou shalt ever know," Lady Buckingham whispered to Emma one day.

Emma paused, waiting for more, but the only sound in the room was the crackling of the wood burning in the small stone fireplace at the head of the Wardrobe chamber.

"Her ladyship is pleased with the lettering?" Trying to connect, she was about to say more when she noticed a single tear sliding down Lady Buckingham's right cheek.

Immediately, her ladyship wiped it off. "My…my…my cold hath gotten the better of me. I must rest."

"'Tis a good idea, madam."

"Thou hast such a simple life, my dear. Thou shouldst indeed be grateful."

Lady Buckingham sounded so wistful Emma couldn't help herself. "I crave your pardon, yet I wouldst give anything to have thy life, my lady!" She blurted out.

"Oh, Emma, Emma, if thou couldst know. If thou only couldst know…" Her words trailed off, leaving the seamstress more curious than ever. But the moment of intimacy was over and Lady Buckingham quickly drew herself up to announce, "Well, 'tis time to go to bed for I must sleep. Goodnight, and if I am well enough in the morn, I shall see thee on the morrow." She nodded curtly and hurried out of the room.

Again Emma couldn't sleep. Within the safe confines of the manor, she had come to feel even more comfortable with the night, often exploring until the early morning hours. The 'Moon Worshipper', her mother used to call her. "Thou shalt have danger with this obsession. Only people connected to the devil or robbers or evil fairies hath anything to do with the night, mark my words. There shall be no good from it," she warned.

Stepping by the kitchen, Emma could hear several of the servants washing the manor's clothing as they gossiped in solemn tones, unaware of her presence. "I tell thee, thou shouldst watch out for Lord Buckingham. Our noble madam shouldst watch herself as well. I dare say he is up to no good deed." All at once their voices hushed and Emma had to strain to hear.

"I shouldn't want to be married to the likes of him. Indeed, m'husband is no prize to be sure, but in truth, he doth not wish to kill me!"

Emma rammed her ear up against the doorjamb. Whatever were they talking about? Then she remembered all the changes she had seen in her ladyship recently and as she crept back to Lady Buckingham's chambers, past the turrets mildewed from heavy rains and early morning fogs, she was surprised how protective she felt.

At her mistress's wooden door she heard voices coming from within, and quickly ducked into a nearby alcove. Suddenly the door swung open and Lord Buckingham stood in the doorway, looking back into the room. "Hark now, me thinks 'tis for thy own good. The doctor hath recommended this potion, therefore, thou must continue to drink it!" As Emma's dealings had been primarily with the mistress of the manor, she had not seen much of her master. Rattled, she was immediately struck by the power and harshness of his voice.

In comparison, Lady Buckingham's pleading voice sounded weak, vulnerable. "Please, kind Sir, it doth maketh me ill, I swear it. Do not force me to keep taking this liquid. It shall be the end of me, I feel it."

Lord Buckingham snorted. "Fie on thee! In faith, thou art my wife and therefore must do as I bid thee!" Stomping off, his boots scuffed sharply against the cold stones.

All protocol evaporated as Emma rushed in, full of concern. "Prithee m'lady, by your leave, if 'tis anything I can do to help," she murmured to her weeping mistress.

Lady Buckingham stopped crying long enough to access the girl. How could she trust a servant, someone from the village? It was unimaginable. But her fears were engulfing her. "Dear, dear Emma, I do need to trust someone. Indeed, I hath no one else. My Lord hath locked me in his manor, privy to no friends, and no one to help me. I do not know what else to do."

"Your ladyship, thou canst most certainly have my trust. I willst not betray thee, I promise on the graves of my family." Something about the seamstress' intensity relaxed Lady Buckingham, and she nodded solemnly.

After that, Lady Buckingham kept Emma even closer to her side. She demoted her personal maid, and insisted on Emma performing higher duties so she could be with her for many more hours than she had before. The maid was bitter, pouting and glowering for several weeks, but Lady

Buckingham stood firm. She needed an ally.

"I fear I shall not be long on this earth," she admitted one evening to Emma as the rain beat against the windows, embedding a permanent dampness in the walls.

"My lady, thou must tell me how I can help, you must. I realize thou ist not happy. Still, thou wouldst not let me help thee." Emma was surprised at her own boldness, but choices were rapidly fading alongside her mistress' well being.

Lady Buckingham hesitated a few seconds before answering. "My Lord is not the man thou thinketh he is." She canvassed Emma's eyes carefully.

"I cannot divulge too much information. In truth, I am not convinced of it completely myself. I only know that he is involved in something evil, a plot against our king, Richard. Now, thou must swear not to tell what I have just told you to any person!"

Emma, caught in mid-nod, flinched at Lord Buckingham's jarring voice at the door. "Lady Margaret, I must see thee at once!" He charged into the room, stopping at the sight of Emma.

"This wench needs to be gone! 'Tis of the utmost urgency that I speak with thee alone!" His darkening face turned towards the seamstress and she froze, unsure of what to do. Should she stay and defend her mistress or should she leave?

Lady Buckingham interrupted her thoughts. "Go now, Emma, I shall be all right, I promise thee," she urged, forcing her anxious voice to sound calm.

As she exited, Emma could feel Lord Buckingham's eyes penetrating through her back. Pretending to go downstairs, she quietly backtracked up to the bedroom and leaned her head against the closed door, listening.

His voice bellowed. "In a fortnight, there shall be a ceremonial dinner in honor of the High Minister from King Richard's court. I expect thee to be a grand hostess. Indeed, thou knowst what to do, you have done so before. I command you to also think of a ceremonial present that wouldst please his lordship. 'Tis important he remember me well."

"And why is that so important, pray tell? Thou hast never cared for Richard the First and his court, and his High Minister even less so. What manner hath changed?" Her voice had garnered some strength.

He strode towards her menacingly as she shrank back into a corner of the room. "Out upon it! Never question my intentions! Thou shalt do only thy wifely duties, nothing more! I expect a perfect meal as is befitting our position. Do not disappoint me!"

Furious at his wife's insurgency, he stormed out of the bedchamber so hastily Emma literally had to leap out of sight. But within seconds, she had scurried back to her mistress, planted on the floor, her hair falling in large wisps around her face, her hands trembling.

"I—I—tr-ried—to t-t-tell him, but I—I fear I couldst not. He—he is f-a-far too powerful for my heart a-a-nd my head."

Dropping down beside her and ignoring all boundaries, Emma wrapped her arms around the shaken woman, holding her new friend until the stammering had ceased.

Several days later, she noticed Lady Buckingham was looking remarkably better. The color was back in her cheeks, the dark circles had completely disappeared, and although some of the nervousness was still there, her physical strength seemed restored. What had happened? she wondered.

One afternoon, as the two of them were discussing a tablecloth to be made for the ceremonies, she could no longer keep quiet. "Tis so good to see thee looking well after appearing so weak and sick."

Lady Buckingham looked stunned. Then, as if thinking out loud, "Oh, my God..." She turned to Emma. "Thou art correct. 'Tis due to the celebration."

Emma gaped at her.

"He doth need me alive for the celebration only." She frowned then proceeded to mutter something else, stopping only when one of her maids entered.

That night, as Emma slippered her way through the unlit corridors, she didn't dare use her walnut oil lamp; these were not safe times for anyone connected to her ladyship. In the blackness, she could feel her fingertips lightly scraping the jagged edges of the stone walls and was thinking of returning to the comfort of her own room, when she heard two distinct voices.

"I told thee, 'tis important to wait until the High Minister has paid us his visit. After that, we shall be able to have our meeting with the French, of that I can assure thee. If all goes as planned, England shall finally be in the hands of the rightful ruler, not this crusading imbecile we have for a king!"

The speaker was unmistakable. But to whom was Lord Buckingham talking? She took a deep breath and silently moved closer.

113

"Attendez-vous! Attendez-vous!" the stranger cautioned.

"Didst thou hear something outside?" Lord Buckingham's voice became guarded.

Suddenly, she was on fire, flying back through the passageways, past the kitchen, and into the safety of her room, where she crawled into bed, pulled up the covers, and tried to soothe her racing thoughts.

"What is it, Emma? Thou looks a sight for sore eyes," Lady Buckingham smiled, looking at the sleep-deprived girl the next morning.

A few seconds ticked before Emma could muster up enough courage. "M'Lady, I have something very serious to tell thee. Please believe me, I wouldst not lie to thee, ever! 'Tis very important that thou believeth me."

"I do believe thee."

As she hastily recounted the conversation she had overheard the previous night, she watched the color slowly drain from her ladyship's face.

"'Tis worse than I had suspected. I must do something about this, I must." The noblewoman looked up at the seamstress, trembling. "Can I indeed trust thee, Emma? Can I?"

Emma nodded vehemently.

"Yay, I do believe so, but if indeed my husband hath gotten involved in a plot I cannot abide, he knows I shalt not support him in this, and for that, he wants me killed. Emma, I fear poison is his choice of death. Remember, thou noticed it thyself. I was feeling so weak; alas, my stomach did ache from what he hath me take. An herbal potion, he named it!" She started wringing her hands. "Oh, Emma, if I die, then there shall be no one to stop him. He...he couldst kill our king!"

Both women studied the floor a good five seconds before Lady Buckingham spoke. "Ah, well on the morrow 'tis the street faire. Perhaps we couldst buy a gift for his Eminence there?" Offering short simultaneous nods, they bid each other adieu.

The faire, held on the local Saint's Day, was glutted with men, women, and children, all dressed in brightly-colored clothing and displaying toothless gums, reminding Emma of the life she was so grateful to have forgotten. Merchants peddled their baked goods, trinkets, and scented water under tented booths, while livestock lazed in the warm sun. Archery attracted a decent crowd, as did wrestling and the long staves.

Walking alongside her ladyship, Emma was given free rein to her spending. No wizened mother, hunched over from years of backbreaking work, clucking warnings, no father ordering her to not even pick at the vegetables because their metal money pot had long been emptied.

The carriage itself felt as if it were one story up from the ground, and when she stepped down onto its black painted steps to enter the faire grounds, she knew this was the true life she was destined to have. Once on the hard-packed earth, however, came a more familiar reality—the constant bombardment of unbathed villagers jostling by her and coaxing her to buy something from their bins.

"Emma, can thee not see something we couldst use for His Eminence? Some painted box, a basket perhaps, or fabric for a new suit for him? What dost thee think?" Away from her husband and in the midst of so many people, Lady Buckingham almost appeared cheerful.

"Be of good cheer! Be of good cheer!" a familiar voice rang out. Immediately, Lady Buckingham's face shut down as her husband rode up to them, his right hand waving patronizingly to the crowd.

"Emma," Lady Buckingham asked, "wouldst thou go to that booth over there and retrieve a painted box for his Eminence, so I couldst put an object from my collection into it?"

Emma edged through the crowd until she arrived at the booth where the painted and metal boxes lay. Much to the annoyance of the vendor, she fingered them all before choosing a large, hand-painted one with a replica of a castle resembling the Buckingham Manor.

"May he someday be punished for his sins!" one woman commented to another at the booth.

"Hush! His lordship is about to pass. Hush!" replied the second woman.

Emma turned her head just in time to see Lord Buckingham steering his horse by their section of the crowd. This is worse than Lady Buckingham had feared, Emma thought. If people on the street were commenting on his Lordship not being trustworthy, then her ladyship's problems were far greater than they had originally thought.

That night, in the privacy of her ladyship's room, Emma noticed Lady Buckingham looking more excited than she had been for quite some time.

"Emma, the box you bought for his Eminence was beautiful to be sure; but I hath decided to use thy own gifts in its stead." Her cheeks were flushed, her hands fluttering.

"Oh?"

"Yes, I should like thee to make a beautiful embroidered pillow for his

Eminence and the planning of it may commence on the morrow. Thou willst have to work very hard; the banquet will be in a matter of four days from now. Dost thee understand?"

"Of course. On the morrow I shall begin it. As for tonight, is thee all right? May I retire to my own room?" Unsettled from the afternoon's realization, all Emma wanted to do was to retreat to her own chambers.

"Of course, of course. Go, my dear." All Lady Buckingham's attention was focused on the making of her gift pillow.

Ambling back towards the kitchen, Emma became aware of some kind of activity in one of the smaller halls. She slowed, took off her shoes, and cupped her right ear just in time to hear a foreign voice. "Monsieur, c'est trés important that we begin our plan, n'est-ce pas?" It was the same man who had spoken before, only this time, he sounded more agitated.

Lord Buckingham was curt. "His Eminence shall be here in four days hence. There shall be a banquet and I have asked my wife to produce a special gift for him, to convince him all is well between us. But two days after he leaves the manor, 'tis the time we shall meet with thy group along the shore, by night, when the moon is young and the darkness sure to protect us. Wait for my message, and the attack shall begin. The reign of Richard I willst end, I swear it!" His voice suddenly crescendoed, echoing throughout the hallway.

Lying in bed that night, it was all Emma could do to refrain from crying. Not only was her ladyship in grave danger, it appeared their country was as well. Tossing back and forth, she wracked her brain, trying to devise a plan, yet it wasn't until she leaned over to pick up a fallen pillow that her mind flickered.

It took only one look at Emma's face the next morning for Lady Buckingham to blurt out, "Emma, dear child, what is wrong?"

"M'Lady, I am but a common girl, a humble girl from a family with no education." Emma was feeling her way.

Lady Buckingham nodded, waiting.

"I hope thee doesn't think 'tis too forward, but there is something else I must tell thee about Lord Buckingham."

"What?" Her mistress asked, instantly unnerved.

"Last night I heard a conversation in the West Hall which hath frightened me on thy behalf, and indeed, on behalf of our entire country." She then launched into what she had ascertained.

Lady Buckingham sat on her high-backed chair, her hand at her throat. "Oh, what shall we do?" She swallowed. "He must be stopped, but by what method? 'Tis urgent I get a message to the High Minister when he is here, but there are spies everywhere. I daren't say anything in front of my Lord. The danger is too great. He wouldst have me killed as it is."

"If thou wilst permit me, I have an idea that perhaps wouldst work." She paused, then, "Doth his Lordship understand Latin?"

Lady Buckingham was taken aback. "Why, no. He is rich in name and title, but poor in education." She grimaced contemptuously.

"'Tis reasonable," Emma ventured forth, "his Eminence wouldst understand Latin; 'tis a necessary part of his position. If I embroider a warning on our pillow, then present it to him at the Banquet, with hope he shall read the message, and thus try to stop his Lordship before any real harm 'tis done."

Her ladyship leaned forward, her eyes intense, then suddenly drew back. "Ah, but I, too, am not versed in Latin. I fear my education 'tis sadly lacking, for indeed, I was raised only to marry well."

Her head held high, Emma announced, "Indeed, I know Latin, Milady. I hath studied it at the abbey for several years, and wouldst be able to translate anything we wish to write."

The expression on Lady Buckingham's face was well worth any imminent danger that might happen; she was finally the object of respect from a nobleperson, and sitting together head to head for another half hour, they carefully devised a simple Latin phrase that could not only be read easily by His Eminence, but would also add a decorative element so as not to cast suspicion.

Watch carefully our shores by night,

When the French invade

"Twill break England's might.

The other seamstresses were not a problem; if his Lordship lacked an education in Latin, they surely did as well. But what Emma did lack was time. After choosing the proper embroidery thread, all her meticulous hand sewing consumed her days and nights, up until the very last square knot was tied, and seconds before the Royal carriage carrying the High Minister arrived at the manor. It wasn't until after she peered down through a narrow wardrobe window, watching each embedded jewel glitter on his purpose robe as he stepped on the red rug leading to the front entrance that she could breathe a sigh of relief.

To her young, inexperienced eye, the feast preparations proved fascinating; from the Master Cook supervising his staff while sitting on a stool in the huge kitchen, to the Chief Carver kissing the carving knife, then kissing his Lordship's napkin before it was presented to Lord Buckingham, she witnessed how the hierarchy was implemented at the long table. Each time the procession of dishes was led in by the Grand Master of the Manor, the cupbearers and breadmasters tossed napkins over their shoulders while serving his High Minister, yet when serving lesser nobility, they made sure their arms and napkins were at their sides, as befitting a lesser rank.

Then came the actual presentation and with it, a fine mist of perspiration and sweaty palms. What if her shaky hands dropped the pillow? As she stood up to retrieve her handiwork from a nearby manservant, she spied Lady Buckingham turning towards their guest. "Your Lordship," her mistress announced, "I hath commissioned a gift for King Richard, to thus demonstrate our loyalty. 'Tis indeed a timely present, and one which shouldst sit well with thee, if thou wouldst take the time to look upon it carefully."

Out of the corner of her eye, Emma noticed Lord Buckingham scrutinizing his wife carefully, his arms crossed over his chest and suddenly she wondered just how far they should go in this endeavor.

The High Minister looked kindly enough, and Emma, taking courage from his open face, took her carefully worded piece over to him. He thanked her graciously, and turning to his host and hostess, declared, "I shalt accept this gift in the name of Richard I, and by so doing, acknowledge thy allegiance."

"'Tis a rare gift, indeed Sir, and one that required thy utmost attention." Lady Buckingham dared not say more; even as she spoke she could feel her husband's dark eyes stationed on her.

The High Minister remained at the manor for another two days, enjoying falconry, hunting, and rich food, and each night, if she happened to pass him in the great hall, Emma prayed for some sign of acknowledgement, but there was none. All she noticed was Lady Buckingham looking more and more desperate, and her heart went out to her brave cohort.

On the last day of his visit, as the High Minister strolled through the main hall en route to his carriage, talking with his host and hostess, Emma took a brazen step. "Might I be so bold, Sire, as to congratulate thy Eminence on behalf of Richard 1. Since 'tis I who hath sewn this noble present in the name of Lord and Lady Buckingham, I wouldst feel honored, indeed, if thou might look upon my work closely, to understand how much time I hath spent sewing this pillow for such a courageous king. Indeed, a king who wouldst fight the enemy at any cost in order to protect England."

She searched the face of his Eminence for any reaction to her speech, but there was nothing unusual there, except perhaps a flicker of surprise upon hearing such an articulate, outspoken village girl. He glanced over to Lord Buckingham, and Emma felt as if she had been kicked in the stomach. Perhaps the High Minister was involved with Lord Buckingham! Perhaps he, too, had plans to betray Richard the Lionhearted and bring England to its ruin! Not waiting for any further response, she retreated into the comfort of the archway shadows.

"Wait, child. Thou hath done beautiful work, indeed. I thank thee for thy interest in thy king." Chuckling, the High Minister moved on, with Lord Buckingham glowering over at her. He motioned to one of the guardsmen with a short, clipped nod, and the armed man rapidly headed towards the seamstress.

She froze, as Lady Buckingham looked on helplessly. When the minister stepped into his carriage for the long journey home, she felt the vise-like grip of the guardsman's fingers on her arm. "Cometh with me, thou wench scoundrel! M'Lord wants thee locked away, safe," he growled.

As a prisoner at the top of an unfamiliar winding staircase, she could hear Lord Buckingham barking at his wife somewhere nearby.

"So, thou thought thou was more clever than I! How dare thee! Thou and thy little servant girl shall not liveth to see the morrow, I can assure thee of it! Thou shalt not get in my way! Making pronouncements in favor of King Richard indeed! England shall be governed by someone who is truly worthy! By my faith, long liveth the Dauphin of France! Down with Richard the Lionhearted! Lionhearted indeed! There is nothing lionhearted about this ruler, I can assure thee!" His words made Emma shudder.

"Spare the child, she hath nothing to do with me, really. She only pleaseth me because of her excellent work. Let no harm cometh to her!"

"Very touching, my dear, very touching, but 'twill do thee no good. When thou hast gone, she shall be gone as well. Truth be told, one less villager shall not harm anyone."

S.R. MALLERY

Emma heard a short scuffle, then, silence. Soon, grating footsteps on the stone floor reverberated louder and louder towards her. Half-choking with fear, she looked around the room, but there were no visible paths of escape, and when the footsteps stopped just outside the door, she began to cry.

Lord Buckingham, dressed in a long riding cloak, suddenly loomed over her. Grabbing her by her hair with one hand, twisting her arm with the other, he jerked her along with him to another room. "Stay there with thy mistress and prepare to die. In good truth, see what it doth mean to favor the King!" he snarled.

In the darkness, Emma heard the gentle rustling of a noblewoman's dress, lost in the shadows.

"Emma, in good sooth, I hath brought thee into a world thee knew nothing about, and for it, thou must die. Please forgiveth me," Lady Buckingham mewed softly.

Numb, Emma let her eyes get accustomed to the spare light, before exploring the darkened room, filled with tablecloths and linens, ready to be embroidered. Without warning she felt a momentary pang of sadness of all that might have been.

Five seconds later, she laughed. "By my faith, all my best thoughts do cometh to me at night!"

She ran over to the only window, larger than the others with wooden shutters and no bars across it. Immediately under the window to the left was an iron rod, embedded in the wall and used for spinning various threads. She proceeded to drag a small stool next to Lady Buckingham over to the window, and standing up on its narrow seat, held onto the wall for balance. Then, jumping off the stool, she hurried back to the tablecloths, beckoning Lady Buckingham to join her. Her ladyship continued to look puzzled until she saw Emma fast at work, tying the linens together to form a crude rope. Soon, the two women were so engrossed in their project they didn't hear the guardsman's jagged voice until it was just outside their door.

"Marry! 'Tis too quiet in there! Wha'st thou both doing?"

Lady Buckingham quickly answered. "We are resting. In faith, we are allowed to rest, are we not, even if we are condemned to die?"

The guardsman grunted and shuffled away as the unlikely comrades persevered, frantically trying to finish before they were discovered. When Emma was satisfied that their rope was long enough, they both ran to the window and looping the linen over the rod, made sure it was tied into a triple knot. In her excitement, Lady Buckingham knocked over the stool by mistake and they paused, suspended, barely breathing. But after a full minute, with no outside sounds forthcoming, they nodded at one another and pressed on.

"Emma, thou goeth first. Thou art younger and everything 'twas thy idea. I shall hoist thee up, and when thou ist safe in the moat, I shall follow thee!" Lady Buckingham's cheeks had regained a healthy, rose sheen.

She was as good as her word. Tossing the long rope out the window, she pushed Emma up and over the window ledge, and as Emma was lowering herself down the other side of the wall, she jumped up to the window, flipping the stool down with a loud clatter. Then, pulling herself up and over the ledge, she began her own descent, a good six feet behind Emma.

They made it down to the water and immediately started paddling— slowly at first, then, due to the frigid water, at an extremely splashy, accelerated rate. They were halfway to the other side, when Lady Buckingham let out a cry of pain.

At first, she had felt a sharp sting on the back of her head. Then came a jab, only harder and fiercer this time. Stunned by the blows, she didn't expect the flutter of the swan's wing as it flapped hard against her shoulders. In her panic, she strained towards Emma with her left hand, while trying to swing at the relentless bird with her right, as she fought her way to the shore. After she reached Emma, the two became a united front, poking and punching at the swan as they slowly continued their swim across a seemingly endless moat.

Shouts could be heard coming from the Manor, and Lady Buckingham recognized the fury of her husband, screaming at the guardsmen to take aim and draw fire. As they neared the shore, suddenly they could hear the faint voice of someone hidden in the bushes:

"Do not tally! Come to safety. We shall protect thee. Do not stop—"

Emma didn't understand, but Lady Buckingham did, and let out a sob of relief. Landing on other side of the moat intact, she turned back for Emma and started to pull her friend up the marshy bank behind her, just as the High Minister and his servants rushed over to help hoist the noblewoman up the slippery embankment.

Halfway out of the water, Emma could hear the whir of arrows whooshing past her ear and thudding into the ground all around her. Suddenly Lady Buckingham wailed, "Oh no, dear God, no!" as the High Minister pried her hand loose from the seamstress' hand, to whisk her away with him.

She kept turning back for Emma, panicked at not seeing her friend. "Wait! Where hast Emma gone?" she demanded.

The High Minister shouted, "We have no time! The carriage is just beyond. Pray, do not go back or we shall all be killed!"

"But I do not see Emma!" She sobbed, trying desperately to pull away from her saviors as she was being dragged off into the carriage.

Through the night air, they could all hear the slow grind of the drawbridge chains being lowered. Torches, held by at least a hundred guardsmen, lit up the moat as the carriage started to pull away with Lady Buckingham leaning out of its window, straining to see her friend one last time.

"Oh no, no." Her whispers faded to silence as the carriage raced away to London and King Richard I, leaving Emma lying on her stomach at the edge of the moat, an arrow lodged in her back.

My mother, never one for leaving stories unfinished, has informed me that these days, when tourists visit the famous stately homes of England, they never miss the Buckingham Manor; it is one of the finest examples of how the nobility lived during the Middle Ages. On this tour, she has proudly assured me, the guides usually take an extra five minutes or so to point out the small gravestone almost hidden on the front grounds, just beyond the moat. If one looks closely enough, with a little help from a tour guide, most people have been able to make out the weathered words on the moss-covered shrine:

"Herein lies Emma at night,
Who did seweth with all her might
To save England it hath been told,
Long liveth Emma the bold
--Lady Buckingham
1455, Year of Our Lord

MURDER SHE SEWED

"Detective Del Riggio, please take a seat."

Shifting her body slightly on top of the uncomfortable vinyl cushion, Carla avoided the jagged, scar-like tear. In front of her, the standard issue police desk loomed large, as her palms moistened and her mouth felt like the Sahara Desert.

"Now, I'm going to call off a list of symptoms, and you tell me, to the best of your knowledge, if you have ever experienced these feelings. Ready?" The psychologist leaned towards her and started in.

"Ever had chest pain?"

"Yes."

"When?"

"Two days ago when I was admitted to St. Vincent's." Carla drummed the metal railing of her chair with the fingertips of her right hand, castanet-style.

"Any difficulty in breathing?"

"Yes, that too." Carla waited for a response. It never came.

"While you were experiencing these two other symptoms, did you also have any dizziness or vertigo?"

"Yes."

"Blurred vision?"

"I—I don't think so."

"Feelings of faintness?"

"Yes."

"Profuse sweating or clamminess?"

You mean like what I'm feeling now? Carla thought. "Yeah, yeah."

"Sudden sensations of nausea?" Dr. Rogette was beginning to look worried.

Thoroughly depressed now, Carla gave a slow nod.

"Now, detective, I realize you've had a couple of deals gone bad recently with your partner. Understandably, you are experiencing some PTSD—you know, Post Traumatic Stress Disorder." He opened up one of his top drawers and pulled out a thick, industrial-looking rubber stamp. Smacking it down hard on the papers in front of him, he looked up at her and blinked.

Carla jumped. "What's that for?"

"Well, you should be hearing from your supervisor on this— soon, very soon I should think." With a wave of his hand, he started sorting papers on his desk. She was dismissed.

"You've got to be kidding. You want me to do what?" Carla stared at her supervisor in shock.

"That's right. I'm ordering you to take a Leave of Absence. Look, Del Riggio, frankly, you don't have any choice. If you don't take it, I suspend you. Period. But because I'm such a nice guy, I've taken the liberty of signing you up for a cruise to the Bahamas. Courtesy of the NYPD. Not bad, huh?" Captain McMann grinned.

"Very bad. What in the world would I do on a cruise?" Visions of Carnival Cruise Line advertisements, with wall-to-wall people aerobicizing across decks while gluttonous couples knocked little children aside on their way to the banquet rooms for a mid-afternoon food orgy, flashed before her.

"Relax, Del Riggio, relax. That's what cruises are for. Just think, no drug busts, no incompetent partners. Just ordinary people acting decadent. How can you go wrong?"

Mary Ellen Stafford couldn't wait to get onto the cruise ship. What a great vehicle for teaching your quilting workshop, her friends had all told her. Hang the workshops. It was a chance for her to get away from her own drab, mundane life.

"I don't get why these murder mysteries mean so much to you," her husband had complained recently, flipping popcorn kernels into his mouth with one hand, fingering the remote control with the other.

"I like a good mystery," she said, looking up from her crime novel. "I like a good mystery, and I like variety."

With a familiar grunt, he changed the channel to "America's Funniest Videos."

Mid-life was hitting Mary Ellen hard.

SEWING CAN BE DANGEROUS

The Cyraneaux Cruise Line was unique in one respect. It offered a more varied program of courses than many of the main stream lines: Refurbishing Antiques, Belly Dancing and now, Mary Ellen's Memento quilt class showing how to make quilts using people's personal clothing, lending an even more homey touch to the curricular lineup. But to Carla, none of these workshops written up in the brochure were impressive. Classes? What for? And quilting classes? Give me a break!

She made her way down the narrow corridor, her black backpack and tote bag slamming into people, her black tennis shoes squeaking against the newly polished floors. Just outside her assigned cabin, she stopped. She could hear someone humming on the other side, and her heart sank. Oh, crap! Some happy person is in there, and I'm expected to make light conversation. I knew this was all a big mistake. She started to use her key when the door burst open.

"Oh, hello! My name is Mary Ellen Stafford, and I guess we're going to be roommates."

Carla stared in horror at the Peter Pan collar and granny-glasses-attached-to-a-chain facing her.

"Hi. I'm exhausted. I gotta get my things together here. Maybe we can chat later."

Mary Ellen's offended look was brushed aside as Carla continued. "My name's Carla Del Riggio, I'm a New York detective on leave of absence, and I really need to have my own space. Understood? And FYI, I hate humming!"

With a quick gulp, Mary Ellen froze, her heart pounding. A New York cop! Of all the good luck! If only this woman weren't so nasty. Well, they did have two weeks. Maybe in time, her new roommate would thaw out.

The quilter finished placing all her clothing and supplies neatly in a small chest of drawers next to her bunk bed. She started to hum again then stopped, with a quick glance up at Carla. By way of a silent apology she shrugged her shoulders and smiled tentatively.

Unmoved, Carla flung her luggage onto her bed, practically ripped it open, then pulled out her vacation clothing. One black skirt, four pairs of slacks—all in dull shades—black shoes, several tops, underwear, and a large floppy hat.

Mary Ellen, more meticulous, unzipped a large rolly bag and proceeded to take out various sewing items. Two acrylic rulers of assorted sizes, a pin

125

cushion stuffed with colored-headed straight pins, sewing scissors, a soft cutting board, some odd pizza cutter thing, graph paper, note cards, and a folder filled with Xeroxed paperwork.

"What's with the pizza cutter?" Carla couldn't help herself.

Mary Ellen smiled. An entrée. "Oh, that's my rotary cutter. It's a wonderful invention for quilters; it enables you to cut very straight, even strips of fabric. You'll have to take my quilting class this week. I always give a demonstration on how to use this."

Carla sat down on her bed with a nod of her head. "Look..." She cleared her throat. "I don't mean to be rude, I just need a lot of R&R, if ya know what I mean."

"Sure, I can appreciate that. It's just that I have always loved detective stories and mysteries, so I guess I got a little carried away at meeting someone like you. I promise I won't bother you too much on this trip." Mary Ellen attempted a tight smile.

Carla felt guilty. "Hey, no problem. I mean it. To show you there's no hard feelings, why don't we go to the dining room together for lunch, OK?"

Mary Ellen did nothing less than beam.

As the two women entered the First Class dining room, they both gasped. Raised-mahogany paneled walls fenced in high-lofted blue and gold fleur-de-lis patterned carpeting, rendering more of a 'Titanic-esque' feel than a modern cruise line eatery. The circular tables were covered in white Damask, with full table settings of elegant silverware, crystal wine goblets, white plates edged in gold, and porcelain centerpieces exploding with spring-like flowers.

Carla spoke first. "Boy, this is something, isn't it?" Mary Ellen agreed and steered them both toward a large sign at the far end of the room that read, "SEATING ASSIGNMENTS." They noticed they had been placed together at Table Number 12, along with about six other people, including a Richard Hempton.

"Ummm. Richard Hempton. You know, I know that guy's name from somewhere," Carla murmured to herself, ignoring Mary Ellen hanging on to her every word.

At their table, Mary Ellen's motor mouth took over. "How are you? My name is Mary Ellen Stafford, this is my roommate Carla Del Riggio. She's from New York." Carla cringed with each new introduction.

"Well, don't this beat all! John T. Porter here," blustered a heavy-set Texas businessman in a tight cream-colored suit and tan leather cowboy boots. He shoved his cowboy hat down under the table away from sight as his timid, fluttery wife smiled in agreement, pulling herself in closer to the table, and checking out her husband every few seconds.

"Hello, everyone. My name is Richard Hempton," a balding middle-aged man proclaimed. "This is going to be the last time in a very long time that I will be able to really enjoy myself. You see, by next fall, I plan on running for the House of Representatives, and although I will be traveling quite a bit, it will be primarily for business."

A politician! That's where I've heard of him. Great! More BS to contend with, Carla thought.

"Hey, I'm Eddie Runyon and this here's Tracey," said a young man sitting next to a thin, giggly young woman. His hair looked as greasy as hers looked clean, and they both had light nicotine stains between their fore and middle fingers. Mary Ellen just hoped they would wait a few years before starting a family. Suddenly, like synchronized swimmers, everyone turned to stare at the only vacant chair.

Five seconds later, a fiftyish looking man slid onto the seat. His mouth folded into a straight line and his head bobbed a quick nod just before he introduced himself. "Hello, I'm Steven Bingham. Pleased to meet you all," he announced. Everyone murmured a greeting in return, then looked down at his or her shrimp cocktail, but Carla's radar felt a slight tug.

The main course of Rubber Chicken Kiev was more than tolerable, so at first, people were too intent on eating to make polite table conversation. Then Mary Ellen broke the silence. "I'm a quilter by profession and will be teaching a workshop on the ship, but my roommate is actually an NYPD detective on vacation!"

Uh-oh. Carla dreaded what would inevitably come next. "Really? Aahhh, Ooooh, what a kick!" people responded, as if on cue.

Oh, God, here come the questions. "Tell me, detective, how much time do you spend per case? I mean, how quick does it take to crack one?" John T. Porter leaned forward, his chin tinged with Chicken Kiev sauce.

Carla sighed. "It depends on the case."

"Well, I'll have you know, little lady, I have a software program on my laptop that could streamline any case you were working on!"

"Oh?"

"Yep. It's called WebPrivateye2009, and it'll get you all kinds of information on anyone you want."

"You mean people with records only, don't you?" Mary Ellen was fascinated.

Porter was having a ball. "I mean, you can be curious about your neighbor, for God's sake—find out his social security number, where to go for unlisted numbers, or whether or not he's been missing his child support payments. You name it, you got it. You can even camouflage your e-mail so no one knows it's you doing the searchin'!"

"Sounds dangerous to me," Carla fired back. "We do use something like that at work, but I think that's too much information for the general public."

She had already set her usual game in motion, 'Where's the poker face?' Looking around the table for reactions, she noticed Eddie and Tracey couldn't have cared less. They and their nicotine fingers were far too into each other. Porter's wife looked uncomfortable with her husband's showmanship, Mary Ellen, of course, was enthralled, Steve Bingham looked ill at ease for some reason, and she couldn't quite make out Hempton's face. The politician's mask was on.

That night, Mary Ellen was impossible. Every ten minutes she would try to grill Carla about detective work. Had she done many stakeouts? Had she killed anyone? What was undercover work really like? Finally, the exhausted cop had to say 'enough was enough, let me get some sleep' as she reached up to turn out the light.

A sealed, plastic sandwich bag started to form tiny beads of moisture as a faceless policeman swung it high over his head.

"No, no, that's destroying evidence. You're supposed to use the paper bag, not the plastic bag!" Carla screamed.

"Oh, really?" The faceless cop stood still, clueless.

"It's all ruined, it's ruined!" Carla repeated over and over again. Numerous hands reached in towards her, then started touching everything in the room. Cocaine vials scattered as the featureless man in blue chuckled and shrugged.

A second later, Carla was screaming. "You blew it! You blew it! Blew the whole case!" The cop remained standing, his head rolled back in one roaring belly laugh.

"Hey, hey, hey! Wake up! You're having a bad dream. Wake up!" The quilter shook Carla awake.

Carla shot upright, layered in sweat. Then she remembered where she was. Oh God, I'm with the Do-Gooder-Happy-Homemaker, she thought, struggling to gain some composure.

Mary Ellen switched on the light. "You want to talk about it? Who's Martin?"

"Martin was my partner for six months," the detective replied. "He was young and inexperienced, and they put him on a drug bust with me. It was terrible. He messed up key evidence and he didn't even realize it. And because of his incompetence, I almost got myself killed."

"So why are you here?"

"I told you. I'm here on a Leave of Absence."

"That seems kind of drastic, all because you had a bad experience," Mary Ellen pointed out.

God help us, we have a police expert in our midst. "I had an anxiety attack if you must know. That's all." She glowered at Mary Ellen. Her roommate finally got the point; you could hear a pin drop in the cabin.

By the time the two ladies reached their full table the next morning, a lively conversation was ensuing between Porter and Hempton.

"Tell me, Hempton, what does it cost to run a campaign these days, umm?" Porter's wife cringed at his crude questions, but Hempton was obviously happy to pontificate.

"Well, let's put it this way. Years ago, before I decided to get into the law, I was in medical school. But the costs then were a drop in the bucket compared to what it takes to run for Congress these days!" Hempton's chest swelled out a good inch.

Everyone else laughed, but out of her peripheral vision, Carla thought she picked up a tiny scowl crawling across Steve Bingham's forehead.

Stop it, Carla, stop it! This is why you're in the shape you're in! Just relax and c-h-i-l-l out.

Mary Ellen's voice cut through her thoughts. "So who's gonna come to my quilt workshop, huh? It's really fun, and it'll be different for most of you. What about it?" She ended her question by turning to Carla.

Carla thought a couple of seconds. This could backfire on her big time, but what the hell. "OK, Stafford, you're on; I'll take your class!"

Clapping her hands in delight, Mary Ellen spent the rest of the meal humming while she picked at her food.

The class was actually better than Carla could have imagined. Mary Ellen was an excellent teacher—funny, full of side comments and careful instructions on how to follow a basic pattern, sew only quarter inch seams, never backstitch like you would in tailoring and always, always "when in doubt rip it out," she declared as she held up a seam ripper. When it came time for her to demonstrate how to use a rotary cutter for the first time in order to cut strips from an old favorite dress of hers, she pretended to cut pizza, Italian accent and all. By the end of the session, she had the entire room in stitches, and in spite of herself, Carla could feel her body relaxing. Maybe her roommate wasn't half-bad at that.

That sentiment didn't last. By the time they returned to their cabin to dress for dinner, Mary Ellen had started up again. "What do you think about that software detective stuff, umm?"

"Personally, I don't like it, and frankly, wouldn't trust it. As I said, we use it at the precinct and P.I.'s also use it, but once the public gets a hold of it, it becomes a violation of people's personal freedoms."

"I just thought it was pretty cool." Mary Ellen looked crushed.

At dinner, it was even worse. Carla felt as if it were a free-for-all, who could fling the most questions at New York's Finest.

"What kind of person commits murder?" Bingham wanted to know.

"Well, all kinds, really. There's no monopoly on killers, y'know. That's why we have detectives and investigators to scope 'em out."

"Or great software programs," Porter chimed in. Carla shot him a dirty look.

"So, for example, anyone on this boat could commit murder?" Bingham inquired, peering over at the detective.

A familiar sensation in the pit of her stomach was kicking in. Cocking her head at a forty-five degree angle, she shot back, "Sure, even you."

Everyone laughed, finished their meal, and waited for dessert to come, but as they all gobbled down their Tiramisu, Mary Ellen noticed Carla glancing at Bingham several times. The quilter couldn't wait until they got back to the privacy of their own cabin.

"So what do you think of our tablemates? Quite a collection, with Porter and his software and that Bingham and his murder questions." Mary Ellen plopped down on her bunk bed, waiting for Carla to elaborate.

Oh no you don't, Carla thought. I'm not trusting anyone ever again. She shrugged. "Oh, they're all right. Just idle curiosity, I guess." Turning out her light, she rolled over to sleep. Totally frustrated, Mary Ellen wriggled around on her bunk bed in the dark, trying to think of something else, but all that popped up in her mind was Porter's WebPrivateye2009 and the soft glow of moonlight filtering in through their two portholes.

Each night, the would-be detective was relentless—a Mixmaster of whirling, non-stop questions. "Did your partner get canned, or did he just get an Internal Affairs probe?" Or, "How long is your Leave of Absence?" and "Will this be a permanent black mark on your police record?"

Finally, one night, Carla had reached her limit. "Mary Ellen, I know this is thrilling for you, but for me, it's been a bit of a nightmare, ya know? I'm sorry, but I just need a break."

By morning, everyone seemed to be in a particularly good mood. The newlyweds were practically planted on each other's lap, Porter was slapping Hempton's back, bragging about his millions in oil and potential campaign contributions, and Mary Ellen seemed to have forgotten the previous evening, and was doing her most Midwestern Cheerful. But after five minutes, Carla realized that Steven Bingham was still absent.

"Does anyone know where Bingham is?" she inquired. They all shook their heads and went back to concentrating on their food. She signaled a waiter.

"Yes, ma'am? May I help you?"

"Yeah. Have you seen Mr. Bingham this morning?"

"No, no I haven't. Perhaps he slept in, ma'am." The waiter was impatient to get back to his other tables.

Mary Ellen, after last night's reprimand, stayed mute. By dinner, however, when Stephen again didn't appear, the police detective sensed something must be wrong.

"I gotta go to the 'can.' Be right back," Carla announced, staring at her juice glass then standing up. Mary Ellen waited until the cop had left the room before getting up and following her at an inconspicuous distance.

Up a level, Carla hurried over to the Administration Desk on the second deck and asked for Steven's cabin number.

"We simply can't give out that kind of information," the woman sniffed without looking up. Sorting through papers one-by-one had suddenly become the most important job in the world.

Carla slammed her NYPD badge down on the counter. Instantly, there was a flurry of movement behind the desk. Papers shuffled for real now, her computer keyboard, a sudden vehicle for frenzied typing, and within seconds, the clerk had come up with the correct room number: 253.

Hanging back at least twenty yards, the quilter could see her cabin mate arriving at the Steward's quarters and knocking on his door. After a quick exchange, they continued up to the deck above. Still attempting to stay incognito, Mary Ellen's breathing had become so labored, she feared she might start belching huge gasps of air if she didn't make a pit stop soon.

Got to start an exercise regimen, she noted as she watched Carla and the steward pounding on number 253. Withdrawing a key, the steward opened the door, and the two disappeared into the room, leaving Mary Ellen to slowly inch up the corridor towards the cabin. Steadying herself, she was about to move again when the steward rushed out of the room and proceeded to dry heave.

That did it. She had to see what was going on. Running up to the cabin, she could hear a few movements inside, just before she stepped into the compartment.

She had never seen so much blood before. Steven Bingham, stretched out across his bed, lay covered in the stuff, as if the sheets had been painted with some kind of bright, acrylic fabric paint, smeared in some areas, pooling in others. His glazed eyes were still open and to her horror, a half-smirk was still pasted on his face.

Bending over the victim, Carla glanced back up at her roommate. "The next time you follow someone you'd better be in greater shape. I could hear your breathing a mile away. Well, now that you're here, are ya satisfied? Not too pretty, huh?"

Mary Ellen put a hand to her throat, swallowed, and shook her head. "What…what do you think happened?"

"I don't know, but I'm gonna find out, that's for sure." Carla went outside the cabin and noticed a very green steward hovering in the corridor. "I need some forensic backup on this," she ordered. "Call Ship-to-Shore, and meantime, get me the Captain. Pronto!"

The Steward ran off as Carla faced Mary Ellen. "You're in the thick of it, now. Ya might as well help me." Mary Ellen nodded, her heart beating so hard she had trouble catching all of Carla's words.

"Without touching anything, look for some kind of murder weapon. He was probably killed with a knife, but judging from the jagged quality of the wounds, it might not be." The two searched the room, carefully stepping over puddles of blood. Nothing seemed out of place.

"He sure was neat for a guy," Carla muttered to herself as she walked over to the side table next to his bed. On top of the table were two books. One, obviously a Bible, the other a Merck's Manual and she was going for a closer look when the Captain hurried in.

"Oh my God," he said, falling back against the doorjamb, sheet white and staring at the body. He took two short inhales-exhales before looking at Carla.

She had already charged into full police mode. "Captain, as soon as the forensic people come, I can leave the crime scene. In the meantime, it would help me enormously if you wouldn't let people know what has happened yet. One, the murderer is obviously still on the ship and that would give him or her the chance to hide the murder weapon, and two, we don't want any panic going on, now do we?"

"But we have to tell people at some point, don't we?" The captain's face was slowly gaining color.

"Yes, but for now," Carla said, turning to her roommate. "I want everything to go on as if nothing has occurred. Mary Ellen, you've got to teach your class today, OK?"

Impressed by Carla's sense of command, she made a slight dip of the head.

Mary Ellen's usual jocularity left a bad taste in her mouth that afternoon, but outwardly she continued doing her schtick, demonstrating how to make embellishments out of dress laces, buttons, or bows.

"OK. Now, remember whenever you use your rotary cutter—remember, this pizza thing here—you have to always push the safety latch up on it after cutting. I'm talking every time, by the way. Do not leave it out without the safety on. The blade is very sharp and dangerous. I've even cut myself on it a couple of times. Everyone show me how to push that safety-latch on and off." The class dutifully complied.

"Now, take your scissors out, and once again, I will demonstrate how to cut around all those hard to rotary-cut places; you know, your seams, your bows, your buttons, etc." She looked around for a couple of seconds, puzzled.

"Has anyone seen my good Gingher scissors? They were here yesterday evening, I'm sure of it." A dozen heads shook no. She muttered, "Oh, well, it'll turn up. I must have misplaced it." She was starting to feel a little better about the world. Quilting was definitely good therapy, and by the end of the class, she had almost forgotten about Steven Bingham.

After the students had filed out, she began tidying things up. Waste not, want not, her mother had always claimed. Organization and cleanliness were next to Godliness, she thought, as material scraps were tossed into large empty coffee cans. A seam ripper, her rotary cutter, and rulers were neatly placed in a row on her front desk, ready for the next day's lesson. She noticed that most of the people had been fairly neat, but off to the left, on one of the side desks, one student hadn't even bothered to clean up at all. Annoyed, she walked over to the messy area to straighten up. Putting things in some sort of order, she glanced over at a box of dresses, wedged up against a nearby wall. Intrigued, she went over to take a closer look at one of the dresses that from a distance, looked quite beautiful—pale mauves, lavenders and blue-grays swirled together in a modernistic, almost painterly style. She picked it up, admiring its texture and colors and thinking what a great addition to a quilt this piece of clothing would make.

Suddenly, she noticed a lump in the pocket, and a dark stain off to one side. Curious, she reached into the cloth-like envelope and started pulling the object out. Moisture from its bottom edge made her hand wet and sticky as the object slipped away from her. Instinctively, her hand recoiled and her stomach wrenched.

The blood covering her fingers had already turned a burgundy color, as opposed to a fresh, bright turkey red. Out of nowhere, she suddenly flashed back to the time she had played with her mother's nail polish bottle, and how it had tipped over, leaving a crimson gooey coating all over her fingers. Quickly shoving her hand back down into the pocket and giving two light tugs, she extracted a sharp, metal object.

Horrified, her first thought was about how her Gingher scissors had never looked so dirty. Snapping back to reality, she tossed them quickly back into the pocket, shoved the dress down into the box, and flew out the door, knocking over a couple of chairs in her wake.

"Carla, you've got to come with me! I found the murder weapon in my sewing room. It's my scissors! They used my scissors!"

"Show me," came the blunt reply as the two sped off to the sewing room, along with an official paper bag one of the newly arrived forensics team had brought.

This time, when the detective told the Captain about the scissors, he simply shook his head. "Detective, it's time to tell the rest of the ship," he commanded.

"Yeah, I've got to start interrogating people. I've also got several items of evidence to examine and catalogue."

Mary Ellen jumped in. "I could help you both, you know." The captain and Carla looked at each other and laughed.

"I found the murder weapon after all! She persisted. "I can certainly help with cataloging, for God's sake!"

"This is not "Murder She Wrote." This is real life, Mary Ellen. I'm a real police officer, and this is a real Captain. It's our job to proceed with this, not you, a quilter for God's sake!"

Back in their cabin, Mary Ellen fumed. Boy! I treat her to a free class, I am always nice to her, and what do I get in return? Boy, I...Suddenly, a box marked 'Evidence,' placed on top of Carla's side table snagged her attention. Getting up from her bunk, she carefully leaned over it and peered in. On top of various pants, shirts, underwear, belts, and ties lay a Merck's Manual, frayed at the edges and coated with dust.

What in the world would Steven be doing with a medical manual she wondered. She reached down into her purse and extracted four rubber postal fingertips she always carried with her for traction on the cloth when she machine-quilted big pieces. Forensic procedures, phooey! Might as well use an old quilter's trick so I won't leave fingerprints, she chuckled as she put a tip on each finger. Who says quilters know nothing about crime! She started going through the thick text, first putting her rubber-sealed thumb down on the page then gently curling the right hand corner up with her rubber-tipped forefinger. But the pages were so thin and old, they stuck together like paper-thin Filo dough layers and leafing through it seemed to take forever.

She was about to give up entirely when halfway in, an envelope floated out of the manual and onto the floor. Excited, she reached down, pincer-grabbed it, and deposited it on top of her bunk bed. The envelope flap was open and on closer inspection, she could see a small stack of one hundred dollar bills and a piece of paper, all clipped together with a hastily handwritten note:

"Here it is, you bastard—
you'll never stop, will you?
Now LEAVE ME ALONE!!"

Blackmail. The hairs on the back of Mary Ellen's neck were not only beginning to rise, they were ramrod straight, at full attention. There was something else. A shredded piece of paper, worn with age and use had also fallen to the floor. She bent down, and scooping it up, opened it carefully, knowing full well it might serve as evidence later on. It was dated May 20, 1959:

> Dear Stevie—
> I don't know how to tell you this. I know you never wanted to be a dad, so I feel there is no way out for me. I had to have this abortion, don't you see?
> Please forgive me, and even though you may never see me again, remember that I will always love you, no matter what happens. And promise me you won't ever tell my mother and father. They would never understand.
> t's all for the best. All my love forever, Maggie."

Hmmm. Steven had been obviously blackmailing someone, and from the looks of it, this abortion happened to an old girlfriend of his long ago. Somehow it was all tied up with someone else on the ship. But with whom? How could she find that out, embedded here in a small cabin in the middle of an ocean, with no resources in sight, and without Carla's knowledge?

She closed her eyes, took a deep breath, and imaged her favorite scene—the Pacific Ocean, with the sound of seagulls squawking lazily as they circled each other, playing tag in a baby blue sky. Instantly, her brain cleared—WebPrivateye2009.

"Well, little lady, fancy seeing you," John T. Porter chuckled, straddling his doorway. Behind him sat Mrs. Porter on one of the beds, curlers wound tight on her head.

"Sorry to bother you," Mary Ellen began, "but I was wondering if I could possibly look someone up on your great detective software?"

Porter's smile broadened. "Why sure, it'd be my pleasure to show you." He ushered her into their room and sat her down on one of the desk chairs. A minute later they were booted up, ready to go.

On the WebPrivateye2009 website, Porter typed in his name and password, then switched places with her so she was in front of the computer. On the screen there were two columns labeled 'Regular Search' and 'Professional Search'.

"What do these two headings mean?"

"Well, 'Regular' is for people like you and me and if you want to pay more, you can go into 'Professional Search' and get even more information."

"You mean like what Carla was talking about in her department or what the private detectives use?"

Porter nodded. "OK. Now, who shall we begin with?"

"How about my cabin mate, Carla Del Riggio?" They both looked at each other and grinned. He pointed; she punched keys. Click-click-click-click-click-click. Instantly, Carla's address, phone number, and police identification number cropped up.

"What's next, little lady?"

"Let's find out some of her history…where she went to school." This was so cool!

"OK. Go over here on the sidebar to the words Educational History. Now click."

Click-click-click-click-click. Suddenly Carla's entire educational history popped up.

She had gone to PS 143 in the Bronx up through 8th grade, then moved on to Bronx Science before attending NYU in Forensics Pathology. Mary Ellen was impressed; Carla's tough exterior masked a very intelligent person.

"Would you mind loaning me this laptop just for a couple of hours?"

Sitting back, Porter tilted his head to one side, his eyes narrowing.

"Ah, I realize you don't know me from Adam, but I would sure appreciate it." Mary Ellen practically batted her eyes.

Porter assessed the quilter for a few more seconds. "Oh, what the hell. Sure you can, honey. Get your own account, though. I'm not giving you my password, although I suppose if you steal the thing or break it, I can always write it off as a business expense!"

Ten minutes later, Mary Ellen was alone in their cabin, planted in front of the computer, trying to remember everything John T had just shown her. She went to the website and whipping out her credit card, set up her own account, going for the more expensive Professional Search. When the advanced software came up on the screen, she did the preliminaries.

Bingham's name, address, phone number, email address:

sbziploc@gmail.com. She laughed out loud. What kind of character would think of an e-mail like that! She continued. OK, OK, we go here, then here, and OK, OK… There! Steven Bingham's entire life was up on the screen. She scanned the page. Grew up in Wichita Kansas, local high school, got a scholarship to Brighton Medical School. OK, smart boy. Transferred out of med school into a different division called medical research, three years into his med program. Why? OK…

Bit by bit, she was scrolling down the page to the bottom when suddenly she paused, her brain percolating.

"When I was in Medical school years ago, before I decided to go into Law, the costs were a drop in the bucket compared to what it takes to run for Congress these days." Hempton went to medical school, too. Let me try him.

She cleared Bingham and started in on Hempton. His e-mail address was not as silly: rjhempton@earthlink.net. Continuing, she ticked all the appropriate keys and got his history. Prep schools all the way. Of course. She recognized several of the well-known names. College: Brighton Medical School. The same school as Bingham. Interesting…

She could feel her pace quickening. Never finished med school, but there was nothing that would indicate why. Then she went back over to the educational sidebar and hit another key listed: Reason for Leaving. She waited a couple of seconds. Then, it flicked on: Reason for Leaving: Expulsion.

Expulsion. Why would he be expelled? She was wracking her brains on what to do next, when the phone rang.

"Hey little lady, how's it goin'?" John T. sounded a bit nervous.

"Great, only I forgot the next step if a school has a reason for a dismissal." Mary Ellen blurted out.

"What the hell are you lookin' up if I might ask? And what program are you in?"

"I ordered the Professional Search one. And, well, don't tell anyone, but I'm looking up someone on this ship."

Porter's tone switched from mildly interested to intrigued. "Oh? Which one?"

"Well, if you must know, Mr. Hempton," As soon as she said it, Mary Ellen regretted having mentioned his name.

There was a slight lull. "You might try punching in the F10 stop on the top of the keyboard—it should take you one step further. But remember, little lady, all this info should be confidential. You get it?" All of a sudden, the gregarious Texan had turned prudent.

"Of course, of course."

He could hear her doing a couple of more clicks. "Hey Mary Ellen, are you still there?" All his charm had evaporated.

"Yes, yes." She scanned another screen filled with details—who Hempton roomed with, what car he drove, license number, etc. etc. She was about to hit Exit when her eye fixed on the lower right-hand section. 'Reason for Expulsion: Attempted Abortion without License.'

"Oh, my God," she muttered.

"Oh my God, what? What is it?" Porter demanded.

"It's complicated, but I think I might know who killed Steven Bingham."

"Yes, I heard he was dead. What's going on? Now, honey, don't do anything foolish, ya hear?"

"Yeah, sure. Thanks for all your help." Hanging up fast, she elected to go back to the locked sewing room for another look at the scissors before relating her suspicions to Carla. Just in case there was any evidence they might have missed.

Extracting a forensic paper bag from Carla's leather briefcase, she hurried along to her workshop station, excited and pleased with herself. I'd make a pretty darn good detective if I do say so myself, she mused, visualizing Det. Mary Ellen Stafford in gold embossed letters on a black lacquered plaque on top of a police office desk somewhere. Next to a Dunkin' Donut and Starbucks coffee, and…

"Mr. Hempton, please sit down," Carla said warily. After a trying morning of interrogating disgruntled vacationers, she was worn out.

"Yes, yes, can we get this over with soon? I have to make an important call at four p.m. and I want to read some material before I do it." Hempton kept looking around him impatiently.

"Just a few minutes, if ya don't mind. Did ya know the victim other than our table conversation?"

"Of course not. No, no, no, I never saw him in my life. What kind of question is that to ask someone in my position?"

The red flags inside her head were already up and fluttering. "Please just bear with me a minute. You say ya didn't know him before the cruise ship?"

"I never met him before. And if you try to link him to me, I will have my lawyers come down on you so fast it'll make your head spin!"

Whoaaah, Nelly! What's goin' on? Carla thought. "All right, calm down, Mr. Hempton. We're through, for now. You're free to go." She watched him leave and quickly turn left into the corridor as she tapped rhythms against a chair rail, deep in thought.

Meanwhile, Mary Ellen, passing by en route to her workstation, couldn't help but notice how red Richard Hempton's face looked as he exited the 'interrogation room.' Angry red, she speculated. What happened? she wondered.

I'm not going to tell Carla about Hempton yet. I'll just go see if the murder weapon is still in the workshop, then bring all my info back to her. Mary Ellen gloated at the idea of being the one to solve the case. Carla would be so grateful, she might even offer her an assistant's detective job, or at the very least, a special recognition certificate.

Her daydreams buzzed around her as she opened up the sewing room, but once inside, she focused and charged over to the box where the dress had been housed. The dress was still there, but there were no bagged scissors anywhere. Carla must have nabbed them to be cataloged.

Turning back to her overly organized desk, she sensed something else was missing, but began her usual preparation drill anyway. Rulers, check; masking tape, check; seam ripper, check; rotary cutter…where in the world was the rotary cutter?

Wham! From out of her memory bank flashed an image. She was ten-years-old and she had just been hit on the side of the head with a soccer ball, and all she could remember was pain and this boy Billy Thomas, close at hand, sing-songing nasty comments.

Wham! It happened again. This time, through her stinging tears she could see Richard Hempton coming after her again. She dodged just right of his fist, and ran to the door, trying to scream, but no sound came out. Scrambling to another exit, she discovered the side door had been locked from the outside. Slowly, she turned to face him.

Panting and wheezing, he took out a tiny inhaler and sucked in two puffs of ventolin; enough time for her to find her strength. "Why are you doing this? Why me? What did I do to you?"

"You're connected with that busybody detective, that's why. Don't worry, I'm gonna get her too after I finish with you. Nobody is going to stop me from being in Congress! Nobody!

"You killed Steven Bingham! Admit it!"

"He deserved it, the bastard. He was ruining my life! Wherever I went, there he was, blackmailing me. All because long ago, so long ago... How was I to know she would bleed so much? It wasn't my fault, I tell you! It wasn't!" He looked so desperate, for a moment Mary Ellen almost felt sorry for him. But his mood flipped. Lunging at her, he shoved her up against the wall, then spun her around so that he could hold both her hands behind her back with his left hand as he fumbled with something in his pocket with his right.

Sss—snapp! The sound was so familiar. "Remember, class, when the safety latch is off, the rotary cutter is dangerous!"

Hempton drew his right hand out in front of her, then over towards the left side of her face. With one smooth stroke a neck could so easily be sliced. She closed her eyes and thought about how wonderful her husband and kids were.

Crack. Mary Ellen could feel Hempton collapse behind her, the rotary cutter clattering on the linoleum floor. She looked up to see Carla in a swat-team stance, legs apart, both hands on the gun. Behind her, the tall Texan was holding onto the doorjamb, issuing a slow, deep, wolf whistle.

Still in shock, Mary Ellen couldn't move as people streamed in, demanding to know what had happened, and each time someone asked, Carla would answer simply, "Ask Mary Ellen. She solved the case!"

At dockside, the last day blended into a series of yellow sticker tapes, uniformed crewmembers, and cops everywhere. Passengers couldn't wait to rush off the ship to tell their family and friends about the double homicide, but in their cabin, Mary Ellen and Carla took their time, silently packing their bags.

Finally, Carla spoke. "If I come to the Midwest, how 'bout givin' me another quilt workshop?" She winked at her roommate. "Maybe my new partner and I could use a creative outlet to balance out all our anxieties."

"Oh, you plan on trusting another partner again?" Mary Ellen raised one eyebrow.

"Sure, why not. And what about you?" Carla turned to face her. "You know, I could put in a good word about you to my supervisor. Go back to school. Think about Forensics. It's a growing field. "

The quilter smiled, but shook her head. She had already decided to switch to romance novels.

PRECIOUS GIFTS

The air thickened as a heavy blanket of rain clouds threatened to let loose a downpour at any moment. Out of the stillness, a quick, sharp breeze kicked up little spirals of dust from the earth, making the cornfield rustle with activity. Gears clicked softly, as the rat-tat-tat-tat of a needle dove in and out of a patchwork quilt so large, it seemed to completely envelope the small woman hunched over a metal machine, lost in her own world.

Despite the increasing wind, there was no stopping, or even slowing down of the needle. If anything, the rhythm only got faster. Ignored hungry chickens clucked in the front yard of the small cabin and dried laundry flapped sideways as the cast-iron sewing machine pedal persisted, up and down, more and more frenetically.

On a nearby road, a dark wooden wagon was making its approach, the hooves of the horse trotting in time to the movement of the pedal as the wagon's driver gave tiny clicking noises to his nag, signaling he was serious about getting a move-on.

"What do ya bet your Mama's out sewin' in the cornfield again!" Papa grumbled out of one side of his downcast mouth.

"Papa, why does Mama wanna sew all the time? We don't git to see her the way we used to," his youngest, Martha protested.

Ten-year-old Paul chimed in. "The other day I was goin' out to fetch the firewood, and I saw the dirty dishes in the sink and no Mama anywhere! An' when I holler'd for her, all I heard was the sewin' machine!"

"Oh, you mean the 'Devil'?" Papa snorted.

The children stared up at their father, startled by his tone. But he was already deep in thought, remembering that infamous day when they had all gone to the 1872 Washington Territory State Fair. There, they had passed jelly booths, pig demonstrations, horse-trading auctions, and farm equipment trade-ins. Armed with twelve of her most delicious fruit pies, Mama was hoping to take home at least one blue ribbon. For two consecutive days she had rolled dough, stirred pots of bubbling fruit glaze, and hovered over their small oven, until the delicious aroma wafting in from the kitchen became almost unbearable. Her only break came when she caught the children and even Papa trying to dip their fingers into the warm pies. "Leave them alone! Leave them alone! You're not going to take away my ribbons!" she had wailed, wringing her flour-coated hands.

By late afternoon, they were all exhausted and ready for their cabin. Mama was discouraged because she was returning empty-handed, Papa was annoyed at the prices and the children had seen and tasted enough to last them for quite awhile, at least until the next year's fair rolled around.

Just as they were about to climb onto their wagon, a woman bustled by. "Did you see the new Singer Sewing Machine Exhibition? It's Mr. Singer himself, visiting us all the way from New York City!"

Before anyone could stop her, Mama had darted off towards the 'sewing' tent, where a small crowd had already assembled.

"Step up, little lady, and see my new Singer Perpendicular Action Sewing Machine demonstration! Step right up; you won't ever go back to hand sewin' again!" Isaac Merritt Singer's Shakespearean-trained voice bellowed as he beckoned to Mama from across the tent. Then, placing a flirtatious arm on the shoulder of a young woman he had retained to show off his machines, he urged everyone to 'gather 'round.'

Mama, edging her way through the crowd for a better look at the new wonder, saw a pretty young girl of around twenty, down in front next to Mr. Singer, seated on a new bench, her bodice tight, her back arrow-straight, poised to sew. While the few men in the crowd seemed particularly appreciative of her form, Mama's focus was solely on the machine itself.

The model's black shoe tipped the foot pedal forward, thrusting the needle up and down with a clicking noise that instantly had the eager crowd oohing and ahhing. And when she held up the seams she had just completed, everyone cheered.

Before he could come out with a "What's all the fuss about?" Papa caught sight of Mama's face and froze; in all their time together it had never shown so much animation. Suddenly he felt replaced.

"Mama, can't we please go home now?" the children were unanimous. Ignoring their cries and looking only at her husband, Mama spoke up. "I'm gonna git me one of these, you know."

"What, are you crazy? How much do they cost?"

"It doesn't matter; I'm gonna have it, make no mistake about it."

Papa stared at her uneasily for a few seconds, shifting from one leg to another. "Well, I suppose it wouldn't hurt to ask how much they are..." The children's mouths dropped. Papa giving in this easily? What was going on? Before they knew it, it was ordered and the contract sealed, for the whopping price of seventy-five dollars—ten dollars down, sixty-five dollars due upon delivery.

The family's return trip to their farm was long, bumpy, and stagnant from the angry silence up front. The children, nestled in the back on a pallet, kept rubbing their burning eyes, but with only the owls and coyotes to serenade them, all resistance faded and soon, they drifted off into a much-needed sleep.

And then came The Wait. For Mama, each day felt like an eternity, sticking in her craw and driving the children outside from morning until dusk. Papa remained outside as well, fantasizing about a quail expedition in nearby territories as he did his chores. But finally, the mail carrier appeared with a well-traveled letter. Barring any unforeseen Indian attacks or other mishaps, the sewing machine was due to arrive the following week.

"You know, I heard 'bout a settler who killed a couple of Chinooks gist last week. There's bound to be trouble. It just might disturb the comin' of your contraption," Papa announced, puffing on his pipe and assessing her reaction.

"It'll get here, it'll get here. We haven't really had any trouble with the Chinooks, now have we?" Mama snapped back.

Shrugging, Papa turned away.

For the next few days, Mama bustled throughout the cabin, possessed by a new-found energy. Decisions had to be made as to the best placement of 'it'; hours were spent rearranging chairs first here, then there, dragging their clothing bureaus around, and shifting their supper table over against a wall. Sounds of heavy objects scraping against the wooden floors became a daily occurrence, yet she never seemed satisfied. Once she stood back and surveyed each room, she would sigh, and begin the entire process over again.

Finally, the moment came. Sitting down to supper one evening, they could hear a single-teamed wagon chugging up their road. The children looked at Papa, who was riveted on Mama. In an instant, she was jumping up and galloping out the front door, down the porch steps, and over to the approaching wagon, her skirt and petticoat making full arcs as they swished on either side of her.

"Hey, little lady, I can see you're all fired up about this here machine. Best thing money can buy, I can tell ya that! The machine to beat all machines. It'll make your life a lot easier, that's for sure!"

As if the salesman had to convince Mama! She was already running her chore-worn hands over the frayed horsehair blanket cover. She had started to pull it off when the salesman stepped in and took over.

There it was. Shiny, black, embellished with beautiful gold lettering, and supported by intricate ironwork around the pedal and below the mahogany base. Mama sucked in her breath. It was even more spectacular than she had remembered. The salesman signaled to Papa standing on the porch, to come over to help him remove it from the wagon, and between the two of them, they managed to hoist it off and carry it over to the cabin.

"Where do you want it, little lady?" the salesman inquired.

In unison, everyone turned to Mama.

"Well, I've done a lot of thinkin' and I've decided it should go in the main room where I can get to it real easy," she gushed.

After they had planted it in Mama's designated spot, the sales man mopped his forehead. "Whoosh! It sure does look pretty sittin' there. Just take good care of it. If you knew what I went through to bring it out here, you'd treat it like the Queen of Araby!"

"What kind of trouble you have?" Papa leaned in, his eyes instantly alert.

"Oh, injuns mostly, up the next valley. I had to hide the wagon behind some rocks to wait for a couple of their scouts to pass before movin' on. They sure did look mean, though, like they was just itchin' for trouble if ya know what I mean."

Surprised, Papa took a step back. The Chinooks, avid traders with the white settlers for years, had always remained peaceful, trusting, filling their bellies full of the salmon that swam up the well-stocked Columbia River.

"Yep, seems there were a couple 'a settlers, mean men, who killed an Injun and his family. Now there's talk of revenge, and…"

Mama wouldn't let him finish. "What if they come and burn down the cabin or the barn? Why, they would destroy my beautiful sewin' machine!"

Papa stared at her for a couple of seconds, one cheek muscle twitching.

"Well, if that don't beat all! You care more for your blasted machine than you do about your own home! Don't that take the puddin'!"

Mama crossed her arms over her chest and the salesman cleared his throat while the children made imaginary drawings on the floor with the tips of their shoes.

"Well, suit yourself. Where d'ya want to put this thing?" Papa continued, his voice flat.

Mama clapped her hands. "I know. In the cornfield! We could hide it in there, 'specially before harvest. The corn's so high, no one would see it from the cabin!"

"How you gonna protect it from the rain?"

"Well, lemme see…why, we could use that heavy covering we used last year for the plow. That seemed to work gist fine!"

Suddenly, the salesman took an active interest in his own shoes. Domestic arguments were definitely not part of the delivery package. A couple of seconds later, he begged off, claiming he was exhausted from his long journey and where was the barn they had promised him he could sleep in for the night? Mama nodded and handed him the balance due, then Papa led him down to his sleeping quarters in the stall next to their only mare.

Early the next morning, the two men carried 'The Devil' out into the cornfield and watched Mama plop down and begin mending a pair of Papa's torn pants. By afternoon, the salesman had departed and the mended pants replaced by some new curtains for the cabin. Soon, every spare minute she had she was sewing in the field and although the family did miss her, they all agreed the cabin had come alive with quilts, pillows, and curtains. In addition, everyone got new clothing and at week's end, even Papa had to admit maybe it was a good thing after all.

But as with any addiction, she couldn't stop; sewing granted her far too much pleasure and soon, a disgruntled Papa began spending more and more time away from the cabin. There was always an excuse—pheasants to be shot for supper, a deer waiting just beyond the bend. As his trips extended, Mama's good-bye waves turned increasingly absent-minded, and after six months, their time together was more often than not choked with silence.

Kolote closed his eyes. His stomach, fluttering like small butterflies that hover over the fields, suddenly surged, churning its way up into his chest and throat. His father had reportedly prepared him for this day, the day when he would be old enough to launch his own Spirit Quest, but although his entire life had been a foreshadowing of this moment, now that it had arrived, it was too difficult to face. If only he could be a little boy again, safe in their Longhouse, surrounded by comforting horsehair blankets and familiar foods roasting over a smoky fire.

"My son, now you must go forth into the world, to places you have not yet seen. Do not travel up the river, but instead, go into the forests to find your yuhlmah. There, you shall search for your Spirit Helper who will then guide you into manhood." Tyee turned away, stifling his disappointment with his motherless son, a boy who, unlike the other young braves from the village, had always appeared so fragile, so uneasy, and so fearful of everything.

Kolote nodded dutifully, ruminating about all the fasting he would have to do for several days while traveling over unknown terrain. As he slowly walked away from the village, he could hear a baby crying in its papoose, its mother chanting a soothing song and from out of nowhere, he wished with all his heart that he could be the one in her strong arms.

Unexpectedly, he shivered. Dark gray, swollen clouds had gathered over the tops of the trees and picking up his pace, worry covered him like a blanket. What if there was a heavy rainstorm? He searched for shelter, but spotted only thick underbrush and moss-covered trees.

The wind began taking on a life of its own, whooshing, swishing, never settling down for more than a few seconds. Cold, Kolote had to stop. He yanked out part of a bearskin from a large sack he had brought to keep him warm, then, in an effort to create body heat, jumped up and down a few times. At first that worked, but once he became chilled again, he panicked.

Up ahead was a clearing and he started running towards it, but when a large, knotted tree root caught his foot, he went flying, his arms and legs spread out like a soaring eagle. Still sprawling towards the earth, he could see the rock he was about to land on and by the time his head hit it, he could hear a crunching noise inside his skull. Then, there was only black.

When he opened his eyes, there was no time awareness, simply darkness and the fact that he was alone, freezing, and nauseous. He tried to sit and nearly keeled over, his head bursting with a rhythmic throbbing. Cupping his hands over his eyes to ease the pain, fresh concerns only aggravated the pounding. Dizziness cascaded over him in waves, and soon he couldn't distinguish between what was inside his head and what was happening around him. Crawling on all fours, he managed to make it into the clearing, where he headed towards an adjacent cornfield.

Close by, within the warmth of their cabin, Mama tried stifling her resentment. Papa had set off again, informing her this time it would last for several weeks, and that she had better be more conscientious about household chores by the time he returned. Wide awake in their bed, she could barely contain herself.

"He doesn't git it, he just doesn't." she fumed. "I won't go back to gist doin' chores. If I don't always have every dish clean and put away, then my family will have to understand. I won't give up my sewin'! I won't!"

Hooting owls kept her thoughts active, restless. But just hearing the wind begin to whip up the leaves, she turned grateful to be inside, snuggled up under her newest quilt. At least she wasn't outside, where the late summer nights were beginning to carry a nippy edge to them.

At dawn, Kolote woke up, trembling uncontrollably. His head still ached, but at least he wasn't nauseous and the world wasn't spinning. Looking down at his right hand, he noticed dried blood and when he reached up to his forehead, he could feel a crusty scab already forming. He entered the cornfield gingerly. Yesterday, from a distance he had noticed a white man's cabin, but today, in the midst of the field, he saw only rows of corn bursting out of their husks just above his head.

The sun was out in full, and with its slow burn, his shivers were diminishing until he heard someone approach. Instantly, he froze. The woman's song sounded resonant but different from the familiar Indian chants he had grown up with. But it was the other sound a minute later that puzzled him so completely. Rat-tat-tat-tat— Rat-tat-tat-tat. What was that? he wondered.

Chest pounding, head throbbing, he attempted to walk as quietly as possible toward the clatter. Rat-tat-tat-tat. He could feel his balance shifting, but caught himself from falling over by reaching for a corn stalk. Then, holding onto some ears to keep steady, he curled one stalk backward for a better view. Inching forward he could see the shape of a woman hovering over an object and as the air lay calm, the woman held up some sort of cloth object in front of her.

Kolote gasped in amazement. Colors that reminded him of late spring flowers blossoming were on this cloth, and in spite of himself, he smiled. Then the woman caught sight of him. No one moved. Narrow blood vessels rose then pulsed inside Kolote's neck seconds before he fainted, hitting the earth with a dull, lifeless thud. Mama instinctively jumped up, ready to run towards him, but stopped; he was an Indian after all. When she proceeded, it was with caution.

With her quilt wrapped tightly around her, she tried hard to stay utterly silent. Maybe he wasn't really unconscious; maybe he would jump up to attack her. But he didn't move and soon, she was standing directly over him, peering down.

His delicate body and splayed feet, deformed from years of squatting, was intriguing enough. But as her eyes traveled up his torso, clothed in the simplest of bearskins, his head, with its peculiar flatness to his forehead, fascinated her the most.

Suddenly, he startled awake, very much alive and doused with fear. But the pale, yellow-haired white woman had kind eyes and after she started to make little shushing noises while stroking his face, he slowly began to relax.

"What are you doing here?" Carefully enunciating her words proved useless; the language barrier was far too great. He could only gaze back at her with a slightly baffled expressions, his pupils like droplets of black coal.

Without warning, he shivered and immediately, her maternal instincts took over. Pulling the quilt off her narrow shoulders, she carefully draped it around his body and took a step back as he fingered the cotton texture, marveling at how different it felt from the heavy dog-hair blankets of his village.

"You look so thin. Wait, I'll be back shortly," Mama promised, holding up one finger as a gesture for him to be patient. Somehow, he understood and drifting off to sleep again, he awakened in the late afternoon to the smell of something hot and delicious in a porcelain cup placed next to him. He shifted onto his elbow and ignoring all tribal customs, devoured the soup, smacking his lips with unabashed pleasure.

"So you like our food, ummm?" Mama chuckled, ladling more soup from out of a large cast iron pot and filling up another cup for him. He nodded and downed another portion.

"You can stay in the barn until you get well," she reassured him. Noticing his confused stare, she held onto his sack and motioning for him to follow her, steered him towards the barn. The family horse snickered softly, angling for an early supper, but Mama turned a deaf ear and led Kolote straight to an empty stall, well hidden from view. There, she propped up handful after handful of straw, forming a makeshift bed, and when she pointed to it, he collapsed gratefully. She started to leave for bed linens, but Kolote grunted, so instead, she stopped and turned towards him.

"Here," he announced in the Chinook Jargon she had heard only a few times in her life. From out of his sack, he extracted a pile of glass 'pony' beads, the kind his tribe used as a bartering trade system with settlers. Extending them out to her, he carefully placed them in the palm of her hand without actually touching her.

When she smiled, he was surprised to see her eyes moisten. Were all white women as tenderhearted as this one was? he wondered as she exited the barn.

He lay in the hay, satiated, dozing, waking intermittently. When he did sleep, his dreams were filled with colored cloths, a gentle white, faceless female, and cornhusks, floating in and out of his unconsciousness, and when he finally sat up, he felt more at peace than he had felt for a very long time.

"Mama, where did you get these beautiful beads?" Back in the cabin, Paul stood still, feet apart, hands on hips, expecting an answer.

"Hush, never you mind. I picked them up on the road while I was berry pickin', that's where. Now, go to sleep." Mama understood too well the consequence of Papa finding these beads; if he found them, he would insist on knowing their origin. After the children had gone to sleep, she got out of bed and shoving the beads into an empty coffee tin, hid it far back in the larder, behind the flour sack. Nobody would ever look there—that was Mama's domain.

The next morning, her first thought was of her new foundling. At the earliest sign of light, she hurried down to the barn, bringing biscuits from yesterday's breakfast, fresh milk, and several apples.

By the time she arrived, Kolote was already sitting up and looking perky. He dug into his sack, and rifling around, pulled out a brownish-gray small rabbit skin lap robe—thick, warm, and in perfect condition. Mama gasped, clasping her hands together in delight.

"Oh no, you can't give me this! It's just too beautiful!" she exclaimed.

Kolote thrust the robe out towards her while she shook her head no in tiny little movements, so as not to appear too ungracious.

"Potlatch! Potlatch!" Kolote tried to explain. How could he make this white woman understand that in his tribe, the giving of one's own belongings as gifts was as essential as breathing. Besides, the more you gave away, the more prestige you had within the tribe.

"Potlatch, potlatch!" he repeated, nodding his head vehemently.

Mama finally took the rabbit skin. Thanking him profusely, she wrapped it under her arm and scurried back to the cabin to hide her treasure before the children woke up.

A pattern had emerged. Each morning, there would be a little gift left for Mama: more glass beads, a piece of inner Alder tree bark, a piece of Grape bark, even a red onion.

"An onion?" Mama asked. "What should I do with this?" She turned the vegetable over in her hands as it caught the morning's rays. Taking the onion from her, Kolote pointed to the old iron pot she had left next to him from the day before. First, he imitated water boiling in the pot, fluttering his hands, then, peeling off the outer sheaths of the onion, pretended to put them into the pot. Next, retrieving a wild yellow flower from outside the barn, he showed it to her, repeatedly pointing to its petals. Finally, he pulled out his sack of sprig lichen and pointed to her dress, a shade of lichen blue.

Dyes! He was describing dyes! So the next time she couldn't get dyes from the trade post in town she could make her own, using materials she hadn't thought of before. Looking at him, her grin was particularly broad and he nodded, pleased. But in his heart, he knew he had to return to his village; his sojourn had lasted far too long, and as comfortable as he felt with Mama, he kept thinking of his own people and of his father— disapproving, and perhaps even worried.

The following morning, when Mama appeared at the barn door she was met by a downcast Kolote, packed to go. Her shoulders sagged. She wanted their friendship and all the little exchange gifts to continue. Racing back down to the cabin, she returned with a small, lap-size quilt tucked under her arm, and handing it over to Kolote, slowly nodded at his tears.

Then, she did the unthinkable: she hugged him. He sprang back like a wild animal, then catching sight of her expression, looked around to make sure no one else was present, stepped forward, outstretched his arms, and hugged her back.

"Mama, what is going on?" Little Paul's voice at the stall edge ended in a squeak. Mama and Kolote jumped apart like guilty lovers.

"Nothing, darlin'." Mama gulped. "This is our new friend. He was hurt and I helped him, that's all. Nothin' to worry about. But he has to go now, so we're gonna have to say good-bye, all right?" The thought of Paul telling Papa about the incident made Mama's stomach flip over.

Watching Kolote take off through the cornfield, together they could hear the faint sound of horse hooves plodding up the road behind them.

"That's gotta be Papa!" Paul burst out.

Mama attempted a smile. "Yep, it's gotta. Listen, Paul. Can you keep a little secret? Not a big one, mind you, just a little one. Can you?"

Paul's eyes grew larger. "Sure, I can."

"Let's keep the Indian's visit between us, all right? I don't wanna upset Papa any and he might not understand. All right?"

A quick nod and he was off to join his sister in welcoming Papa. Mama sighed. She would just have to trust him.

"Got some pheasant and fish and some fresh flowers for you!" Papa announced, searching his wife's face for a reaction. Getting down from the horse, he hugged Paul and Martha, but over the tops of their heads, his eyes still rested on hers.

Mama came towards him, broadening her smile into a full crescent. "It's good to have you at home. I've made some fresh bread and we're gonna have stew for dinner. It's good to have you home."

Papa breathed a sigh of relief. She had obviously come to her senses after all; maybe a little time apart was all they needed. However, by breakfast, his uneasiness had returned. The night before, their reunion had been somewhat of a reminder of earlier married days, but just before dawn, Mama was already up and boiling water in one of her big old rusty pots.

"In the Name of Thunder, what kind of chore are you doin' so early?" Papa was incredulous.

"I'm tryin' a new thing I heard about. I'm taking onions and lichen and making homemade dyes for my..." She caught herself. Too late. The same old tension sparked instantly. Snorting and buckling his pants belt, Papa raced out of the cabin, slamming the door behind him.

Later, Mama's hands wouldn't stop trembling as she hung laundry out to dry. Why won't Papa understand how important quilting is to me, she fumed. I can't give it up, I just can't.

Martha broke her train of thought. "Mama, can I play in the kitchen and pretend to make a pie?"

Nodding absently, Mama was grateful that at least Martha had something to do. Soon, the morning sun had entered her pores, calming her down and letting in renewed hopes, when all of a sudden, a sweeping shadow loomed over her.

"Where the hell did you get these?" Papa snarled.

Mama gazed up towards him, stunned. Holding the glass beads in one hand and the rabbit skin robe draped over his arm, the veins on his neck were popping. Behind him stood Martha, looking scared and ashamed.

"It's nothin'. Just something I picked up…" She trailed off when she caught sight of Paul ambling up to them, shuffling his shoes in the dirt, like he always did when he got into trouble.

"What in the blazes is goin' on with that heathen? I swear, Matilde, if you don't tell me now…"

Tyee was angry with Kolote. Not only did the boy's Spiritual Quest last longer than expected, the chief had missed his only son more than he had thought possible. Still, when he finally spoke to the boy, it was terse. "A Spiritual Quest is only supposed to be a few days!" he snapped, patting his son on the arm and looking off in the distance.

Still glowing from Mama's warmth, the familiar chill left a particular sting. Replies to his father had never been possible, only feeble nods before walking away.

By nightfall, a meeting was scheduled in Tyee and Kolote's Longhouse, where horizontal timbers connected to pole rafters to form a rectangular framework, and thatched cedar bark and rush matting served as a ridge-roof. In the middle of the main room, a vent allowed any smoke to escape as some of the elite elders sat crossed-leg in a solemn semi-circle.

Two old, wizened women, wearing conical basket caps on their heads, waited on their men with patience and submission, their movements slow, designed for continuity. Kolote had witnessed this kind of scene numerous times growing up, but tonight he sensed something very important was about to be discussed.

"As you must all know, one of our families has been killed by the White Man. Tonight, we shall decide what to do." Tyee's voice was commanding as he commenced the meeting.

One of the elders spoke up. "As it is our custom to hire someone else to do our killing, we should begin our search now." Many of the others quietly agreed, mumbling amongst themselves.

"Yes, we shall look for help elsewhere, and after they are hired, there is a small group of White Men," Tyee continued, "past the Great River, with fields of high corn and small wood houses who would be simple to destroy. They are few in number and cannot fight us well. Let the White Man learn our lessons."

Kolote's head jerked up. Why, they were talking about that kind white woman's area! He had to say something. Opening his mouth, intimidation strapped him in like a tight papoose.

"In the tribe of our neighbors there are warriors ready to kill for us," Tyee went on. "It is time for the White Man to understand that they can no longer hurt our people!"

Small droplets of perspiration beaded on Kolote's flat forehead. "Father, I have something to say…"

Surprised, the elders pivoted their heads his way.

"I wanted to tell my story later this week, but you must hear it now. On my Quest, I found my Spiritual Guide. Someone who has taught me about kindness and giving…" Kolote could feel his father's piercing eyes.

"Yes, Kolote. Tell us," one of the elders beckoned.

"It is a white woman. She…" Explosive voices shook the walls. He waited a few seconds for a lull. Then, "Wait. Wait. Please, you do not understand. She helped me, she took care of me." Tyee gripped his own chest.

"You let a white woman take care of you, my son? How could you do that?" Tyee felt sick to his stomach.

"I had fallen, I was hurt. I might have died, but she gave me food and gave me a place to sleep." Suddenly, Kolote turned defiant. "If it were not for this white woman, I would be as dead as our forefathers," he continued, scooping up courage like an eagle diving for food. "She taught me about kindness. You cannot tell me she is not my Spiritual Guide, my father." For the first time in his life, Kolote faced his father and looked directly into his eyes.

Tyee sat still, intractable.

Another spoke up. "Maybe this woman was good, but I still think we should send a warrior to kill the others."

Once again the room buzzed with conversation, leaving Kolote alone, sitting off to one side. But Tyee couldn't take his eyes off of his child. Like a young bird that in time leaves its nest, it seemed that Kolote had at last, learned to spread his own wings.

Later, when he spoke to his boy, he was uncharacteristically soft, patient.

"Tell me more about this white woman, my son."

Kolote looked up, stunned. Clearing his throat, he started to explain. "I gave several presents as my form of potlatch. She gave me food, and the most beautiful blanket I have ever seen. I believe it has certain powers, like the woven blanket my grandfather gave to me when I was born over twelve moons ago. This white woman could not make such a beautiful covering without magical powers. This, I believe."

The room quieted as all eyes focused on Tyee and his son. Then, going over to his sack, the young brave pulled out the quilt, and held it up high for everyone to see.

"Ahhhhhh. Ummmmmmm" they all chorused. Glancing at Tyree, Kolote's chest puffed out and his heart was full; at last he was getting some respect.

"I want to meet this white woman, to see for myself. Will you take me to her?" Tyee whispered.

For the past few days Papa had taken to sleeping in the barn. First that horrid machine stealing her heart away from him, and now this incident with the Indian. His first instinct was to punish her further, but recognized now was probably not the time; they had all been invited to one of their neighbor's farm for a day of food and socializing, a monthly ritual everyone looked forward to. He didn't have the heart to call it off and make Mama, or anyone else, stay home.

The trip to the neighbor's get-together seemed interminable. Papa, clicking furiously at their horse, kept flicking the mare's hind quarters with one of his homemade switches as Mama nervously checked her jam and jelly pots every two minutes. Paul began an endless round of hiccups while Martha hummed manically.

At the gathering, the women raced through the process of serving their families, then quickly formed a tight circle around Mama. How fast could her machine go? How many things had she made by now? Mama answered each question with a little decisive gesture, as if she were Mr. Singer himself, lecturing onstage about his famous product. By the time the afternoon light had shifted from golden yellow to bluish mauve, she had convinced most of the women there to pressure their husbands into getting one of their own.

Papa, outside on the weathered porch, listened to Indian trouble talk, still annoyed by Mama's posturing inside. But soon, his full attention was drawn solely to the discussion around him.

"Seems those two Smithlyn brothers were up to no good," his host reported. "On their way home, they robbed and killed a Chinookan family. One of the fur traders up the Columbia River said he heard the Chinooks are hoppin' mad about it, too. Gonna do something about it, he told me. Might even hire an assassin! That's what the Chinooks do, you know. They can't do the fightin' themselves, the cowards, so they get others to do the deed!"

Everyone sat still, taking it all in. Finally, Papa announced fiercely, "Well, I ain't gonna let 'em take my cabin or hurt my family, no sir! Maybe if we stick together, they won't try 'n get us. Strength in numbers, y'know?"

Compliant nods were a'plenty, but no words; everybody was too dazed. Indian trouble was so infrequent in their territory. After many goodbye handshakes and hugs, Mama could tell by Papa's look that conversation was out of the question during their ride back home. He wouldn't have answered her much anyway; he was far too consumed with protecting his family.

Tyee and Kolote toe-heeled carefully alongside the Columbia River into the dark green forests and on towards the sun-brushed cornfields. The wind was whirling up into a low pitch in the sky, but the moccasins on their feet cushioned the crunch of leaves as they walked. At night, Tyee knew exactly how to stoke a small fire, just enough to keep them warm, but not so large as to call attention to themselves. As they sat together near the low, crackling flames, Kolote looked at his father and his heart felt full. He admired Tyee's competence, his protectiveness, and his wisdom. And when Tyee looked down at his young son, he could feel his heart opening up just enough to let in love and pride.

The following day, the sun promised to be warmer than most autumn days. Papa stayed close to the cabin, doing odd jobs in the barn so he wouldn't be too far from his family. Mama hurried through her chores then scrambled down to the cornfield, clutching a large basket filled with an almost completed Log Cabin quilt in one hand, an extra spool of thread clenched in the other. Faint, child-like laughter filtered out through the cabin door and windows, making her smile as she settled down to sew, if only for an hour. She fingered the coverlet and took a deep breath, slowing her pace, as she drifted into the familiar peaceful mindset she had come to know so well. Made out of their old worn-out clothes, this current quilt embodied years of memories: one of her favorite dresses, Papa's wedding shirt, Martha's swaddling cloth, and Paul's first breeches, the ones he had stubbornly refused to take off right before bedtime. As she stitched, she kept stroking the top and feeling the batting between the layers, still marveling at how fast she could finish a quilt with her Singer.

Softly, Tyee and Kolote paced themselves through the cornfield, careful not to create any extra noise. Rat-tat-tat-tat. Rat-tat-tat-tat. Tyee froze, then turned to Kolote, his neck, half-twisted upward, curious, alert, but Kolote motioned for him to press on, bending each bursting corn stalk slightly, making sure the stems didn't snap back at them after the husks had flexed like bows in the wind.

They needn't have been so careful; Mama's concentration had blocked out all sound. When the chief and his son approached her from behind, Tyee was surprised at how petite she looked. Could this possibly be the spiritual guide his son talked about? What kind of powers could someone that small have? And a woman! He suddenly noticed Kolote nodding enthusiastically, then pick up speed.

Closer and closer they padded until finally, they stopped within a yard of her. It was at that exact moment, Mama decided to take a quick break. Stretching her arms out towards the sky, she opened her mouth to sing a church hymn as she stood up to revel in the beauty of their ripe corn undulating gently in the fall breeze. Instead, she let out a shriek.

Papa came racing from the barn, his heart bursting out of his chest. He scoured their property for Mama, but of course, she was hidden in the cornfield with that damn machine. Sprinting towards the field, he knocked over a bucket of water that she had forgotten to bring back into the cabin, and dragging it with him for a couple of paces, cursed the day that Isaac Merritt Singer had ever been born.

Mama recognized Kolote and smiled. Extending her hand out to her new friend, Tyee jumped forward using his warrior pose, but Kolote pressed him back. "Do not worry, my father. This is my spiritual guide. It is all right for her to touch me." Tyee dropped his arms, retreated several feet, and waited.

Striding over to the sewing machine, Kolote pulled the quilt up and out from under the needle, demonstrating to his father what he had been talking about. Fascinated, Tyee gestured for Mama to continue sewing. She sat down obediently, shoved the quilt back below the needle, and started stitching. Rat-tat-tat-tat.

Papa paused at the edge of the cornfield. Rat-tat-tat-tat. Well, she must be all right if she's sewin' again. He turned on his heels for a return trip to the barn when suddenly, the tingling on the back of his neck made him pause. Spinning around again, he inched up on his toes to peer through the high corn, but was met with only a sea of stalks. Cautiously, he maneuvered closer to Mama until the machine clattered as if it were next to him. Just then, a gust of wind blew several of the hanging cornhusks back so far they almost doubled over and he caught a good look.

There was Mama, bending over the machine, talking and laughing with two Chinook Indians! He instantly went into fight-or-flight mode, ready to pounce, but to his amazement, the machine stopped, Mama pulled out a quilt and, wrapping it around the older Indian, gave a little laugh before hugging the younger one. Papa, his feet glued to the ground, stared as the older Indian nodded and bowed to his wife. Then, pulling a hand-basket out of his large sack and placing it on top of the iron device, Tyee said something in Chinook Jargon and bowing once more, exited with his son through the south end of the cornfield.

With the corn still at a ninety-degree angle, Mama spotted Papa, gasped, and braced herself for a full tirade. Instead, he remained silent. Then, after several seconds, he spoke. "Seems like you might have saved us from an Injun war." Looking directly into her blue, apprehensive eyes, he grinned for the first time in months and by the time the corn began its rustling again, they were already leaning into one another, holding hands, and conversing in soft tones.

A few days later, the sun positioned itself in a windless sky, warming up Papa as he marched through the cornfield to Mama's favorite spot. Attached to his belt was a small wreath of Juniper leaves swishing and crackling as he walked, and in his arms, a large bundle of threadbare clothes, ready to be cut and pieced into a quilt. He stopped just shy of the 'Devil,' and placing the wreath gently on top of the mahogany casing, laid the clothes neatly in the Indian basket, whistling a childhood song he had suddenly remembered.

At that exact moment, nestled inside his Longhouse, Tyee wrapped his new Log Cabin quilt more securely around his shoulders as he and the other elders sat knee-to-knee in a semi-circle. Everyone had turned to him, eyeing his movements and anticipating major plans for revenge. Instead, with a studied calmness, he opened up a nearby horsehair sack and drew out a long, feathered pipe. He was prepared to talk peace.

LYLA'S SUMMER OF LOVE

August 1969

Face down on the floor in the darkened room, surrounded by tiny light bulb shards, the girl seemed smaller than she actually was. Her fine, shiny hair, made crusty by dried blood, appeared dull, disheveled. Still, Yee's forensics team at first glance commented on what a babe she was.

"Turn her over carefully, so Captain Maynard can take a look." Yee was matter-of-fact. Nothing ever bothered him. Meantime, the low hum of verbal forensic note taking served as a steady background noise.

Face up, even through the bruises, cuts, and swelling, you could tell how stunning Lyla was. A perfect '10' body, clothed in a tie-dyed T-shirt and blue jean cut-offs, she looked like someone you might care about.

"I see some blood in her hair and around her nose. Multiple jagged stab wounds. At least six. Two on her back and four on her front. She's also been hit on the face…further tests will tell us more." Yee had already become detached. To him, her body was only for professional purposes now, much like an artist concentrating on his nude model's form and structure, totally ignoring his libido.

"There's something else. Here's a note we found next to her." Yee pointed to a small, yellow piece of paper as the room fell silent.

H ❏ J A C ✝ T ♂
L Σ M + I Ⅎ ⧣ K
u N ⊯ F ∀ T ⋈ J
± W Y ∞ s Σ V ■
℧ F ℞ ⅄ ⊃ ★ ♛ b
w q ☯ m ↗ L T ♨

Signed ♂ The Zodiac

"The Zodiac again?" Captain Maynard looked glum.

No one spoke for a few seconds. Then, guiding his small, narrow flashlight in a circular pattern around the room, the captain focused in on a small table in one corner and steadied his hand.

Covering the surface of the side table, drug paraphernalia, caught in the thin beam of light, showed boxes of Zig-Zag papers, a couple of alligator roach clips, plastic baggies loaded with weed and pills, crumpled Kleenex sheets, and a beer can intermingled with two colored bandanas. A drug stockpile collecting dust.

Captain Maynard snapped on his gloves before offering anything. "Check out this note with the guys up in the Sacramento Bureau of Criminal Identification & Investigation. Let's make sure it's real." He paused. Then, as an afterthought, "We've got to get this guy. He'll be writing the newspapers again. Soon."

April 1967

Up in his San Francisco State college office, Professor John Cummings stared down at the pile of student papers and sighed. How many times could he read through this stuff without going out of his mind? Year after year, history class after history class, it was all melding together. Soon, he wouldn't give a damn about anything.

Being married to Susan for twenty-four years didn't help either. The perfect wife; the perfect mother. The frigid wife; the tiresome homemaker. The perfect high-society party hostess; the endlessly acerbic personality. Lately, these phrases had begun circulating in his head, no matter how hard he tried to squelch them.

He stood up. On, the hell with it! I'm going out for a walk, he thought. Sorting through the papers on his desk, he made sure his top right-hand desk drawer was locked before turning off the lights.

Strolling down Schrader Street, then crossing the "Panhandle" part of Golden Gate Park, he could feel himself perking up. Hippies were everywhere; Edwardian clothing, long paisley dresses, tie-dye skirts, sandals, dirty blue jeans, East-Indian earrings, long hair on boys' heads and short hair in girls' armpits, all made for great sightseeing. It never failed to amaze him just how far these kids had strayed from his own generation. He was both fascinated and envious.

He continued walking until he reached the front door of the I Thou

Coffee Shop. Outside, a line had already formed, and giving out his name to the hostess, he lit up a cigarette and leaned against the side of the building, just taking in the day's semi-fair weather and hoping for a new lease on life.

"Hey, Prof, when's the next meeting of the SDS?" asked Tom Wallenstein, a particularly annoying student in his History 101 class, shuffling by, his shirt hanging halfway out of his pants.

"Don't you ever read your SDS bulletins, Tom? It's next Thursday at 8 p.m. Be sure to be there." Amenities weren't a high priority today.

"Thanks. I know I gotta clean up my act. See you there, man. Later!" Tom clumped away, happy to have run into his teacher. Everybody liked the Prof. He was like one of them—a true liberal—vehemently against the war in Vietnam, and a chapter head of the local Students for a Democratic Society organization. No establishment there; around him, you could just relax and be yourself.

The line dwindled down to two couples just as some dark clouds were rolling in. By the time he was inside and seated at a table, a few sprinkles were already flicking against the windows as he snubbed out his cigarette and opened up a menu. Feeling better, when one of two waitresses finally ambled over, he actually tossed out a big grin.

"Hey, Prof, how's it goin?" The waitress couldn't have been more than seventeen.

"Good. Good. Thanks for asking. How's by you?" He glanced up at her, then across the room. He had felt a pull.

In the only booth, a lone girl was sitting, reading a book. He had never seen anyone as beautiful—long, shiny blonde hair, parted perfectly in the middle and big doe-brown eyes were only part of the package. A cherub-shaped mouth, very pale yet luscious skin, and an amazing body wrapped in a form-fitting paisley hippie dress, made her look like a Mod-Squad Peggy Lipton, with a touch of Veronica Lake.

He had to meet her, get to know her. Watching her as she read, when she paid her bill and started to leave, he quickly grabbed some cash from his pocket, plunked it down on the table, and followed her out.

He could see her dawdling along the Panhandle on the Pell Street side, maybe twenty yards from him and suddenly he decided to trail her, if only to enjoy how she moved. She seemed to float; a waif in the midst of a chaotic hippie world. At Clayton, she turned left, then left again at Hayes, stopping in front of The Blue Unicorn, but when she entered, he returned to his car and straggled home, unable to get her out of his mind.

"What's the matter, John? You look as if you swallowed a cat!" His wife, Susan, never minced words.

"A strange expression, if ever there was one. No, I'm just tired, is all. I have a lot of stuff to catch up on for school. I'll be up in my study."

Susan shrugged. So what else was new? She did a reverse turn and disappeared into the kitchen.

His study was professorial—floor to ceiling bookcases overflowing with worn books, magazines, and newspapers. Disheveled papers, stacked high on his large mahogany desk, had reached chaotic proportions, and with his Underwood typewriter and lava lamp (a gift from one of his students) close at hand, he sank down into his leather armchair, closed his eyes, and sighed. He could still picture her.

When his private line rang, he practically jumped out of his skin. "Hello. Professor Cummings speaking," he breathed into the mouthpiece then listened to the voice on the other end. "I'll get it to you when I get it to you. Be patient!" he grunted, suddenly flashing on his college roommate returning from one of the elite Yale Skull & Bones meetings. There had always been 'in' and 'out' cliques at school back then, so when he dated, then married the prominent Susan Livingston, the shy, awkward history major suddenly switched paths, and thus became privy to the inner circle and all its implications. It had seemed so important back then, but now, twenty years later, all he could think about was how much he could use a good, stiff drink. Trudging downstairs, he helped himself and by midnight, was passed out on the living room sofa.

The next day, he survived his classes, but he still couldn't get the girl out of his head; he needed to see her one more time. So at 4:15 p.m. he started out, hoping to catch a glimpse of her at the I Thou Coffee Shop.

He didn't have to go far. She was seated on a bench in the Panhandle, looking incredible: A vision in a wide straw hat, bell-bottoms, and a rose-colored tank top. As he approached her, he was searching for a catchy line, but couldn't think straight. She was too damn distracting, particularly up close.

"Hi, I'm Lyla. You're the Prof, aren't you?" He could feel himself melting as her big brown eyes reeled him in.

"Yes, yes, I am. How do you know me?"

"Everyone knows who you are. You're the eight hundred pound gorilla around here, don't you know that?" When she smiled, he wanted to stroke her face.

"I've only seen you once before. How come? Are you a student at SFS?" He was trying to connect.

"No. I was, but then I realized I didn't need to go to school. So now I'm living by myself and doing my own thing." She spoke these lines as if she had rehearsed them before.

"What's that, if I may ask?"

"Macramé. I'm a macramé artist, among other things." Her tone had picked up some confidence.

"Oh. Is that that ropey stuff?" God! That sounded so patronizing! He cringed.

But she didn't seem offended. "Yeah. That's it. Hey, I live nearby. Do you wanna see my studio?"

This was way too easy. "Sure, why not?" He could feel his pulse race and as she stood up, he resisted the urge to put an arm around her waist.

Sandwiched in between crumbling Victorian houses, Lyla's loft on Page Street was a true artist's lair. Depending upon the time of day, high ceilings hovered over long, dusty windowpanes that let shafts of light filter through in variegated patterns. By 4:45 p.m., the rose-blue light had dissolved into a mauve color, casting a particularly subtle tone on all the macramé wall hangings nailed up in her living room area. Twisted, bejeweled rope and yarn were woven together like spider webs, creating intricate designs enhanced by delicate colors. Rock group posters in psychedelic colors and ameba-shaped letterforms covered the wall nearest the kitchen, while another wall was home to black and white photographs of assorted people. On the floor lay three or four large overstuffed pillows edged with gold tassels, along with a legless sofa bed covered with small East Indian-styled pillows—perfect for 'crashers'.

"I...I like your work a lot," he remarked with a half wink. Anything to get in her pants.

"Oh, yeah? Well, coming from you, that says a lot!" Her youth made her even more impressionable.

His eyes zeroed in on her neck. "You even have a macramé around your neck, I see." He needed to keep her interested. "What's that large jewel in the middle of it?"

"Oh, that. It's a precious stone, a ruby, given to me by someone in my past." Her face suddenly shut down.

"May I see it?" He gently reached for the choker.

"Oh, no," she insisted. "This NEVER comes off—not for one second. I even shower with it."

A pregnant silence forced him to look away, but before he could muster a comeback, she asked, "Hey, you want some vino? I have a bottle in the fridge." He nodded and she traipsed off to the kitchen area. When she returned, besides the wine and glasses, she had a plate of cheese and crackers. How civilized. Not a total hippie. Undoubtedly, good breeding.

Three sips in and he looked at his watch. "God, I've got to go. I have an appointment. Sorry. A rain check, perhaps?" he waited a beat. Then, "Would you go out with me?" Fingering his wedding ring, he felt so nervous, so old.

"Sure, that would be a blast!" she beamed. Obviously undeterred by his marital status, maybe she liked the age difference, he thought as they made their arrangements for that Friday night, 9 p.m., her apartment. He sighed. He could always make up some excuse to Susan. She was so predictable, and regular weekend nights with her theater and opera crowd allowed him total independence.

As he knocked on Lyla's door, 9 o'clock sharp, he could feel his palms sweating. Unbelievable! I haven't been like this since I was a teenager, he reflected. Soon, he could hear light, padded footsteps just beyond the door.

The door opened, and his eyes nearly popped out of their sockets. All she had on were blue jean overall cut-offs. That was it; no shirt, no bra, nothing else. It was a perfect end to his day. Instant testosterone managed his movements now—in two seconds, he had his hands all over her, steering her towards the bed.

At 1 o'clock in the morning they were awakened by the sound of a neighbor's laughter outside the apartment.

"Christ!" he blurted out. Glancing at the time and pulling on his clothes, he leaned over to kiss her goodbye, promising, "Don't worry, I'll call you soon!"

Their next date was at his favorite hangout, The Matrix, on Fillmore Street. As Jefferson Airplane played, Lyla looked around, soaking up the atmosphere. Everyone seemed high, whether on alcohol, pot, or LSD. Small round tables stood on top of a sawdust-covered floor, and the lights were turned low to create a soft ambiance. Small clouds of smoke swirled up like mini-tornado funnels, and the clanking of beer mugs resonated across the room. But it was the wall of hieroglyphs that really blew her away; she was just about to make a comment on it when he interrupted her thoughts.

"I just love this place! Can you imagine? The owners thought up the idea of the wall of hieroglyphs. That's my area of expertise, you know." Apparently he liked showing off.

"What do you mean?"

"Well, I've studied these Egyptian letterforms verbatim and sometimes I trace them just to relax."

"You have a strange way of relaxing!" She started to laugh at him.

"OK, OK. Let's relax a different way. Do you want to go back to your place?"

She giggled. "Talk about a one-track mind! OK. Let's…"

He didn't let her finish. "Oh, God, I forgot. I've got to go to a quick meeting at school. Can I come back in, say, an hour and a half?"

"Wait. What kind of date are you?"

"I promise I'll make it up to you later." He had already risen.

Make it up later to her, he did, and for many months beyond that, like clockwork, interrupted only by his SDS and college meetings, and occasionally by his wife, but clockwork, nevertheless. The explosive sex was far better than he had thought possible.

But one Saturday afternoon in bed, John grew pensive. "Tell me about your family. If we're going to be with each other, I should know more about you."

"There's not much to tell. My mom has never had an opinion about anything. She's definitely under my dad's thumb."

"Well, what about your dad? What's he like?" He delighted in probing; his Socratic classroom techniques had been a part of him for too long.

"I really don't want to think about him. He was always a cold son-of-a-bitch to me when I was little and as I got older, I didn't like who he was and how he acted towards me. Besides, he was always getting away with things, too." She turned towards the wall.

"Tell me, what things?" Tact was low on his totem pole.

"Leave me alone!" She flung off the covers and disappeared into the bathroom, leaving him with one eyebrow raised. Obviously, a nerve had been struck.

January 1968

The winter morning certainly proved milder than anyone could have anticipated. After weeks of rain, the sponsors of the Human Be-In were ecstatic. All the Haight shopkeepers had closed their doors, excited, albeit nervous about the upcoming event, and even the newspaper, The Berkeley Barb, usually condescending towards such happenings, was overwhelmingly supportive.

"Prof. We've got to go to this thing. I mean it! No excuses this time. I want to share my world with you. Anyway, don't you want to see Alan Ginsberg and Timothy Leary do their thing?"

John sighed. Nothing was worth a fight.

The Be-In was all set for 1 p.m., but by 9 a.m., they could hear people arriving. At first there were scattered voices outside her apartment building but soon, a wall of sound emerged, as thousands gathered, then headed towards Golden Gate Park Stadium.

Dragging him by the hand, she led him to the stadium, where they were surrounded by multitudes of hippies and freaks. Bright, flashy banners depicting marijuana plants and the latest LSD tablets, White Lightning, blended with robes, Edwardian clothing, T-shirts, corduroys, long skirts, paisley blouses, and the ever-present sandals—sandals in the summer and sandals with socks in the crisp, cold air. Colorful flowers, fruit, incense, along with tambourines, congas, and cymbals colluded into an all-pervasive atmosphere of Free Love.

Speaker after speaker, rock group after rock group held the crowd of thirty thousand captive. There was Ginsberg reciting the "Hari Om Namo Shuuya" chant and Leary declaring that "Turn on, tune in, and drop out" was the only true way of the world now, while joints passed freely and the few policemen present looked the other way.

Back in the Haight as the sky darkened, Lyla, smoking a joint and humming a Beatles song from the "Revolver" album, turned to John. "Hasn't this experience been transcendent? Can't you feel the love pouring through your entire body?"

"I guess so. I also feel hunger. Let's go to the Matrix for a bite."

Her jaw tightened. "You SOB. Just like my dad! Always knocking me, then trying to make up for it later. You..."

Suddenly, extra police descended on the area, randomly picking up stragglers for 'loitering', and carting them off to jail.

"Hey, hey, hey HEY! What the hell are you doing?" John protested as he tried to loosen his handcuffs." He looked over to Lyla with her own hands tied behind her back. She was crying softly.

He softened. "Babe, don't worry." He managed a comforting tone, but Susan and job security were the only real things on his mind.

Forty-nine people were housed in jail cells that night until 4:30 a.m., thirty-one males in one holding cell, and seventeen females in a neighboring cell. It was a depressing night, filled with "Those are the 'Pigs' for you!" "All we want is peace, man," and "America's not the place I thought it was."

Lyla kept straining to hear the Prof's voice, but it never came. Finally, dirty and starving, she was released with the other women, but before she left, she questioned the night watchman about a John Cummings.

"Oh, he was released earlier last night." He stared at the beautiful girl.

"With all the other guys?"

"Naw. He was let out immediately. Captain's orders." He chuckled and shook his head.

Outside, on the police station steps, Lyla paused. Why would John get special treatment? Because he's a professor and the rest aren't? But Professor O'Brian was there along with the other men arrested. Well, maybe, maybe he was released, too.

She went back inside, making her way through the prostitutes, petty thieves, and drug addicts.

"Did Prof. O'Brian also get released?"

The busy night watchman was beginning to get irritated. "Naw, your Professor Cummings's a special case. Now, run on home little girl, and don't bother me," he snapped. Suddenly, it occurred to her how little she knew about her lover.

By 11 a.m., the Prof stopped by, hoping for some attention. But when he entered her apartment, he saw Lyla in tears. A half torn-up letter with the opening words, 'I'm so sorry,' lay on the coffee table, inches away from a large glass of Chardonnay. Seeing him, she immediately reached over, grabbed the letter and threw the two pieces into the trashcan.

Angling in to read the return address, he muttered," What's gotten into you Lyla? Why all the mystery? Who's the letter from?"

"They're from my father."

"They're? You mean there are others?"

"Yes. But I don't even bother to read most of them." Her jaw was set hard.

"Listen, you've got to work out your anger at your dad. You're an adult, after all."

"Please don't lecture me. You're not at school now." As she got up to throw out the trash, John reached out to her, but she dodged by him and continued on out into the hallway.

Shuffling over to the refrigerator, he pulled out a bottle of wine, and pouring himself a tall glass, settled in for rest of the afternoon on the couch. When she sat down next to him, she made sure there were a couple of pillows between them. Then she lit up a joint of Mexican Brown and switched on the TV.

He immediately started in. "What a waste; a goddamn waste. I've got too many other important things to do, I…"

"Hi, I'm Patricia Wilkinson, part of the news team at WBBTV in Yorktown, New York. I'm here in Huntington, New York, waiting to get an interview with the CEO of Dow Chemical Co, Mr. Jonas T. Ashton. Mr. Ashton, do you have anything to say about the napalm bombings in Vietnam that have killed thousands of people? What do you have to say? Mr. Ashton—Mr. Ashton…"

A distinguished middle-age man, sporting an expensive three-piece suit and an unexpressive face, automatically dismissed all microphones as he climbed into the back seat of a Lincoln Continental Town car. Then it cut to a commercial.

Riveted, John sat still for several seconds before turning back to Lyla, pointedly staring down at her lap.

"Hey, Babe, come closer." For the first time in months, he was feeling affectionate. She eyed him cautiously before edging over.

A minute later, she stated flatly, "I'm off to bed. See you later." He nodded. Whatever.

The bathroom was still, save for the leaky faucet. Drip-drip-drip-drip-drip. Transparent beads were slowly sliding down towards the drain as Lyla stared at the oval tin can resting on the tile counter next to the sink. Drip-drip-drip-drip. Inside the can, White Lightning pills from the Human Be-In peered up at her as she paused, unsure of her next move. Her last LSD trip, hidden from the Prof, had been bad. A real nightmare. No way did she want to repeat that performance, but now, the thought of blotting out everything was far too enticing. She breathed in, then, picking out a tab, quickly popped it into her mouth. There. That's done. I'll go and lie down for a little while.

Twenty minutes later, when John went looking for her, she was lying under the covers. "Hey, Babe, where did you go?" He pulled the blankets back and stopped, horrified.

She was curled up in a fetal position, shivering, clutching at the bedding as if it were her lifeline. Little kitten noises were mewing out of her throat, but when he reached out to soothe her, she snarled, in full self-protection mode. Leaping out of bed, she ran down the hall, hyperventilating as she tried to unlock the front door.

"What's wrong, baby, what's wrong" His body landed hard against her back as she fiddled with the chain, and although he issued soft, cooing reassurances, she batted at him twice before taking off into the kitchen where she started pulling pots and pans down from their racks. Finally, he grabbed her, forced her into the shower, and turning on the warm water, ignored her howls until the soothing wet curtain covered her body and her sobs slowly dwindled into silence. Later, tucking her into bed, he wondered why the hell he was still with her.

January 1969

During the day, Norm Quentin was quiet, awkward. Sears Roebuck white shirts, black slacks, and a pocket protector housing a neat row of pens and mechanical pencils all screamed 'nerd,' making him the butt of jokes at his office. But at night, when his real work would begin, he could perform all his duties without any interruption. A CIA member since the early 1960's, it was inconceivable to him that anyone would not give total allegiance to his or her country. Anything less should be labeled as treasonous, so when John Cummings informed him he wanted out, Quentin went ballistic.

"I can't take it anymore. I don't care what you say. This is not what I bargained for when I signed up with you people years ago. I was just a kid. What did I know?" The Prof pounded his fist against the side of a building.

"Don't you remember our agreement? Aren't you forgetting your reputation as the great American Liberal? We can expose you at any time, you know."

"I know, I know! You guys have me in a vise. I just can't handle the pressure anymore."

Quentin chuckled. "Maybe if you got rid of your little hippie girl, things might be less—well, less complicated, shall we say."

"Shut up about her. Just shut up!" That's my business!"

"You do realize, don't you," Quentin persisted, "she's nothing but trouble. We know all about her; far more than even you know. I'm telling you, she's more trouble than she's worth. If I were you, I'd dump her."

"Well, you're not me, are you? Just leave me alone! Talk to Ashton. He's the boss. He's the one who got me into this business years ago. Maybe, he'll let me go." As John charged off, he left the agent alone, shaking his head in the shadows of their designated alley.

May 1969

At 3 a.m., overactive hormones jolted Susan awake, shrouding her in a fine mist of perspiration. As usual. This time she glanced over to his side of the bed. Empty, of course. *He's with her again. Who the hell does she think she is?*

Undoubtedly one of his students. God damn him! How typical! This time, I've got to do something...

Chambers & Co., nestled between the Tanner Coffee Shop and Lee's Cleaner's, offered little diversion for people buying a cup of coffee just before they picked up their laundry. Caked grit on a smoke-smeared windowpane barely camouflaged a second-rate private investigative agency that lured desperate housewives craving revenge on their foolish husbands. Susan Livingston Cummings was no exception. A faint smudge of frosted lipstick on the Prof's collar the night before was the final straw.

"My fee, Mrs. Cummings, is the usual per diem. Here's my invoice." A hung-over Joe Chambers handed her a piece of paper as she nodded and extracted an envelope of cash from her pocketbook. This time, she was determined to nail the bastard.

"How are you going to do it? Follow him secretly, like in the movies?" Her patronizing tone was a little overbearing.

"Actually, I was thinking of auditing one of his classes first, get to know him a little," replied Chambers defensively, proud of the unique approach he took with his cases.

"Just remember. No matter how charming or clever he is, don't let him fool you. He's only out for himself." She snapped her purse shut and stood up to leave.

Two days later, sitting in a packed lecture hall, the P.I. observed the Prof. adjusting the microphone on the podium, seconds before the lecture began. Cummings was amazing. Anecdotal details supplemented a fascinating slide show of ancient Egypt and afterwards, when the students surrounded their teacher like bees buzzing over a honeycomb feast, probing him with questions and totally at ease with him, he was charming. More than that. He reeked charm.

It was getting late when Chambers sauntered out of Pratt Hall and headed towards Fillmore Avenue and his favorite watering hole. He could relax and start his Prof. John Cummings campaign master planning, his favorite part of every job.

He entered the Matrix and walked over to the bar. Placing his jacket on top of the counter, he extracted a pad from his briefcase and etched out some notes for several minutes before stowing it away again. He was on his second drink when he looked up to see the Prof. settling down on a neighboring barstool and ordering a drink.

"Hey, you look familiar. Have we met before?" John was cordial.

"Yes. I just audited your class—great lecture, by the way," Joe added.

The bartender slid a mug of beer over to the Prof, who then held it up as a salutation. "Are you interested in history, Mr…?"

"Pete Hamilton." Joe always had a ready alias. "Yes, I'm interested."

"Well then, you've come to the right place. I…" He was interrupted by the arrival of a beautiful young blonde girl, dressed in black bell-bottoms and a slightly sheer white peasant blouse. "I'd like to introduce you to a friend of mine, Lyla. Lyla, this is Pete Hamilton. And visa versa."

After several handshakes, John indicated Joe should join in, ordered another round, and located a small table in the corner for the three of them.

Settling down with their drinks, Chambers turned to Lyla. He was trying hard not to stare too much at her exquisite face. "So, are you a student at SFS?"

"No, I'm not." Period.

"That's a very pretty thing around your neck," he managed to say.

"Thanks." Lyla kept looking up at the Prof.

"Yeah, that's The Necklace. It never leaves her neck. Isn't that right, Babe?" John was stroking the handle on his mug.

Lyla nodded, her face turning pink. "It's symbolic to me, that's all. It's not a crime, is it?"

Chambers didn't know what to say. They didn't seem that much in love.

By the sixth round, the men were slurring their words. "Hey, you know, my girl is the original hippie girl," John garbled. "She's stayed with Ken Kesey on his La Honda compound and even with Timothy Leary back east. She tells me she knows Chet Helms and Bill Graham up in San Fran, and that she was privy to the first few posters made for the Avalon Ballroom." The Prof. was flying high.

"That's old news, Prof. Now I'm doing my own thing." Lyla looked hurt.

"Right, your big art career. Of course, you're the best macramé artist on the planet, and we all know how important macramé is for the evolution of mankind!"

"Go to hell!" She grabbed her drink and stalked off.

Through an alcoholic haze, Joe made a mental note. Maybe the old guy would go back to his wife, after all. He smiled and reached for his mug.

John laughed and checked out his new drinking companion. The two men nodded at one another, and with the immediate acknowledgement of the vicissitudes of all women, became instant comrades, making the Matrix their permanent watering hole during the coming months. There, John regaled the detective with great stories and Joe did think once or twice about taking Susan's money as he downed beer after beer.

June 1969

"Why don't you come with me to an SDS meeting? You'd get a kick out of it and you'll see some good-looking co-eds." John tried to gently push Chambers up the street with him.

"No. That's a little too much for me. You go, and enjoy." There was only so much the P.I. would do.

The meeting hall was packed with students and hangers-on, the hardened 'revolutionaries' up front, ready to change the country at any cost. They listened to John intently, taking notes, much like the students at one of his large lectures. But the outer layers of people were the most lax and far more interested in each other—how to pick up chicks or guys, and what kind of munchies were available.

Suddenly, several policemen infiltrated the room, declaring a 'round up' of subversives. They marched past the outer circles and headed directly for the middle with the true followers. Blocking protesters, they took out their clubs, swinging them high overhead as a warning.

John stood planted in the center, and like the great captain of a ship, refused to let his people go under. "Everybody, everybody! Remain calm. Nobody is going to hurt you. I am here for you. But stay CALM!"

The police, recognizing his power, wormed their way over to him. They muttered a few words in his ear as they carefully handcuffed him before the inner core began their protests.

"No, no, don't worry. We are all in this together!" John smiled, offering a gesture of reassurance. Watching some other people being handcuffed as well, his soothing tones helped to maintain peace, and as the police led them all out of the hall, the peripheral crowd started cheering and applauding in support of their great chieftain.

One of the members remembered Lyla and ran to her apartment. Knocking on her door, he yelled," Open up! Open up! The Prof's in trouble."

She flung the door open, wide-eyed, and within seconds, was charging over to the police station with the SDSer. But seeing the same night watchman from the year before at his desk, she shook her head. It was deja-vu in spades.

"Well, well, well; same old, same old. You here about your precious professor again?" Amusement wrapped across his face.

"Yeah, where is he? Is he OK?"

"Of course he is. Whatever his connections are, the Gods are looking out for your guy. Don't you worry about him. He's been released already!" The Watchman raised one eyebrow. "Maybe you should rethink your boyfriends, sweetie," he cautioned, observing her frightened eyes.

July 1969

The music had been loud all evening at the Matrix; by 11:00 p.m. sharp, it was blasting. Psychedelic lights and colors swirled throughout the room, spinning everyone's head, whether they were stoned or straight. Soon, the hieroglyphics on the back wall appeared connected—codes intertwined like colonies of mutant ants following their queen, bustling towards a special meal.

John sauntered in with Lyla and surveyed the room as a waitress sidled up to them both with a circular tray balanced on her left fingertips and a pen clutched in her right hand. Lyla was slightly wasted, but he was on high alert. A barmaid led them over to a far corner table, hidden by a large post, and motioned for them to sit down.

Lyla immediately leaned against John and closed her eyes; the night had started early for her, and she was more than ready for bed. Annoyed, he gently removed her head from his shoulder, shouted a few words to her over the noise, and got up to go to the men's room. After he returned, he eyed the club, nodding to the music and trying to look cool. As if by magic, Quentin appeared and took two steps towards their table, but stopped when catching sight of Lyla. He about-turned and shifted away from them.

She waited a beat before asking John, "Who's that?"

"Who's—what? What are you talking about?"

"The man who was just here. He obviously knew you." She was wide-awake now.

"You're stoned. I don't know what you're talking about." Suddenly something on the table next to them seemed to fascinate him.

"The man who was coming to our table was looking directly at you, like he was going to say something. And for your information, I am not that stoned!"

"OK, OK. Let's get out of here." Steering her away from Quentin's position at the bar he ushered her out of the club.

Back in her apartment, Lyla wouldn't let it go. "Prof., you knew that guy. I know it. What's all the secrecy?"

"What secrecy? You're getting so whacked out on this LSD stuff, you're getting psychotic, you know that? Hell, I might as well go home to Susan!"

Before she could protest, he made a beeline to the street, slamming the front door on his way out and leaving her open-mouthed.

But he didn't go home. Sitting at his favorite table back at the Matrix, John realized how much he needed a break from his life. *The women in my life are gonna kill me! I don't really need Lyla. And for that matter, I could certainly do without Susan. Oh, to hell with everyone. I wonder where my new buddy is?* He searched the room for Chambers, but when Joe did arrive, he wasn't alone. Accompanying him was a man with salt and pepper shoulder length hair, sporting a blue shirt, a grey and black herringbone vest, blue jeans, black jacket, and cowboy boots.

"Prof., I'd like you to meet a friend, Mark Cowling. He works for the San Francisco Chronicle, and has been telling me some juicy tidbits about the Zodiac case."

John brightened. "Sit down! Sit down!"

A half hour later, amidst blaring music and a smoky lightshow reflecting off the beer mugs, the three men stayed thick in discussion, oblivious to everything around them.

"You have to admit, the Zodiac's damn good at what he does," Cowling offered.

"Yeah, but let's not celebrate the man," Chambers said. "After all, he's already killed, what? Five people? He's been clever all right, but I do believe he's going to get tripped up one of these days. What do you think, Prof?"

"I think the man's brilliant. I particularly enjoy his codes. That's an added treat. I mean, the ancient Egyptians had their hieroglyphics, the Pakistanis and Indians had their Indus scripts, and there were the Linear B clay tablets of the Minoan civilizations. Why not have your own code?" He stopped, self-conscious.

"No, don't stop, Prof. I agree. Now, this is something only the San Francisco Chronicle and the SF police know…" Cowling leaned forward, drawing them closer. "Apparently, the way he killed his victims on the lake was a little different than most of his other ones. For example, he stabbed the woman in the back and the front. Weird, huh?"

The three men grew quiet, absorbed in their own images.

Quentin knew that if the moon were full, its darker shadows would most likely cast better areas for hiding things and people, so when he arranged the meeting with his supervisor, Ashton, he actually researched a good night on the Lunar Time Table.

"OK. Now what's the problem?" Ashton kept his hat low over his forehead as he inched further back into the orchestrated shadows.

"This Professor, this John Cummings, says he wants out." Quentin couldn't conceal his contempt.

"So? He's not all that important to us, is he? He and I go back a long way. He was my roommate at Yale, you know. Maybe I should cut him some slack; I can appreciate his feelings."

Quentin grunted. "I told him if he didn't cooperate, we would expose him for all he's worth!"

"Quentin, don't be so dramatic, for God's sake! After all, we're not the Nazis, the last time I checked. Let the man go. He was never all that important, anyway. Besides, we've got bigger fish to fry."

"But, sir. I don't think we should let this one go. You know who he's been seeing, don't you?" Quentin angled towards the CIA veteran and touched his cashmere coat.

"I know who he's with, dammit. But I said drop it! And by the way, never touch me!" Ashton's voice had chilled a good twenty degrees.

Quentin stepped back two paces, flustered. He glanced at a car going by, then back again, but his boss had vanished.

The hell with Ashton! he ruminated. He's getting way too soft, anyway. Could be those rumors of him leaving Dow Chemical are true. But somebody's got to fight for our country. I guess it'll be me keeping an eye on the Prof and his loose cannon girlfriend, he thought, returning to his bare-bones walk-up.

August 1969

These days, going over to Lyla's was thoroughly depressing. The Haight was a mere shell of its former self. Many neighborhood stores stood empty, the few opened ones overlaid with window bars or nailed wooden planks. On the street, most people were no longer hippies and freaks; the amphetamine and heroin users, pushers, and the homeless had taken over, constantly in search of shelter. By the time he reached her place, he was primed for a tiff.

"That's right, Prof. Tear me down again, like always. I don't know what you're doing with me, man. Why are you still here?" Even with dilated pupils and unkempt hair, she looked amazing.

He hesitated. He really didn't know why he was there; he couldn't quite explain it himself.

August 1969

"I know all about your little chippie, dear!" Susan made a mock-toast to her husband later that evening as soon as he walked in the door. Her afternoon had included a tell-me-what-you-got-now-or-else showdown with Joe Chambers.

"Susan, I've got a splitting headache. Not now!"

"Of course, not now, not ever. A has-been, holding onto his youth by climbing into bed with his co-eds. My, my, how *original*." The last word was more of a snarl.

SEWING CAN BE DANGEROUS

He could feel his chest tightening. "Well, I see you've gotten a head start on your nightcap," he sneered.

"That's right! Just twist the whole thing back on me." She downed a large shot. "Maybe you'll find out I'm not such a doormat, after all."

The vise was squeezing his upper body. "Are you threatening me?"

"Just wait and see. Time will tell." She threw her head back and laughed, spilling her drink down her Evan Piccone blouse.

He had difficulty climbing up the stairs up to his study after that, and when his private phone rang, he almost didn't pick up the receiver. Please, not Quentin. Please, not Lyla. Peace. I just need some peace.

"Cummings?" Quentin was curt.

"Yes, what is it?" John could barely speak.

"Maybe Ashton's inclined to let you go, but I'm not. I mean it. You produce those papers or else…" Click.

His breaths were coming in little shallow hiccups. Maybe I should get checked out. This could be a mild heart attack. Maybe…

The phone rang again, turning his last hiccup into small whoop. Automatically, he reached for the receiver.

"Prof. I really need to see you. Pleeeeeeeze come!"

"Lyla, I don't think…" The Indians were circling the wagons.

"Come on, Prof. Come just this once for me."

Entering her apartment, he moved like a robot, numb, expressionless. But just seeing her lying on the couch, he could feel the anger surge. "You've become a total acid head, pissing away your life like all the rest of your generation," he snarled. "Here, I want you to hear this. This, from one of your sacred sources of pot. Here, here. Listen to what it says."

Grabbing a package labeled Sacred Seeds, he started reading its cover. "A little warms the heart, too much burns the soul."

"So, what the hell are you talking about, man?"

"You don't get it, do you? You don't get the idea of moderation. That's because your brain cells have already atrophied, and your synapses can't connect anymore!" He turned away in disgust.

"That's a load! You're still stuck in the 1950's, man! So anal. And seeing some of the things I've seen lately, maybe you're more establishment than I had thought."

"What the hell does that mean?" His tone sharpened.

"I…I don't know. I'm just talking. "She paused for a few seconds. "It's just, well, you won't ever try any stuff with me, not even marijuana brownies. I wanna feel like you're with me, you know? I mean, sometimes you drink like a fish. But this is the 60's. Why not try getting high my way?" She turned petulant.

If only the chest pressure would stop, he stewed. Perhaps I am having a heart attack. Oh, why can't Ashton get me out of this? I just want out. I want out with Lyla, I want out with Susan. Oh, God. The hell with everyone.

He looked over at her, shook his head, and sighed. "OK, I'll try a tiny bit of acid. Then after that, leave me be."

Lyla flung her arms around him and as they held onto each other several seconds, it was a reminder of old times. Then, trotting off toward the bathroom, she returned with her enamel tin can. It was empty.

"Uh-oh. OK, I know where I can get more of these guys. Come with me." She smiled mysteriously; she was in control again.

"Where the hell are we going at 9 p.m. on a Tuesday night? I think I should be getting home." He could feel his pulse throbbing through his ears.

"Oh, noooooo you don't. Not this time!" Lyla took him by the hand and started pulling him after her. Still holding hands, they rounded the corner and went up a flight of steps into a dilapidated apartment building. Once inside the urine-stained vestibule, she led him downstairs into an L-shaped basement apartment with a solitary light bulb just inside the front door. The window, covered with an ornamental iron burglar grill, sat half-hidden from the street. An old mattress lay on the floor in a far corner, and a small table was placed off to one side, covered with drug paraphernalia, a beer can, several crumpled Kleenex, and a pair of scissors. The only things he recognized were three of her macramé pieces on one wall, arranged in order of size—papa-bear size, mother-bear size, and even a baby-bear size.

"What the hell kind of place is this? This is creepy, Lyla. I don't need this now. Let's go, please!"

"I know. It's not my apartment. It's a friend's, but it's my hangout sometimes; that's why some of my pieces are on the walls. Please. The police will never find us here. There's only one neighbor and she's never in. Please, please?"

He was so tired of fighting them all. So tired. Maybe just half a tab and then I can go home and sleep for a week.

He stepped forward and she popped five tiny pills into his mouth. They both stared at each other, their arms down at their sides.

"What now?" He broke the silence.

"Now, we wait."

A minute passed. Two minutes. Three minutes. Four minutes. This isn't so bad, he thought, relieved. But when the room started taking on different dimensions, he was confused. Did the north wall come in two inches, or was it his imagination? No, wait. It did move. Or did it? He wasn't sure. The macramés were activating into tiny movements. How come he didn't notice that before? Oh, my God! Are those Black Widow spiders or just Daddy Long Legs? Wait. That wall is definitely coming in towards me. I can see it now, and why didn't Lyla warn me about the spiders? That bitch! She's no better than Quentin! You can't trust anyone! You can't...

"John! Are you OK? I think you're having a bad trip." Lyla's voice was beginning to quiver.

"What?" His voice crackled through the hollow room.

"You just called me a bitch! And who is Quentin?"

He stared at her. Her head looked enormous and her mouth, so distorted—a spotted grouper about to surround its prey amongst the corrals. Hey! You're ugly, you're evil! Why are you doing this to me? You're one of them, sent to kill me! You're..."

"John, get a grip! You're really, really scaring me now. Let's get someone." Lyla's wide eyes took up one quarter of her face.

The spiders are building a Cat's Cradle of tangles. If I look away, maybe they won't be there when I turn back. Crap! They're still there. Now they're multiplying. Oh, God. Oh God!

"What spiders? Please, please calm down!"

He saw her as if for the first time. "Yeah, that's right. The Ken Kesey/Timothy Leary girl. The original hippie. The one who is also spying on me. The one who thinks she knows all about me."

Lyla came towards him with her arms outstretched. "Yes, I'm the hippie girl, the one who loves you. I don't care what you're into. I..."

Suddenly, his large hands were around her neck, choking her, her macramé amulet intertwined with his thumbs.

"Pl-e-uuh-uh-uh,"eeked out of her throat like a human tube of toothpaste slowly being squeezed out.

He released one hand, yanking her necklace off onto the floor, and as she tried to duck, his other hand swung up and smacked her face on the right side. She let out a scream and ran for the front door, but the lock wouldn't release and catching up with her, they both tumbled together onto the floor against the wall, arms flailing, legs kicking—octopus-style.

"Stop! Stop! It's me, it's Lyla!" she shrieked. But he was beyond that now. His face twisted with rage as he seized her by her hair and punched her mouth, knocking her several feet away.

She lay still while he grabbed an umbrella lying nearby. As he raised it up over his head, it broke the exposed light bulb, shattering glass all around them, and for a split second, he studied her inert form. *Gotta stop her. Gotta stop them all!* Groping the wall in the dark, he made it over to the table and reached for the scissors. *Gotta stop them. Gotta...*

Scissors in hand, he worked his way back to the door until he could feel her body at his feet. Kneeling down, he touched her soft hair and cheek. The swelling had already begun and he could feel her directly beneath him as the scissors entered her stomach and chest. *One—you'll never get me—two—they can't get me—three—oh, God—four—oh, God!*

He sank back on his haunches, tingling. The room was spinning and he thought he could hear someone gasping for life, but it was only his own breathing. All of a sudden, he felt so exhausted. Even more exhausted than when he was a teenager with Mono and he could barely make it to the bathroom. *I need to sleep,* he reasoned. *Sleep...*

When he woke up, he had a throbbing headache and had to strain to see in the semi-dark. What time was it? And where was Lyla? He glanced over to his left and saw a large shape resting on the floor. "Lyla? Is that you?" He inched over to her.

She was so still, so soundless. Reaching out to her, his hand touched moisture. *What the—!* Something was terribly wrong. He stood up and tried turning on the light switch, but nothing happened, so he reached into his pocket for a box of matches he had on him from The Matrix. Striking a match, he turned to face Lyla. She lay stagnant, in a crumpled position.

"Lyla? Lyla?" He could see clearly now. *Oh, God! Was he having a nightmare? Or did he? No! No! NO!"*

His mind raced. *My life is over. Over!* He held his hands over his eyes, struggling to think. After a long two minutes, two words popped into his brain without warning. *The Zodiac.* The Zodiac killed two of his victims by a knife—two hits to the backs and several more to the stomach, the journalist had said. Maybe, just maybe…A pair of scissors? He glanced down. On the floor next to him were the scissors, still slightly warm and sticky.

He gathered them up, turned her over and shuddering, drove two more thrusts into her back. Then he carefully wiped them off, put them in his right jacket pocket and was exiting when something caught his eye.

The light was beginning to filter in through the window, causing a bluish tint everywhere and giving the ruby in the center of her precious amulet a purplish glow, like a piece of coal still smoldering in a turned-off barbeque. Her umbrella in hand, he quickly scooped the necklace up and tossed it into his other pocket before hurrying out the door.

Back at her apartment, he cleaned himself, got into another one of his outfits, and dumped the bloodstained clothes into a garbage bag. Then, carefully wiping down every surface, he searched for diaries, a personal telephone book, and any other incriminating evidence before sitting down at her desk and pulling out a part of the San Francisco Chronicle from his jacket.

He had already hatched a plan. Extracting a pencil and piece of paper from her top desk drawer, he meticulously began tracing one of the Zodiac's codes from a newspaper section, taking his time in order to get it right.

August 1969

Blinding flash bulbs aimed at her body made talking to the detectives difficult, but John managed to display an appropriate level of shock.

"Prof. I'm so sorry. Is there anything I can do?" Chambers inquired.

"I really don't want my wife Susan involved in any of this."

"Of course. Do you know who Lyla's family is and where they live?" Once a P.I., always a P.I.

"Her name's Lyla O'Neil. You'll have to go from there."

Back in her apartment, John made it clear to Captain Maynard that his wife was not a part of this and his relationship to the deceased was a private matter. At the same time, he dropped some important names to the captain who nodded knowingly.

"Hey, I found a bundle of letters in her closet," a rooky detective puffed up his chest.

Curious, John couldn't restrain himself. "Let me see that," he blurted out pushing past several of the others.

The detective revealed the return addresses— always the same: J.T. Ashton, 154 West Elm Street, Scarsdale, New York. Oh, my God! ASHTON!

"I found her birth certificate in a cardboard box." The rooky swelled with self-pride.

John strode over and peered at the document. "Lyla Ashton, born Corona, N.Y., 1949. Mother's Maiden Name: O'Neil. Father: Jonas Thomas Ashton." All this time. Ashton—my God!

"Come on, Prof. Let's get out of here and get a drink." Chambers knew that was the way to relax him, but after an hour or two at the Matrix, the two drinkers had had enough and started to exit the club just as open faucets of rain pelted them.

"Man! I forgot a jacket and umbrella tonight. It's awful out." Chambers began to shiver.

"Here. Take my-my-thingy...I mean—my jacket. I gotta umbrella-for-the-rain-go over my head." Sloshed, the Prof took off his jacket, handed it to Chambers, and staggered off towards his car.

The P.I. slipped on the jacket and tried to hail a cab. No such luck. He wanted to form a whistle with his lips, but he was too wasted. He thrust his hands into the pockets to keep warm, hoping for a vacant taxi to show up soon. Poor Prof. Terrible. The Zodiac's at it again. Poor Lyla. Poor...

His left hand closed around something in the left pocket, the right knocked against something brittle. What the? Even in the rain the ruby amulet sparkled, emitting an infinitesimal flicker and the scissors looked too clean.

"The Necklace. It never leaves her neck..." And scissors?

Within 72 hours, Quentin and Chambers were standing side by side, watching John being led off to jail, his head down and the handcuffs reflecting the last of the late summer's sunset.

Chambers turned towards Quentin. "Did you know him?"

"In a way. You?"

"In a way." The two men wouldn't admit to more.

The Prof started to get into the squad car then paused. Looking back in their direction, he figured they both might have shown up.

Quentin approached the car. "You poor dumb bastard," he said softly. "You could have gotten out in the end, you know. Ashton would have let you get out, especially because of her. You poor, dumb bastard!" he repeated as the black and white sped away.

NIGHTMARE AT FOUR CORNERS

Curiously enough, it was Helen's housekeeper who first noticed a couple of things out-of-whack: a portable phone shoved deep into the sofa cushions, a shower cap left carelessly on the dining room table. Small things, unworthy of most people's attention. Yet Little Wind had a sixth sense. She realized her boss was headed for trouble long before anyone else did; still, she kept silent. After all, it was not part of the Hopi tradition to offer opinions unless directly asked.

But when Helen couldn't even pull on her own panty hose without ugly, guttural sobs permeating the bedroom, Little Wind came running. The Native American didn't need any explanations; wrapping her bronze arms around her distraught employer, she simply held on until the sobs slowly dissolved into soft whimpers.

"I can't take it anymore!" her employer finally managed. "My life seems so pointless. The kids are gone, my husband has his own life. What should I do? I've lost, well—me."

Little Wind broke the boundaries. "You must follow your heart—it is telling you where to go." She sat very still and straight, as if she were still there on the reservation her people had originated so long ago, with the southwest wind gently undulating around the pueblo structures, echoing through the canyons of smog-less air.

Helen's friends and family had cautioned her about hiring a Native American Indian, especially from the Hopi tribe. They were all too proud, too distant, they warned, but Helen wouldn't listen to any of them, and now, having once trusted her own instincts, she took another chance. Subjects that had always remained taboo were finally discussed, and Helen was left with a flicker of hope.

The next day, much to the chagrin of her psychiatrist, she cancelled all her appointments, hummed while she showered, and searched for the phone number of an old newspaper editor with whom she had worked years before. She was returning to journalism.

"I'm going to try and write an article for my former editor," she muttered, half to herself, half to Little Wind as she faced a couple of family photos up on the wall. Her housekeeper stepped in to take a closer look, but all she could see were various white people receiving awards.

Helen continued. "I can do this! After all, I come from a family of prize-winning journalists for God's sake. Actually, that was my goal many years ago. Now I'd be happy if I could just get a good by-line."

Little Wind drew a deep breath and returned to her ironing.

After twenty years, the *Marvelton Times* had changed exponentially. Industrial cubicles, outfitted with brand new PC's were covered with a mauve colored fabric that deadened every sound, from the steady stream of telephone calls to the constant hum of keyboard clicks. It used to be so much noisier, Helen mused as she was ushered into Michael McGruen's office.

"Well, well, well. Helen, you look great!" Coming out from behind his massive desk, Michael bear-hugged his former employee before she sank down into one of his leather chairs.

"What's it been? Ten years, twelve?" He sat on the edge of his desk, rubbing his hands together.

"Twenty. Look, Mike, I won't waste your time. Frankly, I need to work. I will do any assignment—anything, just so I can get back into the swing of things. When I worked for you right out of college, before kids, you told me I had a lot of potential, remember?"

"Whoa, whoa—back up a bit, will ya? That was twenty years ago, Helen! What have you been doing in the meantime, playing mommy and housewifey-poo? How do I know if you still have 'it'?" Mike was suddenly all business.

Red-faced, Helen cleared her throat. "Look, if I come up with a great story, will you at least give me a shot at it? Please, c'mon, please, Mike, for old times sake?" Her soft, pleading eyes reminded him of earlier attractions.

"Jesus, Helen. Let me think about it, OK? Meantime, it would certainly influence me if you did come up with a good story. See what you can do, all right? Now, remember, no promises. Just wow me!"

These days her ranch-style house, so vibrant when the kids were young,

187

now felt particularly hollow and with her husband Bill still at work, the only signs of life seemed to be coming from Little Wind's bedroom, next to the kitchen. Tiptoeing in that direction, Helen could hear her maid's monotonal, hiccup-like chant interspersing with a light bell tinkling over and over again. Just outside the door, she stopped and peered in.

Sitting on the bed, cross-legged 'Indian style,' Little Wind had gathered around her an assortment of weird looking wooden figurines, each one more distinct than the next. The figure she was holding had five or six little bells around its neck and each time she shook it, it would jingle, and with each new jingle, came another round of chanting.

She was transfixed in her own world and Helen, embarrassed by her intrusion, started backing up slowly when suddenly, she stalled, mesmerized. The small room was indeed a shrine to Native Americans— beads draped over a chair and towel rack, and several menacing masks hung on the walls alongside posters of Arizona and New Mexico. Peripherally, Helen spotted at least one full Indian dress hanging in the closet. She continued her retreat but it was too late. Little Wind had already glanced over, her face a collage of surprise, annoyance, and relief.

"Don't go. It's all right. I'm glad you saw me." She got off the bed and stretched her hand out to Helen.

"I'm so sorry. I really didn't mean to intrude. I just wanted to share with you my possible wonderful news. By the way, what is that you're holding?"

"It is one of my Kachina dolls. Very sacred. Very important to the Hopi Indians. Something the white man will never understand. You see, I still communicate with my family, and I have tried hard not to lose the Hopi ways. It is difficult to explain, but these Kachina dolls bring us hope, or good luck, or whatever we need. I thought you needed help. Do you understand?"

Helen nodded, fascinated.

"In our religion, the Kachinas are supernatural spirits that live half the year in the San Francisco peaks of Arizona. They come down to the Hopi villages and live in the bodies of different men. So, for six months, these men are not who they really are; they become the Kachina spirits. They put on masks and dance different ceremonial dances, and this then helps bring good things to the village.

"Another old custom is that these Kachina-men spend a great deal of time carving Kachina dolls to give to the children of the village. There are about three hundred different Kachina dolls, each one representing a different Kachina spirit." She eyed Helen carefully for any negative reaction, then, uncharacteristically, winked.

On the way back to her bedroom, Helen could hear one last jingle from the Kachina doll as Little Wind put it away for the night, and crawling into bed, she felt oddly peaceful. Maybe tribal ancestry was watching over her somehow.

After that, a pattern formed, with Helen stopping by the little room next to the kitchen before retiring to her own bed each night. Knocking on her maid's door, she was always told to enter to listen to Indian folklore tales. One night it might be learning all about the Four Corner region, where Utah, Colorado, Arizona and New Mexico all intercept—a deeply spiritual region called the 'circle with the four O's'. The next, it could be all about how Kachina dolls were only carved by the village men, never the women.

One night, Little Wind edged the conversation around. "If you are still looking for a good story, I have one for you."

Helen cocked her head slightly. "Oh?"

"Yes. About ten years ago, someone from my reservation was accused of killing a white man, but he didn't do it. No one would listen to him at the time, so he ran away from everyone, leaving his family in pain ever since. They know he is innocent, but no one ever believed them. He is still in hiding, unable to ever see his loved ones again." She paused, her voice thick.

"Did this person's relatives hire a decent attorney?"

"You have to understand, my people are not listened to like your people. Indians will never be taken seriously."

Helen bristled slightly. "I can't believe that's true anymore. Why, it's politically correct to bend over backwards toward Native Americans, don't you agree?"

"If you say so." Little Wind didn't seem convinced.

"You know, to tell you the truth, I really think you need a good detective rather than a newspaper person. Do you have any documentation?" Despite herself, Helen could feel the old investigative juices percolating.

Reaching into her closet, the Native American brought down an oversized cardboard box from the top shelf and together, the two women placed it onto the bed. Crammed inside were many Hopi trinkets: baskets, dolls, blankets, and feathers. Little Wind had to shove her hand down deep in order to bring out whatever it was she was looking for, but finally, she extracted several manila folders, filled with old, frayed newspaper articles and legal documents.

"This person must be a part of your family, right?" Helen gasped. "I mean, why else would you have kept everything all these years?"

Little Wind looked up with narrowed eyes. Could she really trust again? Softening, she let out an involuntary sigh. "Yes, that was my brother, White Eagle. He was just eighteen when all this happened, and it has destroyed my family. We don't know where he has gone, only that he is innocent. Please, can you help us? I don't want to go to a detective. We tried that, and it led us nowhere. Please help me, Helen, please."

Helen paused a beat. "I wouldn't even know how to write something like this."

"You said you wanted to be a serious reporter. Well, maybe you could hire a detective. It didn't work for us, but maybe for you. Here, I have some documents from the original investigation and some local newspaper articles written at that time. Would you at least read them?"

When a pile of yellowed papers was placed into her employer's hands, Helen quickly noted a police report, what looked like several eyewitness accounts, and an old, dusty videotape.

In her room three hours later, she was still reading about how White Eagle, Little Wind's brother, had been accused of going off the Indian reservation and killing Sherwood Kensington, a white man who had been attempting to stop the local government from securing water rights for neighboring Indians. It seemed any Native American Indian would have a legitimate beef against this agitator. Helen was hooked. Even if White Eagle was not innocent, a strong urge to get in touch with him overpowered her, like when she was in college and stayed up night after night, researching her journalism papers.

She took out their laptop and logging onto the Internet, surfed for anything to do with Hopi Indians. Among a myriad of related articles, she entered a chat room, sponsored by the American Indian Movement, or AIM, a legitimate, spiritual Indian group, claiming to have helped in various Native American causes. Keying in her own email address, she requested contact with White Eagle. I must be insane, she thought. It's been years. Who would ever know what I'm talking about? Still, she continued, probing into a decent detective out in the Nevada and New Mexico area, someone who might be more familiar with the reservation problems. She got several names near where they were going to stay, jotted down one or two of them, and took off, scouting for her new-found colleague.

Little Wind was busy folding laundry and softly humming one of her chants when Helen approached her. She turned around. "Well, if you do need someone, I can put you onto the detective we tried at the time. He was supposed to be good and he knew the area real well, but he didn't do anything for us. I mean, he was kind of nasty to us." Her voice was bitter.

"It's a start, and if we don't like him, we don't have to hire him, do we?" Helen put a hesitant arm around her new confidant.

"What do you mean, we?" popped out, along with one arched eyebrow.

"We're both going to Arizona. C'mon, I bet you would like a chance to visit your family, and I will need an interpreter. I'm paying you your salary the whole time, so what do you have to lose?" She grinned at Little Wind's reaction.

Helen's husband Bill was surprised at his wife's latest venture, but absentmindedly supportive. After carefully packing their best camera with the telephoto lens, stocking the refrigerator with gourmet take-out frozen foods, and hugging him with a promise to contact him every few days, she uttered a rushed good-bye.

But it was in the rental car, winding their way up State Highway 264 in Northern Arizona, that Helen visibly caught her breath. She glanced over at her companion, who nodded and remarked simply, "Yes, there are no words…"

Before them, pitted against a brilliant blue southwestern sky, lay the famous three mesas of the Hopis, with their flat-topped centuries-old Oraibi pueblo on the third, Black Mesa, as everyone called it. Surrounded by dry rocks eroded by years of wind, rain, and a hot, blazing sun, the pueblo was the oldest inhabited village in the United States. It was also the hamlet where the Hopi ancestors had stood their ground against the greedy Spanish Conquistadors, a historical fact that still made them proud.

Out of the corner of her eyes, Helen could tell Little Wind was crying, but chose not to invade her employee's space. She was learning about these people and their dignity; to probe any further would only be the white man's clumsy, inappropriate way.

Up the road lay a tiny, makeshift western town, covered in a fine layer of sepia dust. Little Wind called out, "This is it! This is where we should stay. The detective used to be here, and so was the local sheriff."

After checking into their motel, Helen looked up the original detective in the local directory and found him to be still in business. Using her most autocratic voice, she phone Clyde Washburn to make an appointment as soon as possible. The fact that he immediately answered himself indicated no secretary on hand and probably little client revenue.

His thick, country twang instantly brought a crystal-clear image, and in his office the next morning she wasn't disappointed; the voice and look definitely matched. The cowboy hat, pushed back on his head, gave a finishing touch to the Western shirt, string tie, and tan-hide boots. He started out friendly enough to Helen, but as soon as he caught sight of the Native American, his tone altered considerably. Little Wind was right, maybe in Los Angeles people were more politically correct, but out here, people like her were still thought of as second-class citizens.

Before Helen sat down, she instinctively wiped off some dust on the seat of the chair, an action that made Clyde snort and growl his first couple of responses. Little Wind's heart sank. This was going to be more difficult than she had thought.

"OK ladies, what is it you want?" Clyde lit up a cigar and waited.

"Well," Helen started in, "we are here from Los Angeles. My friend and I want to reopen a case you handled about ten years ago."

"And what case is that?" He emitted a loud sniff.

"Do you remember a case about a young Hopi Indian man, by the name of White Eagle, being accused of killing a local white man named Sherwood Kensington?"

Clyde suddenly looked nervous. "Yeah, of course, who wouldn't around here? So what of it? What's this got to do with you two?" His hostility was definitely auguring in.

"Well, my friend here knows the family of the missing Indian boy, and they believe he's innocent. Is there any way I could get you to locate the boy, or at least reinvestigate what might have ha–"

Clyde was already up on his feet, dismissing them with a right-handed wave. "Geez, now why would I want to go back to this after all these years? Huh?"

"Because I am a person of means, Mr. Washburn, and I can pay you a lot of money." Helen waited for a reaction.

He sank back down in the cracked, leather chair and after a few seconds, spoke. "Well, if I did take on this case, I'd want five hundred dollars up front and a hundred dollars a day in expenses. And I'm tellin' you right now, I'm not welcome up at the Mesas. They don't want no white folk up there, so we'd have to use your friend here to help us. Understand?"

Little Wind broke her silence. "I do understand Mr. Washburn, and I am ready to translate. I have relatives who still live on the reservation and I know they would be very helpful to us. They just want their son found and have his name cleared."

"OK, OK. Now, if you'll just give me my deposit, I'll begin today if ya want." He was already dusting off a metal container labeled 'deposit slips' from a nearby shelf. Helen sighed, dashed off a check, handed him copies of their documentation, and left with her partner.

The next morning the detective didn't mince any words. "These transcripts here make it kind of unclear the whereabouts of your relative. I mean, he said he had an alibi and it sort of checks out, but then there are three witnesses who swore he was off the reservation at the time. Two more people claimed they saw his pick-up truck, speedin' up the road toward Sherwood Kensington's house that morning, and a videotape that shows some Indian firing a rifle at Kensington. Even if your man's innocent, there's powerful evidence against him. How 'bout that?" As he leaned forward, both women coughed through his cigar smoke haze.

"I know my brother, and if he said he didn't do it, he didn't do it!" Little Wind looked fierce.

"Now calm down, calm down. I didn't say I didn't believe him, I just want you both to realize there's powerful evidence against this fella. What I'm gonna do is find out from the locals all about Kensington. Maybe there's a motive that'll stand out more clearly. Meantime, you can contact your relatives on the reservation. As I said before, the Hopis sure don't want the likes of me up there in the Mesas, and they sure don't want you, neither." His eyes shifted over to Helen.

Up towards the Mesas, Little Wind exited the car and walked the last quarter mile alone, as Helen sped back down to the town. Word had already gotten out about Little Wind's return, and as she arrived, dozens of family and tribe members closed in around their long-lost relative and friend like ants surrounding the last morsel of food left on a picnic table.

The hotel manager wasn't as welcoming to Helen. She openly sneered when asked questions about Sherwood Kensington's death.

"What do I care? It was all about some dumb Indian. Now, I know you're here with one of them, but I'm just tellin' you what it's like out here." Helen watched the blousy, overweight woman swat at a fly that had landed next to her plate while picking out pieces of her chicken sandwich from her front teeth.

The manager continued. "But if ya want more info, you can always try old Earthman. He was living up on Old Oraibi at the time. Maybe he knows something. Knock yourself out!"

She pointed towards an old, ramshackle, vine-covered adobe structure down the street and Helen went off, energized.

Just outside its front door the reporter was about to knock, when an undefined sound came from within. Leaning sideways towards an open window, she tripped over a rusty tin can, catching herself just in time on an old crate barrel, filled with stagnant water. Once her heart stopped pounding, she slowly angled back to the window. The next step was to position herself behind a nearby shrub and take out her husband's camera from her backpack. Then, peering out through his state-of-the-art telephoto lens, she spied a sun-leathered Indian standing in the middle of a sparse room.

On a small table to his left lay some tools—neat, organized, facing him like surgical instruments in an operating room. To the right of him was a large metal bin, filled with chunks of Cottonwood, which he kept extracting for his whittling. Bits of wood kept flying through the air, creating a semicircular pattern of chips on the floor around him and soon, all Helen could hear was the rub-click, rub-click sound of a chisel against wood.

After a while, she could see a shape emerging from out of the wood. First, a headdress, then a crude, unsettling mask resembling a Wolf-man. Then shoulders and arms appeared, carrying what looked like a bow in one hand and a spear in the other.

Rub-click, rub-click, the noise repeated, and with each few clicks, another body part would emerge. At last came the base of the fringed dress and boots and Helen rotated her focus lens ring nervously, aiming for a better look. As if by osmosis, the old man looked up and swiveled his head in her direction.

She could feel his direct gaze boring through her lens at her and instinctively, she jerked her head back. Then, listening to his slow shuffle over to the window ledge, he suddenly called out, "Who's there? What do you want?"

The game was up. She sheepishly ventured out from behind the bush, ready to explain herself, but there was no need; Earthman was always grateful for an audience. Within minutes, he was going on a tirade against Old Oraibi.

"I knew too much. I saw what happened, and they knew I might tell, so they got rid of me. I was one of their head Kachina spirits for years and still, they threw me out!"

Helen leaned in eagerly. "Tell me, did you know my friend's brother, White Eagle? Do you know what might have happened to him?"

Earthman was stunned. After all these years, someone, a white person, actually wanted to hear from him. Ten years ago, you couldn't pay the police enough money to listen to him; everyone was in too much of a hurry to indict that poor boy.

Watching Helen get out her notepad and pen, he grinned and eased himself down on a stool. "It started many years ago, even before the incident," he began. "There's a Hopi ceremony that's different from other tribes…"

Marked Wings and White Eagle clutched each other in fear. It was almost time for each of them to go their separate ways into the Kiva and meet with their individual Kachina Spirits for the first time ever. The older boys had scoffed, but to an eight and nine-year-old, the anticipation was agonizing. If only they could go in together, maybe it wouldn't be so terrifying, but that was not the Hopi way.

White Eagle was a good boy, always willing to help out; Marked Wings, on the other hand, was reckless, and often didn't do what he was told. When the other villagers considered shunning him, as was expected in their village when a child was bad, his mother lowered her head, unable to hide her shame.

That day White Eagle was fortunate. He was assigned Earthman, then a man in his early forties, who was dressed up as a clown Kachina, the "Koyemsi" Mudhead Kachina. He circled around White Eagle, making funny sounds and waving his arms energetically. White Eagle started to laugh and he almost fell over. This wasn't so bad, the young boy thought. What was all the fuss about? This doesn't scare me at all. He's so funny, this Kachina. The ceremony was short, and at the end of it, White Eagle was handed a Kachina doll representing this clown. Giggling with delight, he walked away from the Kiva, dying to compare notes with Marked Wings.

But Marked Wings' experience was a different story. Being a mischievous boy, the elders felt that he should be in the presence of a Kachina that would make him respect authority, and although everyone in the village knew Sly Dog had a drinking problem, it was decided that he was safe enough around a small boy, if only to discipline him—within reason.

That day, when Sly Dog stepped into the Kiva dressed as Wiharu, the White Ogre/White Nataska Kachina, his blood-shot eyes spoke volumes. In full dress, he charged towards the frightened boy huddled in a corner, his arms flailing and half-choking noises spewing out of his mouth. Then he began hitting Marked Wings for real with his walking stick, instantly producing huge welts on the boy's back and arms that would last for weeks. Marked Wings tried to shield himself with his hands, but he was no match for the all-powerful man/Kachina.

Sly Dog was never seen again. But his presence lived on inside Marked Wings forever, the terror of that day slowly festering until it smoldered into a deep hatred that colored everything the boy did. Impish before, now he was cruel and harsh and the more White Eagle begged his friend to talk about it, the more he was met with impenetrable stares.

As time went on, the boys pursued opposite paths. White Eagle, an excellent law student, specialized in Indian rights. Alcohol became Marked Wings claim to fame. By eighteen, he was a full-blown alcoholic, bitter towards everyone and in particular, White Eagle. In fact, some people maintained that if it hadn't been for Kensington, the two young men wouldn't have had anything to do with each other at all.

Sherwood Kensington was a commanding and simultaneously, loathed man. It became apparent that after months of difficult negotiations regarding water rights between his company and the tribal elders, that this was one white man who would do anything to undermine the health and welfare of the local Native American population. So it puzzled White Eagle the first time he saw Marked Wing's beat-up old Dodge barreling up the canyon road that led to the Kensington estate.

In spite of himself, White Eagle felt compelled to tail his childhood friend, recognizing that history often trumps logic. At the top of High Ridge, he parked his car behind some thick shrubs, got out and quietly took soft, Indian-style steps towards Kensington's mansion. When a couple of voices suddenly resonated outside, he quickly hid behind an ostentatious Romanesque fountain, nestled between two cactus plants on the front lawn. After a couple of seconds he carefully raised his head towards the building, to see Marked Wings and Kensington in the midst of a major standoff.

"So when do I get paid?" Marked Wings demanded.

"Hold your horses, you know I'm good for it. I just have a little cash-flow problem this month. Next month will be different, so keep your shirt on!" Kensington's voice reeked contempt. "So, did you get more of the stuff?"

"When I get paid, you'll get it," Marked Wings hissed.

"Listen, you sorry, son-of-a-bitch, I'm the best thing that's ever happened to you. Give it up now, or you'll never get your money!"

Looking as if he were ready to hit Kensington, instead, Marked Wings handed over two plastic bags of white powder.

White Eagle watched in stunned silence as the two men finished their transaction. Then Kensington disappeared into another part of the house, and Marked Wings drove off, leaving clouds of pebbled dust and a contemplative ex-friend.

Obviously, there was no talking to Marked Wings. At that point, their relationship was nonexistent and besides, who knew what the crazed Indian might do. So White Eagle bided his time, watching Marked Wings vanish about once a week for half a day, then stagger home, drunk out of his mind.

It was then that he decided to go to Earthman for some advice. Instinctively, he knew the Kachina would be discreet and besides, he needed someone he could trust. When he arrived, he found the man-spirit amongst some Kachina dolls in the back of his house.

"What can I do?" the young man cried, after blurting everything out.

"That is a hard question, my young one. Perhaps you should go to the reservation police, see what they can do. But you do understand, I must check with the elders first, before you do anything Such a shame, such a shame!"

The elders were unanimous. They overrode their shock at Marked Wings' consorting with Kensington, and decided the most important thing was not to bring any shame on their village. So their answer was no, the police should not be involved. Earthman argued with them for two hours, but it was of no use; he was completely outnumbered. They had decided to keep their lips sealed.

Two months later, on a crisp, January day, White Eagle noticed Marked Wings standing across the center of the village, sputtering with anger.

"God damn him to hell! Who does he think he is? Well, he ain't gonna cheat me anymore. If he don't pay, he don't live!" Shouldering a rifle, he leapt up into his truck and sped off, depositing a thick dust cloud behind him.

White Eagle sprang into action. Gunning his own car, he followed his former playmate through the town and up into the surrounding hills, hoping to talk some sense into him. Sure enough, Marked Wings was headed straight for Kensington's.

On the way up to High Ridge, White Eagle noticed a family stationed on the side of the road. Two young girls and their mother, shaded only by a small, striped umbrella, were busy selling strawberries packed in pints. Unbeknownst to White Eagle, only seconds before, they had all gone behind a boulder together so that one of the girls could go to the bathroom. So, as Marked Wings drove by, he was totally missed, sealing White Eagle's fate forever.

As he raced up the hill to Kensington's, he heard a shot. Slamming on the brakes, he jumped out of the car, and started to run the rest of the way towards the noise, but it took a full two minutes before he could reach the top of the hill. During that time, a tourist, Mike McCurdy, got a great video of two men on the ridge—an Indian grappling with a white man, with the Indian pulling out his rifle and shooting the white man. The video camera was then shut off, never to include White Eagle dashing up the ridge and coming onto the scene.

The look Marked Wings gave White Eagle when his old friend approached was frightening. "You tell, you die, and your family dies with you, you understand?" White Eagle nodded, and gulped.

"He did me wrong, White Eagle. He deserved to die."

White Eagle found his voice. "Now what are you going to do?"

"I'm leaving Oraibi, I mean it. If you tell the police, I will take your family out!"

Of course White Eagle only told Earthman, no one else. But Mike McCurdy talked plenty, as did the mother and daughters and by the next day, the local community was in an uproar, with the police scouring the area for White Eagle, ready to book him for Murder One.

He didn't wait. He kissed his mother, father, and Little Wind goodbye and took off, ignoring their puzzled, pleading faces. They didn't understand what had happened until everything came out, but by then, he was gone, leaving them all in irreversible pain.

Helen gently coaxed Earthman back to present time. "But with his good character, and the fact that Marked Wings was also missing, why didn't the police ever side with White Eagle? What about the rifle? The shot must have come from Marked Wings and not White Eagle!"

"Bad luck for White Eagle. He was given the same kind of rifle the year before. But it didn't matter; the White Man wanted blood. When the mother and her girls saw the car that was that. And the elders, they wanted no more shame brought on their village, and so they refused to listen to White Eagle's family. They hired a detective, but he was no good; he took their money and did nothing. I argued with the elders. I argued so much, they turned me away and put me out after so many years." His tone saddened. "The funny thing is though, I read in the paper 'bout five years later, Marked Wings died in a car accident, drunk as a skunk. So all these years he couldn't have hurt White Eagle's family anyway, even if he wanted to!"

Helen stared at the surrounding circle of wood chips. Wow, she thought. This could be the best article I'll ever write, but to Earthman, she simply acknowledged, "Now, maybe we can clear White Eagle's name permanently. How can I ever thank you?"

The old man looked spent. "The Gods have spoken through you." He heaved a large sigh then smiled. "Besides, it just feels good to be heard!" Closing the door behind her, more rub-click-rub-click started up instantly.

Back at the hotel, Clyde was surprisingly excited as he and Helen regaled Little Wind with their own individual stories that night. Clyde's news involved forensic evidence, of skin under Kensington's nails at the time of the incident that didn't match White Eagle, of evidence that was buried deep behind the white man's prejudice and a need for immediate justice. Washburn had even managed to locate the son of a local sheriff who, in a newly found fit of conscience, had been willing to talk and promised a reversal of all charges.

But Helen's info made the greatest impact on Little Wind. As she talked about Earthman and her brother's childhood, Little Wind kept nodding and crying, and after four hours, all three of them eagerly opted for a good night's sleep.

Still, Helen couldn't drift off that night; in the dark, she made her way to the bathroom, closed the door, switched on the light, and began writing. As shafts of blue-gray light filtered into the bathroom window, she was still scribbling, and it wasn't until noon the next day, after an anxious-to-get-going Little Wind gently poked her awake, that she even thought of calling her husband.

"Where the hell have you been for the last couple of days? I was getting very worried about you. You promised you would call! And who is WE @www.aim.org? You have gotten three e-mails from this person, and I don't even know who it is!"

Helen's chest was fluttering so fast, she couldn't concentrate on his last few words. "Did you print the letters, or at least keep them?"

"Of course. What's it all about?" Bill sounded petulant.

"I'll tell you when I get back, which will be in a day or two. I love you Bill. Oh, and Bill, I'm writing the best article of my life!" Hanging up, she turned to tell Little Wind the news of White Eagle contacting them.

Back in L.A., Little Wind literally dragged Helen over to the computer to begin their correspondence, and as the sound of "You've Got Mail" popped up, the two women squealed with delight. Little Wind's hand was pressing so hard on Helen's shoulder she had trouble moving the mouse over to the 'read' portion of the mail. Clicking on it, they read out loud:

"The dove is fine. Tell news of family. WE@wwwaim.org."

Together they wrote back, "Family fine, very, very good news for you. No more MW. You will be cleared soon. Write H and LW @ HBLos Ang.com."

Mike McGruen whistled as he scanned her finished article. "I think you may have a winner here, Helen. Outstanding! What a great story. Let's double check all sources, do some editing, and if all works out, probably run it, OK?"

OK? Mike chuckled at her face.

By the next day, Little Wind was in touch with her brother. He had been living under an assumed name out in South Dakota, praying for this day, and although the story later hit the newsstands quickly, the family waited until he was fully exonerated before rendezvousing back at the Oraibi; no chances would be taken this time.

White Eagle wrote Helen separately—grateful letters that touched her more than anything else had for years. She even framed one of them on the wall above her newly built 'writing desk,' and whenever she sat down to compose a new-assigned article, she would glance up at the letter and grin.

Ten months later, when an announcement arrived in the mail about her having won some local newspaper award for her Oraibi piece, Bill promised he would have the photo of her receiving the award inserted in a very expensive, leather-bound frame. Now, where did she want to hang it? To the right of her relatives, or to the left?

No one could understand what was taking her so long to decide and after the framed photo had actually been delivered, she always seemed to find some excuse for not deciding where to place it.

But again, Little Wind knew. As she was cleaning White Eagle's framed letter one day, she thought of Helen's newspaper award photo, stashed carelessly in a half-opened desk drawer collecting dust. Suddenly, she chuckled. She was dusting off Helen's real prize.

A HEARTY THANK YOU

Thank you so much for taking the time to read *Sewing Can Be Dangerous and Other Small Threads*. If you enjoyed it, I would certainly appreciate a short review on Amazon and/or Goodreads. Alas, authors count on people like you!

I would also love to hear from you personally.

Website: www.srmallery.com

Amazon: http://www.amazon.com/S.-R.-Mallery/e/B00CIUW3W8/ref=ntt_athr_dp_pel_1

Twitter: @SarahMallery1

Facebook: http://facebook.com/pages/SR-Mallery-Sarah-Mallery/356495387768574

Pinterest: http://www.pinterest.com/sarahmallery1/

(I have some good history boards that are getting a lot of attention—history, vintage clothing, older films)

Goodreads:
https://www.goodreads.com/author/show/7067421.S_R_Mallery

ABOUT THE AUTHOR

S. R. Mallery has worn various hats in her life. Starting as a classical/pop singer/composer, she moved on to the professional world of production art and calligraphy. Next, came a long career as an award winning quilt artist/teacher and an ESL/Reading instructor. Her short stories have been published in descant 2008, Snowy Egret, Transcendent Visions, The Storyteller, and Down in the Dirt.

Her other books are *Unexpected Gifts* and *Tales To Count On*, both available on Amazon and other outlets. *The Dolan Girls*, a historical fiction Wild West romance, is due out late 2015/early 2016.

THE DOLAN GIRLS

The Dolan Girls by S. R. Mallery has it all. Set in Nebraska during the 1800s, whorehouse madams, ladies of the night, a schoolmarm, a Pinkerton detective, a Shakespeare-quoting old coot, brutal outlaws, and a horse-wrangler fill out the cast of characters. Add to the mix are colorful descriptions of an 1856 land rush, Buffalo Bill and his Wild West Show, Annie Oakley, bank/train robberies, small town local politics, and of course, romance. It's not only a taste of America's past; it's also about people overcoming insurmountable odds.

EXCERPT

S.R. Mallery's Unexpected Gifts
"FROM SONIA'S ANCESTORS' JOURNALS/LETTERS
SONIA'S paraplegic Father --CHAPTER 2: Sam—Living With Fear

"First thing I killed was no kind of thing at all. It was an enemy
soldier, which was a hell of a lot easier to say than the first thing I ever killed was a
man."

--Steve Mason

"Nearing the village, we passed women in their beige tunics, black pants, and Sampan hats, shouldering thick bamboo rods weighted down by buckets of water. Most kept their heads lowered as they walked, but the few who didn't, stared up at us with dead, black-brown eyes and pressed lips. The afternoon was drawing to a close by the time we reached a village compound that reeked of nuoc maum rotten fish sauce and animal dung. An old, leathery woman, squatting by her hooch was our welcoming committee, but once she saw us shuffle by, she scurried back into her hut, clacking loudly in Vietnamese as chickens pecked at rice granules, bobbing their heads up and down in 2/4 time.

Carbini cut to the chase. "First, pull every one of those gooks outta their hooches, then line them up here," he barked.

I watched my troop comb each thatched home, rounding up families of all ages and herding them out into the open like a cattle drive in Oklahoma. I, too, started the mission and stooping into one of the huts, saw a young woman sitting on a straw mat, eating some rice in a black bowl, a young child at her side.

She was exquisite—the best possible combination of French and Chinese ancestry, with such delicate features, she made my heart ache. My immediate instincts were to protect her and her son from Carbini and this horrendous war, but she just gazed up at me, emotionless.

I could hear Carbini yelling orders to get a move-on, and I signaled this girl, this treasure, to follow me. She shook her head vehemently, and curled her legs around her son. I motioned again, but still, she refused. I froze, unable to think, but when Carbini popped his head in the doorway and snarled, "Weylan!" she got the message and followed me out.

Whimpering slightly, she joined her fellow villagers, gripping her child's hand and wiping off a tear that had slid halfway down her cheek. I suddenly pictured slave owners in pre-Civil War days and felt my lunch rise up in my throat.

"Now, get your Zippos ready, men." As Carbini's face flushed red, I sucked in my breath. He caught sight of my reaction and came over. "Weylan here doesn't like my orders. Anyone else here who doesn't like my orders?" Nobody spoke up.

He opened up one of my backpack pockets, yanked out my Zippo lighter, and shoved it into my face. Immediately, you could hear the snap of pockets opening and boots shifting. We were getting ready to Rock 'n Roll.

Carbini was first. He marched over to a hooch, flipped on his Zippo, and carefully lit the underbelly of its thatched roof. It smoldered for a few seconds, a thin, rising wisp of smoke twisting in the tropical air. From that, a flame grew, nibbling at the straw with a low, blue heat before suddenly bursting into a torch, arcing up towards the sky in a yellow-hot blaze.

Carbini turned to us and nodded, his eyes glazed. This was our cue, yet I spun around to search for the girl, who was at the back of the pack, crying softly as she hugged her son. I glanced over at some of the other men, their hands jammed deep into their pockets, and decided to follow their lead. The fire was raging full force on each hooch now, the thatch and bamboo crackling like a 4th of July fireworks display, leaving its reflections in the villagers' eyes and turning the sky dark with thick, bulbous smoke.

"Weylan! You son-of-a-bitch coward! You're no better than the rest of us, you hear me?" Carbini started to charge over, then stopped mid-stride.

In the distance, a large formation of F4's was headed our way, torpedoing fireballs of napalm every several hundred yards and scattering screaming villagers down the main road. We were ordered to take cover, but followed the fleeing Vietnamese instead, charging after them and trying desperately not to show our own fear."

SEWING CAN BE DANGEROUS

13002505R00129

Printed in Poland
by Amazon Fulfillment
Poland Sp. z o.o., Wrocław